The
Death
of
Saints

A Novel by

Adele Simmons

Bel Esprit Publishing
2015

First published in the United States
in 2015 by Bel Esprit
Los Angeles, California

**Kindle & print versions available at www.amazon.com
or
www.TheDeathofSaints.com**

Like us on our Facebook page.

This is a work of fiction. All institutions, names and characters—including those of historical persons—either are products of the author's imagination or are used fictitiously. Any resemblance to actual persons, living or dead, places, or events is entirely coincidental.

ISBN-13: 978-0615967875 (Bel Esprit)
ISBN-10:0615967876

Cover art: detail of 17th century saint woodcarving
Photo by: Roberto A. Sanchez

First Paperback Edition
Printed in the United States

"This book is about the joining of Heaven and Earth,
and the role, in this joining, of dead human beings."

The Cult of the Saints
Peter Brown 1981

"Give me the boy for the first seven years and I will give you the man."   Saint Francis Xavier 1506-1552

New York 1873

Father Kieran Clarence O'Malley sat at the back of St. Stephen's Church. He prayed to Stephen, the first Christian martyr, not as the rector of his congregation, but as a penitent powerless against his sins. Now, he was losing control of the boy and they were all in danger.

A very old woman, head covered in a brown shawl, knelt at the chancel rail beneath the glass reliquary that held the clavicle relic of St. Stephen. The old woman was Irish, unlike nearly all the priest's parish now. A great wave of Italian immigration was pushing to the north and west the last of Manhattan's refugees from Ireland's great hunger.

The old woman crossed herself and stood up staggering a bit. Her lips moved silently as she tottered down the far aisle beneath the Stations of the Cross where a fit of rough coughing overwhelmed her. She wiped the sputum away, then walked warily past Father O'Malley. He saw it was the local midwife Bridey. Bah! Aborter of foetuses and a wicked panderer to the ills of dirty women was more like it, O'Malley considered. She knows more'n she ought. No matter—long as it's more'n she tells. Who'd heed her calumny anyway.

Bridey dipped her fingers in the holy water stoup and crossed herself. She glared at the priest's back and muttered an ancient invective just as the new Third Avenue El rumbled past on Grand Avenue. O'Malley gripped the back of the pew and yanked himself to his feet as the old woman hobbled out and away into grim night.

He knew the boy would come now, was most likely already waiting in the sacristy.

Sister Mary Patrick had beaten the boy badly, his eye quickly discoloring where she'd struck him with her bony knuckles. This time, he'd hit her back, smashing a clay pot against her ear. The boy watched a spreading patch of maroon stain her starched, white wimple. He hadn't killed her, but he ran away praying he had. Behind him, the boy heard little Sister Immaculatta raising an alarm and crying for Father O'Malley to come quickly. The boy ran, slowly enough to mock the old nun within her earshot. His singsong voice rose to a screech at the last syllable just as hers always did. *'Filthy boy. Ungrateful wretch. Abomination. Bastard...'*. He supposed he was all of these things.

He could mimic her perfectly, like cut glass, all of them in fact, not just their voices but their nunnish affectations as well: the way farty, old Sister Bibiana would make a startled *oops* sound and ruffle the back of her skirt; and Sister Joseph Martin barking like a dragoon; Sister Crescentia's ancient body, bent as the Archbishop's crosier, her constant rattling of beads and her drooled Latin; Sister Mariya Evgenia's imperial sweep through the convent halls; and fat Sister Brigid's thick, stubborn brogue. All of these women he carried inside him like graven images.

The boy ran to the secret place where he could hide. All the while, he prayed the liverish, old bitch would die. If there really was a God, she would just die.

Father O'Malley locked the sacristy doors from the inside and opened the large chifforobe holding his vestments.

"Come out," O'Malley said.

The boy lifted the false bottom the priest had installed in the chifforobe and clambered out.

"Is she—?"

"Sister Mary Patrick is being cared for in the infirmary," O'Malley said. He studied the youngster. The old crone Bridey had delivered many such foundlings to the church steps, wrapped in potato sacks, bloody sheets, newspaper; some were dead, most were squalling vigorous recriminations. All of them *filius nullius:* a son of nobody. A hasty sprinkling at the baptismal font and then off it went to St. Eulogius Orphanage on Staten Island.

Except when, sometimes, they'd keep a little cast-off for themselves. Sometimes, when one of the good sisters would get *itchy*, whining in Confession about her empty feelings. Wanting something *more*. It seemed to happen to most of them at a certain age.

So, they'd hold on to a pretty baby for a few years, until circumstances changed, and changed again. *This* boy was one of O'Malley's strays. He'd kept him and reared him, and now would expel him for all their sakes.

"I've arranged for you to go away," Father O'Malley said. "Father Conklin at Good Shepherd Seminary has agreed to take you in."

The boy wailed in protest. "You promised you'd never send me away. *Never.*"

"You can*not* stay here now. What you've done—is dangerous. You'll be safe at Good Shepherd."

"I won't go!"

"You will! Now listen to me, boy. What are you?"

"I am a Soldier of Christ," the boy responded immediately.

"Yes-s-s. And what is the virtue, which saves you from eternal hellfire?"

"Obedience."

"And?"

"Service."

"And?"

"Silence."

"Come with me, boy."

O'Malley grabbed the boy's arm and dragged him into the rectory hallway, to a heavy door at the top of the basement stairs.

"Go down," the priest said with a shove.

At the bottom of the stairs, the boy blinked owlishly at the agitated priest. Father O'Malley retrieved a broken broom handle from under a musty couch. He used it to open the searing hot door of the massive iron furnace, then pointed to a pile of coal beneath a chute in the basement wall.

"Stoke it," he said.

The frightened boy picked up a spade and carefully shoveled coal into the furnace. O'Malley pumped the bellows until the flames inside the oven reached head height and the heat bathed both their faces in sweat.

"Now, pull off them shoes; you don't deserve anything so fine. You'll leave this world as barefoot as the day y'came to it."

The boy sensed his last chance to escape. He knew there was a culvert beneath the floor leading eventually to the street. And knew O'Malley used it sometimes to slip out of the rectory unseen. If he could reach it before the priest caught him, lift the slab, get away through the culvert, he'd be safe, just until things settled down again.

The priest followed the boy's eye to the slab in the floor.

"Try it and I'll strike you down like the fleeing felon you are," O'Malley hissed.

The boy gave up hope of escape and stood in the flame light, making no futile attempt at escape.

"Now. What is the meaning of perfect obedience?" the priest demanded.

"To obey without hesitation, without impious judgment, without fear of worldly punishment."

"And should I tell you to climb, right now, inside this furnace, to lay yourself down amongst the flames, what would you do?"

The boy felt the first real stab of terror. "I would obey, Father."

"Aye, and would you now?" The priest pointed with the broom handle. "Get that crate over there."

The boy scrambled for a rotted wooden box discarded in a corner. He stood still waiting further instructions. "Bring it here. Put it before the furnace opening. And stand on it."

The boy was too frightened now to do anything but what he was told. He prayed perfect obedience would save him. He stepped onto the rickety box in front of the open furnace. The heat from the fire quickly reddened his face.

"Put your hands on your head," O'Malley bellowed. The boy hesitated.

"Now, or by Gawd, I'll shove you in with one kick of my foot and lock the door behind you! You'll melt like tallow and burn, forever and ever, 'til beyond the end of the world! Is that what you want, boy? Is it?!" The priest was shouting now and spittle flew from his lips.

"No, Father, please. I'll be good. I promise!"

"But, will you obey?" The priest bent close to the boy and

put his foot on the boy's wobbly, wooden perch.

"Yes, Father, I swear it!"

"And you will be silent about your miserable sins?"

"Complete silence, Father!"

"And you will be of unquestioning service to Father Conklin, in all he requires of you?"

"Yes, so help me God, Father. Oh, please, Father, I swear before God and all the martyred saints in Heaven!"

"Liar!" the priest bellowed.

Panicked, the boy crouched down on the box and folded his hands in front of his face.

"Please, Father, don't. I thought you loved me. You said you loved me—"

For a moment, the priest's eyes rolled back in his head. Everything was silent save the pop and crackle of the fire, a moment in which the boy knew anything might happen. Perhaps it was his moment to knock the priest down and flee. But then, the priest's eyes rolled forward again, like a shark's, and stared blankly at the boy. Father O'Malley stretched out his arms.

"Come to me, my beloved son. Why do you make me treat you thus? Do you not know the love I bear you?"

"Yes, Father. And... and I love you, too." The boy slid cautiously from the box. "Save me from Hellfire, please, Father. I'll be good. I swear it." He clutched Father O'Malley about the knees.

"There, there. I believe you mean it," the priest said. "Let us pray. We must give thanks, in gratitude for the saving grace of Christ, our Redeemer." O'Malley orated as solemnly as if from the pulpit, "Our Father, merciful King of Heaven, Thou who succors His children, nourishes them from the body of Thine own Son Christ, our Lord and Redeemer. Look kindly upon Thy miserable servants who hunger and thirst for Thy love. Give them to drink from that precious Blood—

"You still wish to be a priest, my son?" O'Malley abruptly asked. His hand was beneath the boy's chin, tilting up that small frightened face. "You've not strayed from your vocation?"

"No," the boy said, "I mean yes. I still want to be a priest. Like you, Father. I want to serve God forever and ever."

"Then you will go to Good Shepherd Seminary," he stated simply. "And you will serve Mother Church with your whole heart, and your whole mind, and your whole body."

Father O'Malley cupped the boy's chin, holding his face captive. The priest looked down into the wide eyes of the powerless child.

"Yes, boy," he whispered with relish. "With gratitude because you love Mother Church, don't you." The priest's pale tongue flicked between crooked, yellow teeth. Spit dried at the corners of his mouth. "Oh, beautiful child, yessss—

"Praise be to Gawd and all the saints," the priest brayed. Again, his eyes rolled back in his head. The white orbs twitched.

"Oh, Gawd, oh, Jaysus. Yes—yesss! Sweet Jaysus in heaven, save me." Prickly, red pimples rose on the priest's scrawny flesh. His tongue waggled in the back of his throat. "Oh, Gawd—" he croaked.

The priest fell onto the dusty couch in a fugue. It was some seconds before his breathing returned to normal and his eyes opened lifeless as a doll's. He watched as the boy rushed into his shoes and inched toward the stairs.

"Go to your room now," the priest said flatly. "Sister Giuseppina has packed your things. We'll not meet again, I daresay." O'Malley spoke more forcefully now. "Mr. Condotti, from the parish Laymen's Organization, happily has volunteered to transport you to Good Shepherd. It's a three-hour ride; you need to hurry."

"Tonight, Father?"

"Right *now!*"

"Yes, Father." The boy, fearing a resurrection of the priest's psychotic wrath, fled up the stairs, through the sacristy and into the chancal of the church. His room lay beyond, in the attic of the convent.

The boy stopped to look up at the crucified Christ hanging above the main altar. Its face was contorted in unimaginable suffering. *Why?* he asked again. Why, since you had all the power, did you *let* them do that to you?

He wanted the priest to look like that. He wanted the *power* to make the priest look like that. If he could have, he would have bashed the old loon in the face until he, too, looked agonized, his mouth twisted, blood dripping from his brow, like the painted Jesus.

Looking over his shoulder to make sure the priest had not yet come up from the cellar, the boy crept to the altar. He stared at the tabernacle where the consecrated host lay, the very body and blood of Christ. The boy's bold thoughts frightened him. He reached up to the altar and grabbed the big, gold candlestick-holder used during High Mass. It was heavier than he'd imagined. He backed down from the altar and clamored to the chancel rail in front of St. Stephen's glass reliquary. He stood there a moment, frozen in the gap between fear and anger. Then he hit the front panel of the reliquary and its glass shattered silently into slivers on the carpet. He was terrified at what he had just done, and what he was about to do.

He dropped the candlestick holder and reached slowly inside the reliquary, tentatively, waiting for the reaction of an angry God. With two hands, he gently lifted the small, filigree ossuary containing the precious relic of Saint Stephen. He opened the little casket and stared at the ancient piece of bone. The boy closed the ossuary again firmly. Relics were the most venerated and powerful of Church possessions; they were the saints' *presence* here on earth, and in Heaven, at the same time. And now this precious relic belonged to *him*.

Carefully, he pushed it beneath his shirt, next to his skin and held it tight with his arm. The boy felt the saint's protection descending on him like a dove. He gathered the candlestick-holder and broken glass and slid it all beneath the pedestal skirt.

He blew out the candles burning by the shrine, then ran as quickly as he could to get his packed belongings, and wait on the church steps for the arrival of Mr. Condotti.

ONE

New York City 1912

An overflow crowd shuffled forward on the sidewalk beneath the Italian Renaissance façade of Carnegie Hall. The line was backed up to Fifty-seventh Street where it turned west and continued around the block to Fifty-sixth, nearly meeting itself like a snake swallowing its own tail.

The evening traffic was its usual commotion of belching motorcars, panicked horses, and careening trolleys. It was chaotic, noisy, and exhilarating.

Inside, the hall was filling to capacity, a hundred and five steps up to the highest balcony where, even there, the acoustics were magnificent.

Cate Gallagher sat down just as Mrs. Harriot Stanton Blatch, whom Cate knew from the Women's Political Union, was concluding her words of welcome to the renowned orator seated on the stage.

"...*political sensibility she brings to social reform and welfare on this, her first tour of the United States...*" Cate was vibrant with the undercurrent which was turning the tide of social revolution in America. The splinter Progressive Party was on the rise with a platform of women's suffrage, social insurance for the elderly, and a national health service plan.

Mrs. Stanton Blatch had provided Cate an excellent seat: fifth row, center. She believed political females like Cate—especially Cate—needed heroes, women of courage to model themselves on. Mrs. Stanton Blatch's mother, Elizabeth Cady Stanton, had been such a woman. Today they were hearing from another. Cate was anxious for the details of Mrs. Pankhurst's ordeal.

"...it is with the warmest regard we welcome Mrs. Emmeline Pankhurst."

Cate, along with the entire audience, stood. The applause was uproarious, the crowd giddy with political promise.

Mrs. Stanton Blatch stood aside as Emmeline Pankhurst, a regal brunette, took her place at the podium. Mrs. Pankhurst had waged the battle for women's suffrage at the militant forefront, in England. Now, with the calm of a seasoned campaigner, she appraised the audience before her, and waited a full two minutes until the applause reluctantly abated. The mostly black-tie attendees resumed their seats and the house hushed. And still she waited, until all could feel the vague unease which ripples through an expectant, silent audience. Then, Mrs. Pankhurst spoke.

"I... am a hooligan!"

Again, Cate and the rest of the house were on their feet in thunderous approval. "And, I am what you call here in America a jailbird!" Mrs. Pankhurst managed to shout over their cheering. "My government considers me a publicly scandalous woman. For which I have endured chains. Insult. And assault!"

The ovation, now, was riotous, particularly so in the balconies. Finally the crowd quieted, and all took their seats to listen closely. When the room was not just silent but still, Mrs. Pankhurst continued.

"Allow me to describe for you the nature of such *legal* assault." Mrs. Pankhurst gripped the edges of the podium and Cate could see the outline of knuckles through white gloves.

"On my arrival at Winston Green Gaol, on Wednesday afternoon, September 22, I protested against the treatment to which I was subjected, and broke the windows in my cell."

Mrs. Pankhurst paused, conceding to a subtle ripple of shock, which flowed through the dress circle. The image of this genteel woman smashing government windows intrigued Cate. She herself could well imagine the fury behind a deliberately flung chair. Such inner fury visited her frequently these days and for good reason.

"Accordingly, I was taken at nine o'clock in the evening to the punishment cell—a cold, dark room on the ground floor, with no furniture in it.

"A plank bed was brought in. I was then stripped to my undergarments, and handcuffed with hands behind, during the day, except at meals, when the palms were placed together in front, like so. At night they were also placed in front, with the palms *out*," she said demonstrating the awkward and helpless position.

"On Thursday morning, food was brought into the cell: potatoes, bread and gruel, but I did not touch it. On Thursday afternoon, the visiting magistrates came. I was given a thin prison shift to wear and taken before them, handcuffed. After hearing what I had to say, I was sentenced to nine days close confinement.

"I still refrained from food.

"About noon on Saturday, I was told the matron wished to speak to me, and I was taken to the doctor's room, where I saw the matron, eight wardresses, and two doctors. There was a sheet on the floor and an armchair on it. The doctor said I was to sit down and I did.

"He then said: 'You must listen carefully to what I have to say. I have orders from my superior officers—he had a blue official paper in his hand to which he referred—that you are not to be released, even on medical grounds. If you still refrain from food, I must use other measures to *compel* you to take it.'

"I then said, 'I refuse and if you force food on me I want to know how you are going to do it.' To which the doctor said, That is for me to decide."

In the audience, many ladies bristled. A number of gentlemen leaned forward in studied anticipation. Cate's mouth was dry and her throat close. Intimations of her own inescapable future weighed on her like winter blight.

Mrs. Pankhurst continued, "Again my response, 'I refuse.' It was then the doctor bowed to me.

"Immediately, as by some prearranged signal, I was surrounded and forced against the chair, which was tilted backward. While I was held down by the wardresses, a rubber nasal tube was inserted. It is two yards long, with a funnel at the end; there is a glass junction in the middle to see if the liquid is passing—about a pint of milk and raw egg..."

Cate was horrified such barbarity was legally sanctioned. If the wife of an influential English barrister could be subject to such medieval treatment, then females were institutionally not safe at *any* level of society. This belief lent the passion of self-defense to all of Cate's political convictions. She had felt that way from as young as she could remember. Her father frequently had allowed her to accompany him to the narrow streets of the meaner neighborhoods of Troy, Poughkeepsie, and Nyack. To Cate, he looked a giant, standing on a barrel or crate, pleading the rights of the working-class family. He lived his convictions on street corners, in union halls, at political rallies, on strike lines. A dozen times over he could have been killed when violence broke out. He didn't care. He was a patriot. Cate was very much like him; but she did not have his courage. Nor even Mrs. Pankhurst's. No claim to moral authority whatsoever. Only outrage and fear.

During the thunderous conclusion to Mrs. Pankhurst's address, Cate moved quickly in a futile hope of avoiding the crush. She was recognized by many who'd followed her recent trial and criminal conviction, in the newspapers. Although this crowd was sympathetic to her cause, there were others, many others, who considered her immoral for her outspoken advocacy of birth control, and were anxious to see the full measure of punishment, five years at hard labor, meted out at her sentencing in less than a month—unless, she did as she was being urged to do. *Unless*, she agreed to—

Cate put the cowardly thought away and aggressively wove her way through the Carnegie Hall audience. Mrs. Stanton Blatch had invited her to the reception room of the Hall where Mrs. Pankhurst was already swarmed by a small group of invited well-wishers and reporters from no fewer than a dozen New York dailies. The two distinguished women were posing stiffly, shoulder to shoulder, for several press photographers who were loudly instructing them not to move.

Cate waved from a few feet away, catching Mrs. Stanton Blatch's eye. "Do come here, my dear," she said, after several, long, immobile seconds. She fluttered her fingers like bird wings in Cate's direction. "So happy you could attend. Emmeline, this is the remarkable young woman I mentioned, who has begun the Family Aid Society downtown. The Women's Political Union is assisting her with legal counsel. Emmeline, may I introduce Miss Cate Gallagher. Miss Gallagher, Mrs. Emmeline Pankhurst."

"How do you do, Miss Gallagher. A great pleasure to make your acquaintance." Mrs. Pankhurst was impressively tall.

"How do you do, Mrs. Pankhurst. Welcome to our shores," Cate replied.

"Thank you, my dear. I've heard very encouraging reports of the work being done by your Family Aid Society. I'd very much like to hear more about it."

Cate noticed several of the press scribbling furiously in their notepads as the room hummed with recognition of *the Gallagher woman.*

"We do feel it's important work," Cate said eagerly. "Particularly in view of the great opposition we've recently experienced from the authorities. The Postal Inspector has had most of our publications banned from public mailing, and our offices have several times been raided by the police."

"But, Miss Gallagher remains stalwart and *undaunted*," Mrs. Stanton Blatch chimed. "Don't you, dear. We, at the Political Union, are very pleased to be associated with her organization and to lend our financial and legal support during her civil difficulties."

"Actually," Cate said, "Mr. Comstock's laws have done us a great favor by bringing our work to the attention of the public. There's power in public awareness." Cate sensed now was the press opportunity she'd hoped for.

"We see so many preventable deaths due to a myriad of unaddressed social ills: child labor, over-population, lack of hygiene education, ignorance of basic reproductive biology, and terrible methods of self-induced pregnancy termination.

"The unsafe living conditions of Manhattan's tenement slums pale the conditions of Mr. Dickens's Jacob's Island," she said to Mrs. Pankhurst exactly as she'd practiced. "Opposition to the authorities that permit such conditions is the *crime* for which I stand convicted and face horrific imprisonment."

"Here, here," Mrs. Stanton Blatch enthused, provoking a smattering of applause.

"It is precisely those conditions I wish to view," Mrs. Pankhurst announced. "And Mrs. Stanton Blatch tells me you're just the one to act as our guide through those wards. Would it be possible on such short notice?"

"I should be very happy to show you, Mrs. Pankhurst."

"Would tomorrow morning be convenient?"

"Most convenient," Cate said.

"Say, at eight o'clock? Our schedule will accommodate that, won't it, Harriot?"

"Certainly," Mrs. Stanton Blatch preened.

"Where do you suggest we *rendezvous,* Miss Gallagher?"

Cate thought a moment. "Do you think you can find your way to Mott Street between Broome and Grand Avenue?"

Mrs. Pankhurst looked inquiringly to Mrs. Stanton Blatch.

"Yes, we can," she replied.

"There's an old, Catholic church, St. Stephen's, on the corner of Mott and Broome next to the parochial school. We'll have to go on foot from there; the crowd will be dense, but there are several families along the thoroughfare, whom our visiting nurses tend regularly.

"Excellent, my dear. I'll have my driver deliver us in front of St. Stephen's Church at eight sharp, tomorrow morning. And perhaps afterward—the reception?" Mrs. Stanton Blatch looked inquiringly to Mrs. Pankhurst.

"Brilliant suggestion."

"Cate, dear, Mrs. Astor is having a small cocktail reception at five-thirty tomorrow evening. Perhaps you can join us? There are a number of influential people whom I believe would be happy to meet you. It would be an important opportunity for you, my dear. Are you available?"

"You're certain it will not inconvenience Mrs. Astor?" Cate asked making an effort to not seem *too* excited.

"Mrs. Astor is quite fond of young Progressives like you, and of course the struggle closest to her heart, next to women's suffrage, is women's welfare. So, until tomorrow, Cate," Mrs. Stanton Blatch said turning away.

Cate hesitated as a thought occurred to her. "Which Mrs. Astor?" she asked sotto voce.

"Pardon?" Mrs. Stanton Blatch asked.

"Which Mrs. Astor? There are several."

"Why, Mrs. Ava Willing Astor, of course. Her home is on Fifth Avenue at 65th Street."

"Oh, yes, of course. Thank you." Cate was still not quite sure which of the exalted Astor women she was to meet the following evening but she, like most New Yorkers, knew the Astor mansion on Fifth Avenue. Ultimately, she decided, it didn't really matter which of the distaff Astors it was. The name Astor was synonymous with philanthropy, and funds to keep the Family Aid Society afloat were always a primary concern, to say nothing of the public support which she fervently hoped would mitigate the prison sentence about to be imposed on her.

She said good-bye to Mrs. Stanton Blatch who'd already turned her attention elsewhere, then headed for the exit, stopping only to accept her first-ever glass of Champagne, which she tipped up and drank straight down like a good oatmeal stout. Cate had a great deal to prepare for, and the evening was already growing late.

TWO

The morning was a warm promise of sweltering afternoon heat. Already the intersection of Mott and Broome Streets teemed with hundreds of people, and by mid-day would swell to as many as three thousand bodies per square block, the densest population in the history of humanity. Russians, Gypsies, Madagascans, Armenians, Irish and Caribbeans, cheek by jowl with Hungarians, Nigerians, Greeks, Arabs, Poles, Syrians and, outnumbering all, Italians. It was as if the entire globe had dispersed and reassembled itself here.

Mrs. Stanton Blatch's Franklin automobile pulled to a halt amidst a flotilla of pushcarts selling fruit, shoes, ice, buttons, pots, knives, hats, chickens, thread, beer, corsets, olive oil, fabrics, and soap—everything to sustain a thriving marketplace. The Franklin with its polished brass fittings and fat, black tires looked amiss.

"My heavens," Mrs. Pankhurst remarked through the open window. "I've never seen anything quite like it. It really is Mr. Shakespeare's *brave new world.*"

Their driver held the door as Mrs. Pankhurst and Mrs. Stanton Blatch climbed out on the street side in order to avoid the sewage pooled along the cobblestone curb.

"Good morning," Cate smiled. "I hope you're well rested. Shall we begin? Perhaps your car can meet you here again at, say, half-past nine o'clock."

The women made their way west on Broome Street toward Mulberry in a throng, which seemed to have no obvious direction or course. Once they managed to gain the sidewalk they passed a storefront saloon, a bakery, cigar store, chandler, herring stand, tea room, butcher market, livery, and another saloon.

"So much industriousness," Mrs. Pankhurst remarked. "It's as though some mighty, enterprising force is astir in the entire population."

"Yes," Cate said. "It's called survival. These are the fortunate. The ones able to find employment." Above them, in wide-opened windows, were men hunched over sewing machines they'd hauled with them across the ocean from Kraków or Minsk or Riga. From other windows, women shouted to the peddlers below in a half-dozen different Romance and Slavic languages.

Cate spoke over her shoulder as the two older women dodged and elbowed to keep up. "A successful pushcart peddler can earn as much as fifteen dollars a week. But look closely, through the crowds, at the tent squatters in the alleys and the idlers on the stoops. Look even overhead."

The women stopped a moment to observe the scads of people perched like shrikes on every fire escape landing.

"And look across there," Cate pointed. "There. The men foraging trash in the narrow ways between the buildings. Even the ten cents a day to rent a pushcart is beyond their means. Now look. This building here."

Mrs. Pankhurst and Mrs. Stanton Blatch watched as a city worker exited a tenement carrying two child-sized pine boxes, one on top of the other in his burley arms.

"Bound for Hart Island," Cate said. "Potter's Field is there. Children are buried three or four deep in graves marked only by serial numbers. A daily occurrence here for people, who can't afford even that much space for the living, let alone the dead. For most, the simple act of opening one's eyes in the morning requires all the courage they can muster.

"When I first came here from Claverack College, I began to *see* in a whole new way. To look closely through the warp and woof of the tapestry for the invisible ones: the sick, the ill-fed, the prostitutes—even at this hour, some as young as eleven. The old, the orphaned, the inebriated, the dishonest, the malevolent, the deranged, the hopeless—all of whom are assembled here as well. At first, you don't see them at all. Then, they are all you see."

Mrs. Pankhurst and Mrs. Stanton Blatch took in the particulars Cate pointed out as they moved more slowly through the crowds. Their facial expressions were now more aligned with their somber purpose.

"Here we are," Cate said in front of a busy tenement. "Mr. and Mrs. Nicolosi live here. They have five children. Mr. Nicolosi worked as an excavator for the Interborough Rapid Transit until a blasting powder accident took his right hand. Now, they struggle along on what Mrs. Nicolosi and her older children are able to earn taking in piecework. And still she shares whatever she can with those less fortunate. Her neighbors call her a saint. I sent her a note last night to expect us."

Cate led the way into the building entry, which was dark despite the broad light of day outside. Apartment doors, barely eight feet apart, lined the corridor deep into the tenement.

"Be careful," she cautioned. "There are rats. Their nests are overcrowded, so they are quite active even in the daytime." As if summoned by Cate's warning, a huge brown rodent darted aggressively in their path. Mrs. Stanton Blatch let out a horrified yelp and attempted to retreat, but Mrs. Pankhurst, to Cate's admiration, stood her ground.

"Come along, Harriot," she said. "We are on a mission. Please proceed, Miss Gallagher."

"You will want to walk with as heavy a tread as possible," Cate explained stomping her foot. "It helps to keep them at bay."

They stomped their way along the corridor, which led onto the open court of an airshaft, about three hundred feet square.

"These older buildings were originally built for single family residence by the Dutch. They were later reconstructed for apartments around these airshafts, allowing at least a bit of gloomy light to penetrate some of the interior flats, and to accommodate plumbing facilities."

In the square open space, several children were playing a game with sticks and a tin can, oblivious to the stench of seepage beneath four closeted toilets.

"The Nicolosi family lives in the fifth-floor, front apartment," Cate said.

They climbed an open-air staircase, which rose like a bramble at the side of the courtyard. It passed through clotheslines of garments, hanging like tattered pennants in the windless air.

At each landing, Cate stopped briefly for the two older women to catch their breath. They were met by the hollow gaze of dwellers to whom the carefully dressed women were intruders.

Cate knew from her own first experiences in the slums that Mrs. Pankhurst and Mrs. Stanton Blatch were feeling themselves to be both threat and threatened. They instinctively knew it was the better course to keep their eyes down and say nothing as they passed.

At the fifth-floor landing, Cate led them into another hallway even darker than the ground-floor entry.

"Here we are," she said knocking on the door.

"Mrs. Nicolosi, it's Miss Gallagher. May we come in?"

Cate waited a moment more, then knocked again before the door opened and Mrs. Nicolosi's oldest daughter, a big-eyed girl of about twelve, peered out.

"Good morning, Seraphia. Do you remember me?" Cate asked.

"Mamma's not here."

"I sent a note yesterday to expect us. Did she not get it?"

"She got it."

Something in the absence of the girl's usual affable disposition alarmed Cate. "Is everything all right, Seraphia?" she asked.

"She don't come back." Seraphia seemed anxious to get the words out.

"Come back from where, Seraphia? Can you tell us what's happened? Don't be frightened. Is your father here?"

"He's go for the police."

"The police? Tell me what's happened, Seraphia?"

The girl took a deep breath and let the words spill out. "Last night, it was very hot, so my Mamma go to the roof for to cool off. She don't come back."

"Since last night? May we come in, Seraphia?" Cate asked.

The little girl hesitated, then abruptly shut the door. It took a moment for Cate to realize there'd be no further response.

"What do you suppose has happened?" Mrs. Pankhurst asked. "Do you think the mother has abandoned her family?"

"That is impossible to imagine," Cate replied.

"What do you suggest we do?" Mrs. Stanton Blatch asked.

"Well, there is another family we may visit. They live two buildings farther on."

Cate led the way again to the exterior landing, where the women mounted narrow, rusted, metal rungs leading to the rooftop.

"Are we to go searching for Mrs. Nicolosi?" Mrs. Pankhurst asked.

Cate hiked up her skirt and stepped onto the rooftop as she answered. "No. We'll leave it to the police and I'll inquire later. For now, we travel as the denizens do: over the rooftops. It avoids much climbing up and down of stairs, and is a safer route than navigating the dark corridors. We can quickly, and more easily, travel from rooftop to rooftop."

The three women advanced across the hot tar surface to the farther edge of the building roof. The still air was stifling.

"The span between the buildings is only about twenty-four inches," Cate explained, "but I suggest you not look down. Those tenants whose windows face these open boundaries use them to dispose refuse. The rat population spawning down there is enormous."

Both Mrs. Pankhurst and Mrs. Stanton Blatch hesitated, then summoning their courage, peered over the building edge, as Cate had suggested they *not* do. Sixty feet below, swarms of rats skittered back and forth in a frenzy.

"Good Lord," Mrs. Pankhurst cried drawing back.

Mrs. Stanton Blatch paled. "Oh, Emmeline, dear, this is too much—"

Steeling herself, Mrs. Pankhurst replied, "We must proceed, Harriot. It is precisely such horrors we have come to witness." Turning to Cate, she asked, "Does the city government do nothing about such conditions?"

Cate shook her head. "Only sporadically. Lack of sanitation is one of the greatest problems in the slums. Not all of the alleys are like *this*, however. This is actually one of the worst."

Mrs. Pankhurst peered again over the edge. "Do the inhabitants not realize the health hazard such practices pose? Why, it must be piled at least five or six feet high with all manner of refuse." Mrs. Pankhurst squinted. "Someone seems to have even tossed their laundry below. Why would they do such a thing?"

"Sometimes the wind will catch laundry hung to dry and carry it off."

"I see. Yes, that seems to be the case," Mrs. Pankhurst said.

"Watch your step here; there's something sticky on the ground," Cate cautioned. Pulling her skirt up about her knees, she stepped across the empty space to the next roof, then held out her hand to assist the other two ladies. In doing so, she looked to their feet, making sure each had a firm step in crossing.

Something below caught her eye; a swarm of rodents seemed particularly agitated where the lost pieces of laundry lay. Then a shudder stiffened Cate's back, and she squinted in the bright sun at the activity in the half-lit depth.

"Oh, God," she whispered.

Two of the largest rats appeared to be fighting over the sleeve of a shirt. "Oh, God," she said again.

"Why, what is it, my dear?" Mrs. Pankhurst asked.

"It's not laundry."

Mrs. Pankhurst and Mrs. Stanton Blatch followed her gaze to the spot below, where they could clearly see the larger rat prevailing in battle over the gnawed arm of a human.

THREE

Noah Goodwin, Esq.
via Royal Mail Station
District Amritsar
Punjab, India

Professor Asa Goodwin
Dean of Archaeological Studies
New York University
50 West 4th Street
New York, New York
United States of America

Dear Father,
Extraordinary news! Let me first give you our location. We are three miles north of Beas, on the west bank of the Hyphasis, which we think is the Greek name of the Beas River.

For the last three months, we have been excavating the disruptions found in the sedimentary formations halfway up a hillside, and a week ago, the greatest discovery! My deductions have proved correct.

We broke through a wall above a shelf hidden from river view and have found the entrance to an immense cavern, many hundreds feet deep.

There are a number of passageways we've discovered leading to dozens of small cells. These rooms are bare and so low-ceilinged as to require one to stoop nearly double on entering. These cells are a trove of artifacts so far: coins, combs, and vessels. One can only imagine what a proper excavation will yield!

The passages themselves are hewn as straight as could be laid out by a modern engineer. One large room, fifty-by-eighty feet, seems probably to have been used for a *langhar,* as we've found cooking utensils and charring from fires. But no animal bones have been found, suggesting the inhabitants ate no meat, a significant possible link to the Nazarene Essenes.

On many of the walls are inscriptions, which resemble a pre-Vedic Sanskrit.

We have gathered a number of artifacts, which are being shipped to you with this posting, along with several photographs of the site. You will see an accounting of these in the bill of lading.

Additionally, this site may very well be the Hydaspes of legend, the battlefield upon which Alexander faced King Porus.

I need not tell you, Father, of the significance of this find. Surely, it is sufficient to convince Chancellor Perkins and the University Board of Trustees to extend my funding for the upcoming year. I urge you to earnestly plead our cause to the Board, as without additional funding we shall be forced to abandon further excavation.

The rainy season will be upon us in June, necessitating a long hiatus regardless of funding. Without assurance of further funding, any hope of resuming our excavation in October is bleak.

The outlaw Bhils continue to plague and plunder this region at will. Should we have to abandon this site, it will be but a matter of days before this magnificent find is thoroughly looted and precious artifacts bled haphazardly onto the Indian black market. The colonial government's disastrous policy of coercion continues against growing resistance. We certainly cannot look to the Crown, for either protection or support, despite the historical importance of this discovery. Confusion reigns and, as in any dark age, the first to suffer in its wake are the arts and sciences.

I beg you, Father, to do your utmost on our behalf and write me as soon as you've received the financial assurances we require, as we will need to arrange for the security and preservation of this site shortly.

Your loving son,
Noah

FOUR

Prof. Asa Goodwin
Dean of Archaeological Studies
New York University
50 West 4th Street
New York, New York
United States of America

Noah Goodwin, Esq.
Via Royal Mail Station
District Amritsar
Punjab, India

Dear Noah,
    Son, regrettably, I must tell you I have failed in securing the additional funding you require to continue your dig. The University is adamant in directing all available archaeological research funds to excavations at this time being undertaken at Luxor. I am afraid your cause before the University Board is hopeless for the present.

    Nevertheless, do not lose heart. I urge you to join me here in New York, with as much evidence and photography as you can provide. New York society seems caught in a kind of collector's fever for relics, fossils and antiquities of all sorts. Archaeological projects are increasingly benefiting from the interest of enthusiastic, independent philanthropists and investors, many of whom I have become acquainted with socially during my University tenure.

Additionally, summer employment with the city is available at a good wage. Due to the subway excavation, the City Engineer's office is seeking a surveyor to update Viele's 1864 subterranean map of Manhattan.

Do come. Come quickly. All is not lost, I assure you. I enclose an amount which should be sufficient to secure the site against vandalism until after the rainy season, by which time I am confident you shall be able to privately raise the funding you require to resume the scientific exploration of your magnificent find. I will expect you at the earliest possibility.

Warmest affection from,
Your father

FIVE

I t's called a dry Martini," Asa Goodwin informed his
son. "Five parts gin, one part dry Vermouth, and a
twist of lemon. Some prefer an olive. What do you think?"

"Damn good use of gin, I'll say that." Noah Goodwin
drained his glass then replaced it from the tray of one of Mrs.
Astor's passing servants. Father and son stood at the center of a
small circle of men, old-monied monopolists who felt compelled
to occasionally posture themselves as genial philanthropists.

The two Goodwin men bore a striking resemblance,
although there was a twenty-five years difference and the son was
taller.

"To answer your question, Mr. Belmont," Noah said,
"No, I don't find it oppressive at all."

"I don't see how you endure it," Belmont, a portly man,
said.

"Every three or four days we return to the surface camp,
and certainly it's good to see sky and sun. But, you know, I think
the underworld is maligned. It can be an interesting place from
which to come and go. Gilgamesh, a Sumerian and Babylonian
hero, visited an ancestor in the bowels of the earth. And Orpheus
ventured there to bring back Eurydice. There one could find the
Buddhist kingdom of Shamballah, or the lost tribe of the Incas
holed up with their golden treasures."

"Even Christ is said to have descended into Hell," one of
the listeners said. "Theodore van Rensselaer," the man said with

a wry smile. Noah raised his glass toward van Rensselaer.

"But, surely lost treasure is just fable and legend, Mr. Goodwin," someone insisted.

"Oh, no, not so. An Inca General named Rumiñahui fled the marauding Spanish Conquistadores, and took with him the ransom he had been collecting for the release of his king.

"General Rumiñahui disappeared into the remote, mountainous region of Ecuador called the Llanganati. The load of gold, which disappeared with him, is considered the largest, undiscovered treasure in the western hemisphere, valued at nearly twenty million dollars."

"Did you say *twenty* million?" several gentlemen guffawed.

"At today's market value, yes."

"Have you ever considered undertaking such an expedition?" The men listening listened more intently now.

"I wouldn't mind a bit of treasure hunting, once I've completed my current excavation in the Punjab, of course."

"Yes, of course. But *the Incas*—I've always enjoyed Latin America. In fact, we're sailing to Venezuela in the fall. Perhaps you'd join us aboard? We could talk about possibly putting together an expedition. What do you say?" Belmont nudged Noah with his elbow. "Could be a very good wager for both of us."

"Unfortunately, by the fall," Noah said, "the rainy season will have passed, and I'll have returned to my excavation in the Punjab."

"How about this?" van Rensselaer spoke up. "Why not join us for the weekend at our house at Oyster Bay? It's a fairly convivial group. We'll be about twenty or so. A few friends of mine and some of mother's. Your father has been our guest. Haven't you, Professor Goodwin?"

"Your mother is a gracious woman," Noah's father said.

"There, you see. Tell me, Goodwin, how's your poker?"

"I play a bit, but not for years."

"He learned as a youngster, from his mother, actually," Asa Goodwin said.

"Something tells me the poker game has already begun," van Rensselaer said. He lit a cigarette and picked a bit of loose tobacco from his lip. "I'll send a car for you Saturday noon. You must join us as well, Professor."

"Very kind of you," Professor Goodwin replied.

"Good. Then it's done. I look forward to it. Hope you like modern music; we've a terrific Tin Pan Alley trio on for Saturday night. And they've a very pretty girl singer; a Miss LeSeuer—or something like that.

"Now I must find the hors d'œuvre I know is circulating somewhere. Excuse me, gentlemen, until Saturday." Van Rensselaer stepped away, taking Mr. Belmont by the shoulder.

"Yes, I'll see you then, as well," Belmont added as he was led off.

They all sauntered off leaving Noah alone with his father for the first time since he'd arrived at the reception. Professor Goodwin smiled affably then turned a disapproving eye on his son. "Why in heaven's name are you belting back your drinks?"

"Because this is demeaning, Father. Charming my way into the good graces of these people."

"Yes, well, I find your shame admirable but you must understand something. This is not the frontier you're on. Charm is coin of the realm here. Be grateful you've got it. It's how money is raised and business gets done here."

"Well then, how about this for a reason   I *like* to drink." Noah squinted at his father. "When did you start wearing that?"

"What are you talking about?"

"The beard, Father. It wasn't there yesterday."

"It most certainly was. You just haven't noticed." Professor Goodwin put a finger to his stubble of goatee.

"Very becoming," Noah said.

"Oh, do you like it? It is growing in nicely—See here, don't change the subject."

"No, really. It's stylish I think. Suits you."

"You are not taking me seriously, I see. Come along. Have a seat, son. You're starting to tilt." They settled into two spindly *gros de Tours* chairs.

"What's everyone whispering about?" Noah asked.

"What? Oh, yes. There was news earlier. Seems there's been a murder."

"In this polite, tight-arsed little group?" Noah said. "Can't imagine any one of these waxworks, besides van Rensselaer there, mustering sufficient vitality for anything as robust as murder."

"Shhh, Noah, lower your voice. Now, you mustn't joke," Professor Goodwin said. "It seems Mrs. Pankhurst—the tall one by the window—"

"Ahh yes, the renowned and valiant Emmeline Pankhurst."

"—and her friend, Mrs. Stanton Blatch, the stout one next to Mrs. Astor, were taking a guided tour of the lower east side slums and discovered a woman's body."

"*They* discovered a murder victim?" Noah whispered. "Probably more local color than they'd bargained for."

"I wish you wouldn't be flip. A woman is dead, the mother of several children I understand."

"You're right. My apology."

"Mrs. Pankhurst received a note from the young woman they were accompanying: the police have discovered the victim's throat had been cut."

"Yes, well, that is pretty grim. Is there something we should say or do? I mean everyone seems to know. Judging from all the whispering and furtive glances, you'd think *Mesdames* were the culprits."

"I suppose, in a way they are. They're guilty of being the vehicles of the single, most unpleasant topic in society. Not just a death, but a murder! A murder among the lower classes to boot. Unspeakable. And, the unspeakable is always spoken in whispers."

"It's absurd," Noah said not whispering. "Death is the most universal occurrence on the planet. Fear and supersti—"

"Will you lower your voice. See here, I know you're angry about your funding, but getting smashed—Aha, Mrs. Astor, dear lady." Both men stood for their hostess. "I don't believe you've met my son Noah."

"How d'you do, Mrs. Astor." Noah said slurring his *s*'s just slightly.

Mrs. Astor wore black, as would be expected of the

widow of her former husband, John Jacob Astor IV, who'd been one of the fifteen hundred souls lost in the sinking of the *Titanic* that spring. The fact he left a newer, current Mrs. Astor in the form of the enormously pregnant, teen-aged, Madeleine Talmadged Astor, seemed to not make up any part of Mrs. Astor's consciousness.

The tabloid press had made hay with the scandalous divorce and Astor's re-marriage to a girl thirty-nine years his junior. Now that he was dead, Mrs. Ava Astor believing, like Lord Walpole, *all history is a lie,* conducted herself as if the excruciating events of the previous two years had simply never occurred.

"No, we've not met," Mrs. Astor replied. "How do you do, young man. Professor Goodwin, wherever have you been keeping this handsome lad?"

"Eh, in a cave, Madam. In India."

"I daresay."

"Yes, he's just returned. A very exciting find he's discovered. He's taken a position here for the summer, in the City Engineer's office. Surveying, map-making, that sort of thing."

"How interesting," Mrs. Astor replied politely.

"I was just suggesting perhaps we should step out to the terrace. Perhaps a bit of fresh air—"

"Oh, please do. So nice to have met you, young man. Such a lively addition to our little *waxworks* gathering." Mrs. Astor smiled tersely and turned to greet a newly arrived guest.

"Monsignor Palladin," she said. "I'm so happy the Cardinal could spare you. Is he feeling better?"

"Come on, son." Professor Goodwin led the way to the terrace.

"Guess I put my foot in it," Noah said sheepishly.

"You guess correctly."

From the terrace facing Fifth Avenue, the spectacular New York skyline glimmered in the sun starting its drop in the western sky.

"Skyscrapers they're called."

"Amazing. Nothing like this back home, heh, Dad?"

"Oh, I haven't thought of England as home for a very long time. Or India either, for that matter. America is home now."

"Really, Dad? Never going back?"

"I doubt it. I'm happy at the University. It's a new frontier of knowledge. England is a distant memory and these bones are a bit too brittle now for the rigors of India."

"I don't know *where* home is," Noah said. "The place I'll always want to return to."

"That's an easy one to figure out. Home is where the heart is."

"You mean marriage?"

"No, I mean love, actually. Poets speak very highly of it, I'm told."

"Well, I assure you, I *do* love the ladies."

"No doubt. But when you settle on just one—"

"*I want a girl just like the girl that married dear old Dad.* Sorry, don't count on it. Just not the marrying kind."

"Yes, well, you'll not likely find another of your mother's ilk, that's for certain. She was a rare creature. Good American, Texas stock. Sloughing it out with me, shoulder to shoulder, first in the Cape Colony, and then the Punjab."

Noah studied the softening of his father's face. "You miss her, don't you?"

"A great deal, son. There's no land as dear to me now as a certain patch of earth, uptown in Trinity Cemetery. New York is my home now. I can only wish you as much happiness someday."

"Dad, I've never heard you talk this way."

"Yes, well blame it on the martinis. I had two before you arrived. I, at least, know how to hold my liquor. At any rate, tell me how'd the first week on the job go?"

"Pretty routine. But I've been asked to head a project in September that comes with a bonus. An excavation the city is researching now."

"Another colonial burial ground?"

"Something more recent, they think. A fellow by the name of Beach, back in '70, secretly constructed an ornate, experimental subway station with some kind of a pneumatic power source," Noah said.

"Always thought it was a myth: a legendary underground creation with chandeliers and fish tanks, and supposedly, a grand piano," Professor Goodwin said.

"Legendary maybe, but not a myth. There aren't any city records, only journal reports. Beach paid for the entire construction from his own pocket. Enormous hoopla at the time. Then it was bricked up and forgotten. Problem is the location. It may be smack in the middle of the proposed BRT Broadway line."

"What does the city want you to do?"

"Find it. Survey it. Bring in a wrecking crew."

"September, you say?"

"Then back to the Punjab in October."

"With at least a few dollars in your pocket. It all seems to dovetail nicely for you."

"Yes, but unfortunately, *only a few* dollars."

"Well, the summer isn't over yet. Let's see what develops." They were comfortably silent for a while, looking, not at each other, but up at the newborn skyline.

"Dad, about, you know, in there. If I embarrassed you, I apologize. Really."

"No need. I guess I was a bit of a topper in my day as well. Always needed to blow off steam when I came off a dig. And your mother, well, there was a spirited girl. I imagine you come by your temperament honestly."

"I suppose now it's me they'll be discussing in whispered tones." Noah smirked.

"No doubt."

"Well, it's all right, Dad. You've enough solid respectability for both of us. Are there any of these nabobs you don't know?"

"A few."

"Dad, look there."

"Where?"

"That woman. There, with Mrs. Standing Blotch."

"Stanton Blatch. Her mother was Elizabeth Cady

Stan—"

"No, no. The redhead next to her. *What* a beautiful woman. Dad, you'll be happy to know, I think I'm in love. Again."

"Don't be ridiculous—oh, I say. She is quite a looker at that."

SIX

Cate tugged at the tight bodice of her dress with still trembling fingers. Earlier, at the Twenty-second Street police station, she'd seen Mr. Nicolosi in the corridor, sitting hunched on a wooden bench, wiping at tears, with the empty cuff of his sleeve. She wanted to sit with him for a moment, and fill some of the terrible, empty space surrounding him. But the detective assigned to the murder of Felicita Nicolosi, Lt. Dermot O'Keeffe, was impatient to get on with the formalities. He'd insisted someone had to come now and officially identify the dead woman.

So, accompanied by Lt. O'Keeffe—who smelled of Bushmills and *Eau de Cologne*—Cate had seen to the task at the city morgue located in the basement of Bellevue Hospital. She would at least spare Mr. Nicolosi that ordeal, so he could go home now to his children.

She might not have, however, had she known what she was going to see. Cate had, of course, seen dead people before; in the slums, it wasn't an unusual sight. And, during her nursing studies she'd seen cadavers; but never had she seen so violent an outcome as the remains of Mrs. Nicolosi. O'Keeffe lifted the corner of a coarse sheet. The dead woman was as white as the chipped enamel slab she lay on, her skull caved-in from the high fall, her face barely recognizable as a face.

The police said Mrs. Nicolosi's throat had been cut. The truth was the entire neck had been hacked through, but for a single bit of sinewy tendon near the severed spinal cord. It left the head juxtaposed eccentrically to the shoulders of the body. Cate momentarily felt wobbly.

The dead woman's dismembered arm, gouged by rats, lay beside her; the hand was completely missing. Cate was horrified, and at the same time transfixed by the grotesquerie. Mrs. Nicolosi's hair was dripping wet. This confused Cate until she noticed a narrow, rubber hose, coiled on the cement floor, seeping water from its lip. A culvert ran round the edge of the enamel slab top, ending in a drainpipe at the foot.

So, that's what they did, she realized. Cleaned the remains with a hose. Cate stared at the rubber tubing, could not stop staring at it. It frightened her, reminded her of something she couldn't quite place. Not just death, but mayhem, madness. She took a step back as though the thing might slither toward her.

Then it came to her. The feeding tube forced down Mrs. Pankhurst's throat. Cate gagged. The stench of decay and chemicals was intolerable and she couldn't breath.

"This is Mrs. Felicita Nicolosi," she managed to say, then turned and walked away quickly.

"Tell the family," O'Keeffe said loudly, "they should come claim the body."

"What about the autopsy?" Cate turned back to ask.

"For her? Wot for?" he asked passing Cate as he left.

"The investigation," Cate said surprised.

"The families don't like it, all the cuttin', you know. We've got everything we need, all writ down. Good day t'ya, Miss," he said.

"Wait. That's absurd. The woman's been murdered!" Cate protested.

"Well, t'ain't up to me. Maybe there's t'be one. Maybe no. Good day t'ya." Lt. O'Keeffe marched out, leaving the double doors swinging on their hinges. Now, there was Mr. Nicolosi to tell, and the children waiting for word of their mother. There would be no hoped-for mistake as to the identity of the dead woman.

Cate stayed with the family in their flat until Father Costello, the parish priest from St. Stephen's, at last arrived. She was no champion of the Church and it's traditionalist dogma concerning women, but was nonetheless relieved at the priest's arrival.

He was loved in the community. From the pulpit Father Costello preached the gospel of love in a voice so affable it left each man feeling more kindly toward his fellow. Among the parish children, it was well known he gave the most lenient penance in Holy Confession, seldom more than five Hail Marys. But if you hid a sinful deed or thought, he knew it, and would ferret it out. Then penance was levied accordingly: Mass twice a day for a month instead of baseball.

Grateful for his sturdy presence Cate finally slipped away unnoticed.

SEVEN

Cate wanted nothing so much now as to sit quietly in her small parlor. She needed something to eat, to have a bath and a nap on a crisp, white sheet. Today she'd seen too much of human sorrow and evil. Tired as she was, she was determined to still take advantage of Mrs. Pankhurst's invitation to Mrs. Astor's party. She sent a note for Mrs. Pankhurst to Mrs. Astor's address. Cate willed her fingers to stop trembling and finally they did. She brushed her hair, then fixed it securely with a good jade barrette. Without vanity, she could admit to herself that the piles of oxblood hair, the buxom figure she'd inherited from her mother, the length of bone and erect carriage she'd acquired from her father, created a presence which drew attention that she was willing to use for political purpose.

Of her face, her mother had told her on the occasion of her seventeenth birthday, that only a high intellectual brow saved her from the look of a complete voluptuary. Cate had never quite understood if this was intended as compliment or criticism.

That was the year she'd left home for nursing studies at Claverack College-on-Hudson, where, as many of the girls at school had, she'd experimented with the usual fumblings of the beaux come a-calling. In Cate's case, it was a cadet from nearby West Point Academy. He was a tall, blond gallant, two years her senior, who presented all the charm one might require.

Despite having all the natural inclinations of the female *libido*—a word newly popularized in college circles by Dr.

Freud—she'd found it all a bit tedious. On graduation day, she broke his heart with a hurried good-bye, when he'd been expecting a quick *I do.*

The very idea of matrimony repelled her. All those pinched, sallow faces who'd gazed up at her father on his civic soapbox, looking for a hero to save them from social ills they'd not live long enough to see righted. Cate understood clearly her life's mission, and romance played no part. She fastened her shoes and marched out the door.

When she arrived at the Astor mansion, a tail coated butler showed her into an enormous drawing room where perhaps forty men and women stood chatting in small groups. Chamber musicians played Ravel in a corner by the potted palms. Servants in breeches offered canapés and cocktails from heavy silver trays.

She'd had to guess at what to wear, five-thirty being too early for evening wear. She hoped she'd made a good choice in a grey broadcloth sheath, although the bodice was tight, and the fabric heavy for summer. She gave the uncomfortable bodice one last tug, then stepped into the room.

With the standard social smile, which she did not at all feel, firmly fixed, Cate circled the room close to the walls, hoping to catch sight of either Mrs. Pankhurst or Mrs. Stanton Blatch.

At last, she spotted them on the terrace, in a small knot of smiling guests. Cate approached and waited to be noticed. Annoyingly, small beads of moisture formed above her upper lip, and she brought her handkerchief to her face with a hand still none too steady. So many perfumed guests didn't help.

"Cate, dear! You're here," Mrs. Stanton Blatch said. "Look, Emmeline, Miss Gallagher has been able to join us, after all."

"I'm so happy you came. Such dreadful information from the police," Mrs. Pankhurst said. "I sail tonight aboard *Mauritania*, and before I depart I wanted very much to thank you. Please give the family my condolence."

"I will."

"You must write and let me know if there is anything I can do."

Cate knew this was an opportunity she should immediately accept, and as awkward as it sometimes is, she had to take advantage of any offer of help.

"Thank you, Mrs. Pankhurst. There *is* something. I spoke some weeks ago with Mr. Nicolosi, the children's father, about being fitted for an articulating prosthesis. He lost a hand in a work accident, you see, as I said. Unfortunately, the thirty-five dollars cost is entirely beyond the family's means."

"Say no more. You may count on me for a personal donation to the family. Two-hundred dollars?"

Cate was elated. "You are *very* generous, Mrs. Pankhurst."

"Not at all."

"That amount will not only cover medical costs but will sustain the family for a number of months."

"That is my intention. I'll arrange it before I embark."

At that moment, Mrs. Astor approached, and Cate was introduced. Mrs. Astor was surprisingly well informed about the objectives and goals of the Family Aid Society. She held forth for a solid five minutes, during which neither Cate, nor anyone else, interrupted their indomitable hostess.

"Now, you must allow me to make some introductions," Mrs. Astor finally said. What followed was a dizzying twenty minutes of being led about meeting people, one after the other.

"And this brilliant young man, Miss Gallagher, is Mr. Scott Nearing. He is Secretary of the Pennsylvania Child Labor Committee. It's a volunteer society working to solve the child labor problem in their state.

"Oh, yes. How do you do, Mr. Nearing." Cate said. "I've read your book, *Social Adjustment*. It's given me great inspiration."

"I'm very happy to hear it," he said smiling. "And I have read of your difficulties with the Postal Inspector. Hold fast, Miss Gallagher, and I'm certain you'll prevail. Under the Constitution, every citizen in this country has the right to express himself on public issues."

"If only I could convince Mr. Comstock that the legalization of birth control *is* a public issue," Cate responded before she was whisked away again by Mrs. Astor. She was introduced to Livingstons, Drexels, Fisks and Fricks. Nearly, but not quite all, expressed their support of Cate's social reform ideas, and of those, she made a mental note to send the usual letter soliciting funds for Family Aid's operating budget and legal expense fund. Things took a somewhat different turn when a Mr. van Rensselaer expressed, quite loudly, his belief in the improvement of the human race through various forms of selective breeding amongst the inferior classes.

When Cate informed him emphatically eugenics was not a motivating factor in their birth control education, he replied *pity*, and turned his attention abruptly to a passing tray of *foie gras*.

Mrs. Stanton Blatch rescued Cate from this awkward moment. "Come, Cate dear," she said, leading her away. "You've done a yeoman's job here today. Come out to the terrace with me. You look as though you could use some fresh air—why you're as pale as a ghost," Mrs. Stanton Blatch said approaching. "Have you eaten today?"

"No. It's just—"

They'd no sooner stepped onto the marbled terrace than an acquaintance of Mrs. Stanton Blatch approached.

"Harriot, dear lady."

"Asa," she said. "How good to see you, and looking so fit. Allow me to introduce Miss Catherine Gallagher. Cate, this is Professor Asa Goodwin of New York University."

"How do you do? May I introduce my son Noah."

"Miss Gallagher," Noah said. "A pleasure to meet you."

"Come sit, Cate," said Mrs. Stanton Blatch. You look exhausted. You've had a very long day, haven't you? And no food."

"Will you allow me to sit with you, Miss Gallagher?" Noah said, stepping deftly between Cate and Mrs. Stanton Blatch.

"You don't mind if I steal the most attractive girl in the room, do you, Mrs. Stanton Blatch?" Noah said. He led the way to a marble bench along the balustrade overlooking Fifth Avenue. Cate glanced quizzically over her shoulder at Mrs. Stanton Blatch who seemed a bit miffed. Mrs. Stanton Blatch *did* mind, and was about to say so, when she noticed a gesture from

Mrs. Pankhurst. Mrs. Stanton Blatch flustered a moment, then with a pained smile, excused herself and left Noah to make the best of his opportunity with Miss Gallagher.

EIGHT

Noah slid next to Cate on the sun-warmed, marble bench. "You've had quite a day I understand."

"Yes," she said appreciating the note of sympathy in his manner. "Just a moment to catch my breath I think," she said trying not to sound as tired as she felt.

"Do you know many of these people?" he asked.

"Only Mrs. Stanton Blatch and Mrs. Pankhurst, and I don't really know her well, Mrs. Pankhurst I mean. We met yesterday after she spoke."

"Yes, I read the account in the paper. So, you're a suffragist? You must have enjoyed her talk."

"Very much. In fact, I was hoping to have a few more words with her, but she sails for Southampton tonight. Have you been introduced?"

"Not yet."

"And Mr. Nearing. Did you meet him? His work is very important. He's helped pass child labor laws in Pennsylvania and is hoping to use that as the basis for a national child labor law, to be amended to the Constitution.

"It's going to be an uphill battle the entire way, I'm afraid," she said finding her wind. "The issue has already gone before the Supreme Court once. Incredibly, they held child labor laws violated a child's right to contract for work. Completely absurd, as the law holds individuals under the age of eighteen cannot legally contract for, well, for *any*thing."

"You seem quite passionate about it."

"Yes, certainly I am. Someday, when a woman is seated on the Supreme Court—"

"A woman?" Noah chortled. "On the United States Supreme Court. You're joking."

"I am not," Cate said surprised. "Why would that be a joke?"

"Well, because," Noah stammered. The idea, I mean, well—would she wear trousers?"

"Is that where you carry your abilities, Mr. Goodwin? In your trousers?" Cate asked flatly.

Noah thought better of the reply that was on his tongue. "Well, I didn't really mean to joke," he said. "But surely it's an impossibility. Women can't even vote."

"Mrs. Esther Morris was a very competent judge in Wyoming, where women most certainly do have the vote. There's no reason a woman shouldn't aspire to the highest court. Just who made the upper regions of human attainment the exclusive domain of men anyway?"

"Yes, of course you're correct, and I beg your pardon. It's just that, well, the image of a woman on the Supreme Court—it's difficult to imagine. A member of the fair sex, someone as fair, and delightfully attractive as yourself—"

"Spare me your flattery, Mr. Goodwin. And, your condescension, thank you." Cate shifted her body weight, just slightly, giving Noah the shoulder. "Your failure of imagination, is very disappointing," she said scanning the room.

"But Miss Gallagher, it so happens I have a vivid imagination—"

"And just what do you *imagine* might transpire between you and me, since intelligent conversation is obviously out of the question?" Cate felt perspiration form above her lip again; she was parched and hot, and annoyed with the man sitting next to her but felt too wobbly to get up and walk away. What she wanted badly but wouldn't admit even to herself was a gulp of her Dad's old potcheen and his shoulder to lean on.

Noah leaned in closer. "Do you dance? Because, I've heard about a terrific, new spot uptown, the Audubon Ballroom, not far from Brush Stadium. Then a late supper. What do you say?"

"One moment, Mr. Goodwin." Cate felt uncomfortably constrained in her tight bodice, and her voice sounded shrill even to her own ears. She paused to square her shoulders and take a deep breath before continuing.

"I'm afraid you've mistaken me for someone I am not: some little ninny whom you're going to sweep off her feet to a dance floor. And, as for a late supper—with you? Not this side of *Hades*, Mr. Goodwin."

"Miss Gallagher," Noah said in mock distress. "I assure you, I am not the devil you take me for."

"Not the devil, Mr. Goodwin. Just a silly drunk. Now, if you'll excuse me, I'd like to join Mrs. Astor and her other guests, whose conversation will not be about late night suppers, I assure you."

Cate brusquely stood up, as did Noah, when a very odd thing happened. The last thing Cate was conscious of was a strong hand around her waist as sky and marble floor abruptly switched places, and graceful as a lily, she fainted.

NINE

I've never fainted in my life," Cate insisted.

"Well, you have now," said the gentleman checking her pulse against his pocket watch.

"Just lie still for a moment," he said. The man began touching her head like a grocer examining a melon.

"Who *are* you?" Cate asked, confused and annoyed.

"Cate, dear," Mrs. Stanton Blatch interceded. "This is Dr. Harvey Cushing—of Boston. He is a brain surgeon," she said in a tone that implied the absolute power of life and death.

"I see. Well, thank you, sir," Cate said struggling to regain her aplomb. "I suppose if you hadn't caught me, I might well have cracked my skull on the floor, and would actually have need of your particular skills." She began to rise from the chaise longue she'd been deposited on. "As it is, I feel quite recovered. Thank you."

"I'm afraid I cannot claim that heroic privilege. The honor of catching you belongs to this gentleman," he said raising his eyes to Noah Goodwin.

"You're quite welcome, Miss Gallagher," Noah said, which visibly irritated Cate.

"Cate, you should rest yourself for a few moments more," Mrs. Stanton Blatch said. "Emmeline and I must be leaving; I'm seeing her off at the dock. But I promise to call on you in a few days."

"But I was hoping to—"

"It will have to keep for now, my dear. Take good care of her, Doctor. We're expecting important accomplishments from Miss Gallagher.

"And, my dear," she added *entre nous,* "if ever you're in Boston you really ought to see Dr. Cushing's collection of brain samples. I'm sure it sets a world's record for something. Extraordinary, really."

"But, I—"

"Rest, dear. I'll be in touch."

Dr. Cushing placed his hand on Cate's chest pushing her down into the chaise. "Don't try to stand just yet."

"Here, Miss Gallagher," Mrs. Astor said pushing through the onlookers. "Drink this. A dram of cassis, don't you think, Dr. Cushing?"

"Yes. And perhaps something to eat," Cushing said. "I understand from Mrs. Pankhurst and Mrs. Stanton Blatch, young lady, you've had a very enervating day. And haven't eaten."

"A plate is being prepared," Mrs. Astor said promptly. "A bit of cold lobster and fruit, Doctor?"

"Yes, fine. And, perhaps now, if everyone would be kind enough to withdraw and allow Miss Gallagher a bit of air."

Mrs. Astor's guests snapped to, like suddenly animated statues, and the low purr of conversation resumed. Cate was grateful to be spared further embarrassing attention from the other guests. Deflated and depressed, she wanted nothing so much as to make a quick exit with whatever remaining grace she could muster.

"Thank you, Doctor. Really, I'd feel so much more comfortable if I could sit up. Perhaps even stand," she said.

"On condition you drink this right down," he urged.

Cate took a small obedient swallow of the syrupy cassis.

"No, not a sip," he said. "I want you to swallow the whole thing. Knock it right back like a good soldier."

Cate tossed down the liqueur without further protest, then swung her legs off the chaise and sat upright. For a swift moment, she thought to ask for another cassis until Dr. Cushing said, "There's a good girl. Now, I want you to eat. Thank you," Cushing said to the maid holding a small plate, dismissing her with a wave of his hand.

"Just a bite or two, Miss Gallagher. Open wide," he urged, raising a fork to her lips.

"Really, Doctor Cushing, it's not necessary to feed me like a child."

"Now, none of that. The doctor insists." Cate swallowed the mouthful whole like medicine before Cushing could start making choo-choo train sounds.

"Really, Doctor, I think perhaps home to a good night's rest is the best course for me."

Determinedly, Cate stood up, as did Dr. Cushing. "I agree," he said eagerly. "Have you a motorcar?"

"No, I came by trolley."

"Ah! Fortunately, I have the use of a motorcar and driver. Where do you live?"

"In Greenwich Village, but I'm feeling quite well now. I'm sure I'll be able to—"

"Nonsense. Doctor's orders. Head injuries can be quite serious."

"But my head is not injured—"

"Besides, I've been looking forward to seeing Greenwich Village again, that bohemian bastion. What was it I read? '*Short-haired women in exotic Grecian drapery; long-haired men in artists' smocks and open toed sandals.*' We've nothing like it in Boston, I assure you. Curbside poets and, he lowered his voice to a whisper, the politics of free love. Something your Family Aid caters to I'll vouch. Tell me, have you ever heard of trepanning?"

Cate was flabbergasted, her mouth agape. *Two* mashers in one evening, she thought. How can that be!? Here, of all places. And what a frighteningly insufferable toad this one was.

She had it on her tongue to say something shockingly rude to the titillated Dr. Cushing, when she thought better of it.

"Well, thank you so much, Dr. Cushing," she said instead. "I should say good night to Mrs. Astor first. I wonder if you could find her for me, while I rest just a moment more." Cate sat back down on the edge of the chaise.

"Certainly, my dear," he said, quickly looking about. "Wait right here." Dr. Cushing scampered off, small plate in hand.

The moment he was out of sight, Cate stood, turned on her heels and headed straight to the foyer. She was out the front door, down the marble stairs, across Fifth Avenue and onto a southbound trolley as fast as she could hike up her skirt.

The lone churchman among Mrs. Astor's guests had closely observed it all. It wasn't the first time Monsignor Palladin had crossed Miss Gallagher's path, though she wasn't aware of it. Her trial for indecency had some time ago made her an object of his scrutiny.

What did surprise him was her presence at Mrs. Astor's reception. The girl had done well for herself, moving quickly into the circle of so august and influential a person. No doubt, the publicity, or rather, the notoriety her activities generated had won the attention of many of the politically misguided.

Steps were being taken to make a severe example of Miss Catherine Gallagher. And as for her iniquitous, *so-called* Family Aid Society, the Monsignor calculated, cut the serpent's head off and the body dies with it.

TEN

F*arpoint*, the van Rensselaer four hundred-acre, Long Island estate, faced Great South Bay. Noah was happy for a morning out of doors. He watched a fine racing yacht glide gracefully along the blue-gray horizon as smaller sail craft: packets, sloops, and local fish dories, maneuvered in and out of the natural harbor.

He hoped a hike in the wooded acres, while everyone else slept in the many bedrooms of the house—if a thing so grand could be called a house—would get his blood pumping. He'd had astounding good luck at cards the night before; his funding worries were over for some time to come. Then, he'd drunk too much, said God knows what to embarrass his father and stumbled off to bed with the band singer.

Perhaps it was time to cut back. Just a bit. Try to get eight hours sleep once in awhile. Eat better. No more street cart food. Make a fresh start with his newly acquired funds.

The salt in the air cleared his head a bit and made him hungry for breakfast. He wandered back toward the house in hopes of kippers or even mackerel with his eggs, and biscuits, hot, buttered American biscuits, with jam. Noah enjoyed the prodigious American breakfast. He'd recently heard of a colorful businessman, "Diamond" Jim Brady, the richest Irishman in America, whose typical breakfast was said to be eggs, pancakes, pork chops, cornbread, fried potatoes, hominy, muffins, and a beefsteak, washed down with a gallon of orange juice.

Only in America, Noah thought, or perhaps ancient Rome, would such excess be considered a virtue. That appealed to him. He supposed it was the Texas half of him that admired such largesse.

Slipping in through a side door of the library, Noah found encouraging signs of life. A small hearth fire had been set. Morning coffee, cognac, and several copies each of the *New York Times* and a *Post* morning special had been laid out. He poured a cup from the Georgian coffee server and took a gulp of the hot, black brew. The room smelled of oil soap, undisturbed books and flowers enough to masque the things that rich men feared.

"Breakfast will be served shortly. But I can have something brought in here now, if you wish."

Noah turned expecting to see the van Rensselaer butler but instead found van Rensselaer himself. "Good morning," Noah said. "I can wait." He added a healthy slug of brandy to his cup from a thoughtfully placed decanter, despite his recently considered resolutions.

"Hair of the dog?" van Rensselaer observed.

"It works," Noah grunted.

"Yes. Yes, it does."

Noah picked up the *Post* and settled onto a leather sofa with his cup.

"Sleep well?" van Rensselaer asked.

"Quite well. Country air agrees with me."

"And Miss LeSeuer?"

Noah sipped from his cup. "I imagine she did, as well," he said with a small grin. "I'll have to ask."

"An impressive set of lungs that girl has, I must say. She certainly knows how to heat up a torch song," van Rensselaer said with all but a wink and a nod. "By the way, you're a very good poker player."

"It was a favorite pastime of my mother's in India."

"Your mother's little pastime has netted you about twelve thousand dollars. Enough, I would think, to fund your work for at least the next several years. You should be quite grateful—to your mother." Van Rensselaer crossed to a large, red-tortoiseshell desk, and removed a checkbook from the drawer.

"Just luck," Noah said opening the pages of his newspaper.

"Was it luck, do you think? I hope not," van Rensselaer said starting to write. "That would be very upsetting."

"In what way?" Noah asked.

"Well, you see," van Rensselaer said setting down his fountain pen. "My father once told me it's far better to be lucky than smart. That is, human intelligence has its limits. Nothing to be done about it. But luck—there you have the highest indication the gods have smiled on you. I would hate to think, as any man would, the gods themselves favored you over me in our little game last night."

"Well, I wouldn't look at it that way," Noah said affably.

"No, of course you wouldn't. That would be rude of you. But I wonder, *are* you a lucky man, Goodwin? Luckier than I? Were you favored by the gods, over me?"

"What exactly are you getting at?" Noah asked.

"A proposition," van Rensselaer said pulling an unopened packet of cards from his desk drawer.

"Go on," Noah said.

"The money, I'm not at all concerned about. But I would like to know. Are you a luckier man than I? Do the gods favor *you*? What do you think?"

"Another hand?" Noah asked.

"No. Something more to the point. We cut the deck for high card. Double or nothing."

Noah hesitated. In a single evening he'd won a small fortune. Now he was being asked to risk it all.

"You mustn't feel pressured," van Rensselaer said. "Your check is here. I've only to fill in the amount. Twelve thousand dollars is a large sum of money—to you."

Noah knew he was being goaded now. He didn't need twenty-four thousand; except for the fact, had he twenty-four thousand dollars in his coffer, he'd *never* have to come hat-in-hand to these rich snobs again. And his willingness to risk it all would go a long way, in his own mind, toward expiating his sense of having beggared himself for it.

"So be it," Noah said, then drained his coffee cup. He got up and crossed to van Rensselaer. "We'll leave it to the gods." Van Rensselaer pushed the packet across the desk. Noah picked it up and carefully broke the seal with his thumbnail, removed the fresh deck, then placed it on the desktop.

With a small wave of his hand, van Rensselaer gave the shuffle to Noah.

Once, then twice, then a third, final time, Noah shuffled the deck neatly and slid it to van Rensselaer who tapped it with a single finger, giving the first draw to Noah.

"Jokers high?" Noah asked.

"As you wish."

Noah cut the deck cleanly revealing the seven of spades. If he was disappointed, he didn't show it by so much as a hair.

With a faint smile of satisfaction, van Rensselaer cut the deck again with deliberation, and revealed the five of clubs. Without comment, he picked up his fountain pen and filled in the amount on the check. He blotted the ink and handed the check to Noah.

"Thank you," van Rensselaer said, "for a most interesting morning sport. If you'll excuse me now, I'll just see what's keeping breakfast."

Noah watched his host exit, then sat back down with the newspaper. He tucked the check for twenty-four thousand dollars in his pocket and tried not to think about this change in fortune. It wasn't easy. He would keep his word to his father: stay on for the summer and work. Nothing else to do anyway until the rains passed. Van Rensselaer had been right; it was a great deal of money, more than the average man might earn for twenty-five years of daily labor, and it was his overnight, with scarcely a hair turned in effort.

If it is your prarabdh—your karma, nothing can be otherwise. The voice of his little nursery *ayah,* so many years ago in India, still chimed in his head like a silver bell.

Noah flipped through newspaper pages quickly, trying to distract himself from the check in his pocket. A box advertisement touted the *Ziegfeld Follies* at the New Amsterdam Theater, while below, Hart, Schaffner & Marx offered blue worsted serge suits for the exorbitant price of thirty-three dollars. Lord & Taylor was having a clearance sale on ladies shoes reduced from four dollars to three dollars and thirty-five cents.

Between the two advertisements was a news item: a young couple had been swept out to sea while canoeing from Sheepshead Bay to Rockaway; and a notice from the public health service documented an outbreak of tuberculosis amongst the Seneca Indians on the Allegheny reservation. In Manhattan, firemen and police had rescued a subway excavator from underground quicksand near the Brooklyn Bridge.

Noah made a mental note to check the location against his chart notes on Monday. It was because of incidents like this that Viele's map, charted in 1864, badly needed updating. Manhattan was, after all, an island and the shifting of underground springs, displaced by the sinking of mammoth building foundations was an ongoing problem. While most of the island sat on bedrock schist, areas in lower and mid-town Manhattan sat on top of loam, silt, sand, and clay, much to the dismay of more than one building engineer.

He allowed one thought to tumble in front of another, distracting him from the small fortune burning in his pocket. He flipped the paper to scan the print above the fold on the next page. He sat up when he read the headline.

MURDERED WOMAN WAS
MOTHER OF FIVE
Body Found on Manhattan West Side Identified
as that of Mrs. Ercole Nicolosi

Fifth Grisly Female Death in Lower Borough
Over 12 Month Span!

POLICE HAVE NO CLUES
----
by
A. B. Kahn

Police have disclosed the identity of the woman whose mutilated body was discovered the morning of July 11, as reported by this newspaper. The dead woman is identified as Felicita Nicolosi, the wife of Mr. Ercole Nicolosi. The deceased was a thirty-two-year-old immigrant from Catania, Italy, and the mother of five children, aged two to twelve years.

The body was identified by Miss Catherine S. Gallagher, founder of the Family Aid Society, who made the grim discovery while conducting a tour of Lower East Side slum conditions, accompanied by English suffragist Mrs. Emmeline Pankhurst, and Mrs. Harriot Stanton Blatch, daughter of the late Mrs. Elizabeth Cady Stanton, co-founder of the National Women's Suffrage Association.

According to Mr. Herman Hellenstein, coroner for the borough of Manhattan, Mrs. Nicolosi's throat had been slashed before being toppled from the rooftop of her five-story tenement home. When questioned as to whether the death of Mrs. Nicolosi was connected to the recent homicides of four other immigrant women, Mr. Hellenstein stated any such "conjecture" was strictly a police matter. His office has had no further comment. It is pertinent, in this journalist's opinion, to note Mr. Hellenstein does not hold a medical degree from any academic institution and was an undertaker before his appointment by long-time crony Mayor Gaynor.

The exceedingly violent deaths of five women in the space of twelve months is in no manner a matter of "conjecture". It is a fact.

It is a fact the nude remains of Mrs. Susanna Profaci, a twenty-five-year-old Sicilian immigrant mother, were discovered on August 11, of last year, in a forty-gallon oil-drum, at the Manhattan Municipal Building construction site, the condition of the body too decomposed for viewing.

It is a fact Miss Lucy Mendoza, a nineteen-year-old nursing student from Barcelona, Spain was kidnapped, and on December 15, of last year, was found in an alley off Broadway near Lispenard Street. Miss Mendoza had been fatally stabbed through the heart.

It is a fact fifteen-year-old Miss Agnes Lombardi's nude, headless body was discovered on January 22, floating in the water of the Hudson River.

It is a fact the remains of Miss Engratia Ricci, a Sicilian spinster, aged thirty-eight, were found just two months ago, on May 15, in her rooms on Forsyth Street. Miss Ricci suffered a demise so exceptionally grisly the specifics of her injuries defy description.

Five unspeakably sadistic crimes perpetrated by one whose love of cruelty and abuse of the weaker sex has not seen its like since the unsolved Whitechapel murders of the last century.

And what has been the Tammany Hall response from New York City Police Commissioner Rhinlander Waldo and Mayor

William J. Gaynor? To blame each unexplained homicide on local gangsters.

Preposterous! These are not the acts of local hooligans intent on larcenous gain or profit. These are the serial acts of a single, deranged mind preying, with depraved and murderous intent, upon our weakest and least protected constituents.

It is interesting to note Hizzoner's inaugural address consisted of these few but telling words: "I enter upon this office with the intention of doing the very best I can for the City of New York. That will have to suffice; I can do no more."

Well, Mr. Mayor, your best does not suffice. Your pious pretensions are a hollow sham. Your ineptitude and that of Police Commissioner Waldo is a disgrace. Your inaction, in the face of such sinister deeds, is a dereliction of duty surpassed only by Mr. Waldo's former stint as Fire Commissioner, during which one hundred seventy-five immigrant women died in the Triangle Shirtwaist factory fire: another colossal failure of duty to the hardworking, immigrant poor. For shame, Mr. Mayor. For shame.

Noah dropped the newspaper in his lap, considered what he'd read, then picked it up and re-read the second paragraph. He had little interest in New York politics, but Cate Gallagher intrigued him. She was a beautiful, buxom woman; that had been the first thing he noticed. And, she was something else, too. Something which challenged him. Like a wall over which he had to see. How? he wondered. Did he climb it? Tear the wall down? Dismantle it brick by brick? Ram it in a full frontal attack?

No, surely that wouldn't do. Here was a challenge requiring finesse, a subtle seduction, a delicate breech of resistance. The thought fascinated him. Noah stared at the newspaper and mused how best he might further his acquaintance with Miss Gallagher.

"There you are." Professor Goodwin stuck his head in the library doorway. "Are you eating?"

"What—"

"Breakfast is served."

"Yes. I'll be right there. Then what do you say we head back to the city early, Dad?"

"If you like."

"You should read this newspaper piece. Remember the girl at Mrs. Astor's?"

"Oh, yes, the pretty one. Miss Gallagher."

"I wonder if I might not be of assistance to her, in some way. Oh, and Dad," he said reaching into his pocket and pulling out van Rensselaer's check. "I've something interesting to show you.

ELEVEN

Monsignor Palladin also put down his newspaper and considered what he'd read: another of Abraham Kahn's disturbing diatribes. Already this morning he'd received a telephone call from Mayor Gaynor urging Cardinal Bernard to denounce the *Post's* inflammatory editorial policy. Monsignor Palladin assured the mayor His Eminence, the Cardinal, would give it his full attention.

In addition to being a Prince of the Church, Timothy Cardinal Bernard was also the Archbishop of the Archdiocese of New York. As his chancellor, Monsignor Palladin's job was to write the Cardinal's speeches, draft the documents he signed, approve his schedule of public ceremonies, appoint those to be promoted to church posts—and those to be dismissed, designate Church patronage, regulate access to the Cardinal's presence, and control the Archdiocesan treasury. For eight years, Monsignor Palladin had served the Cardinal single-mindedly, making Palladin *de facto* the second most powerful clergyman in New York, and therefore, in the country. It was a fact which was not lost on the diocesan bishops who, while higher in Church rank than Monsignor Palladin, knew it was through his singular hand the Cardinal's considerable power was wielded.

Palladin stared at the offending editorial and bristled in righteous indignation. Abraham Kahn was fast gaining a reputation in certain quarters as some kind of social *sage*, and in other quarters, as a dangerous, muckraking Semite, particularly dangerous in this, an election year.

Pressure had been applied to the *Post's* owner, Mr. Oswald Villard; appeals were made to his good Catholic conscience. Kahn was known to secretly be an ungodly *Bolshevists*. It was Villard's religious duty to discharge Mr. A. B. Kahn.

But Villard stubbornly cited the American press's constitutional first amendment right to free speech. And this Jeffersonian philosophy of *separation of Church and State* that everyone was yammering about! It was that erroneous political interpretation which had stripped the Roman Church of all its foreign principalities, one-by-one. A misbegotten concept perpetuated by a cabal of international atheists.

The Monsignor wasn't surprised at Villard's response. After all, what more could be expected of a co-founder of this—*this* National Association for the Advancement of Colored People, a conglomeration of Jews, ignorant coloreds, Socialists, and misguided, sentimental citizens who called themselves members of the Progressive Party. Monsignor Palladin shuddered to think what were the sexual mores of such *progressive* men and women.

And now, this speculation about the connection between these five dead women—God rest their souls—and those two illustrious, stalwart Catholics: Mayor William Gaynor and Police Commissioner Rhinlander Waldo, both sterling examples of Roman Catholic conservatism. Had they not recently brought to justice the *Car Barn Gang?* Even Kahn's own newspaper lauded their apprehension of murderous gunmen Frank Cirofici and Whitey Lewis. How dare this reckless ideologue disparage their competence and integrity.

Monsignor Palladin deplored any threat to the hierarchical order of things. In his deeply-rooted Jesuitical view of the world, it was this hierarchy which kept the world in check. The traditional authority of God's will on earth is vested in those best suited to the task. Any threat to this authority will not be allowed! He had vowed exactly that, just the week before, at the diocese's monthly Knights of Columbus breakfast. Following which, over a thousand dollars—*a thousand*, in a single morning—

had been collected in campaign contributions by Tammany precinct captains passing a hat amongst attendees. Now, *these* were men who, unlike Villard, understood the critical importance of the upcoming election to the natural hierarchy of rightful authority. And, if Mr. Villard could not be convinced to act, then some other means of exposing Kahn's turpitude would have to be found. On this, the New York church and the Tammany machine were in complete moral accord.

Monsignor Palladin looked up at the clock on the wall of his cathedral office. Eleven o'clock on Sunday was the High Mass at St. Patrick's. His Eminence, Cardinal Bernard was the celebrant, with the Monsignor his deacon. He had fumed too long over the disturbing newspaper piece. He'd have to hurry now across the Cathedral courtyard to the sacristy. He must ablute his hands and vest himself before His Eminence arrived. Two altar boys would attend him, laying out the proper color vestment for the liturgical date: a red chasuble for the feast day of a martyred saint; white for a feast of the Blessed Virgin, a nuptial Mass, Easter and Christmas; violet for the days of Lent; and black for the requiem Mass and Good Friday.

When Cardinal Bernard arrived, he would be assisted by the Monsignor in vesting for Mass at the Cathedral's magnificent high altar beneath the Great Rose, stained glass window. All of the solemn, ceremonial rituals would be carefully observed: the Gregorian choir would sing the Mass, the domed nave would fill with the sweet smelling perfume and high ascending smoke of precious myrrh and frankincense, the faithful would be sprinkled with lustral water, the brass collection plates would be passed, not once but twice, the Holy Eucharist would be dispensed, all prayers, epistles and gospels would be chanted in high ecclesiastical Latin.

And later, when the Cardinal and his chancellor sat down together in the Cardinal's dining room—as they habitually did on Sunday afternoons for the lamb, mint jelly and new potatoes to which the Cardinal was partial, Monsignor Palladin would begin the grave discussion of how best to deal with the problematic A. B. Kahn.

TWELVE

"Come in, Mr. Goodwin. What can I do for you?" A. B. Kahn gestured to a tattered, leather chair in his office.

"Thanks for seeing me," Noah said.

"That's what I'm here for," Kahn said. "To serve the public. Says so on the paper's masthead. Dentyne?" he asked offering a piece.

Noah shook his head and sat. Mr. Kahn tossed the little wrapper in the wastepaper basket, and with a sweep of his other hand, cleared just enough space on his desktop to prop his feet up. He tilted back as far as he dared in his dilapidated swivel chair.

Noah calculated Mr. Kahn to be a wiry, late-thirties, with brown, myopic eyes and flecks of gray in his trim moustache. He was surprised to see the heel and sole of Kahn's left shoe built up a good three inches thicker than the right.

"Polio. I was six," Mr. Kahn said.

"Was I staring?" Noah asked. "I guess I was."

"Don't worry about it. Now, that's out of the way; what can I do for you? You said it was about my piece in Sunday's paper—to do with the immigrant murders."

"It's actually more about Miss Gallagher."

"About finding the body or the Federal charges?

"What Federal charges?"

"Look, Mr. Goodwin, I'm a busy man. What about Miss Gallagher?"

"Well..."

"So, you know her?" Kahn asked assessing the stranger. What kind of crackpot may have walked in here now, he wondered. Gruesome murders always brought out the loonies.

"We've met, socially. The day she discovered Mrs. Nicolosi; is that the dead woman's name?"

"Yeah."

"The day Miss Gallagher discovered the body. We met at a party given by Mrs. Astor."

Noah paused waiting for some kind of response, of which he got none save a gimlet eye. "Anyway, I wondered could you tell me anything more about her? These charges—"

Kahn was silent a moment longer as if coming to some conclusion. He lit a cheroot with his pocket flint-lighter then sat up in his chair. "Sending obscene material through the mail," he said.

"Her?" Noah exclaimed.

"Well, it's not quite what you think." Mr. Kahn rustled through a heap of journals and periodicals on the floor near his chair. He handed Noah a pamphlet; the title read *The Married Woman's Guide to Personal Hygiene, Health and Conception.*

"She wrote it," Kahn said. "All fine and dandy, as she pointedly omits the words *contraception* and *birth control*, the advocacy of which is a felony under state law.

"But, she mailed the pamphlets across state lines to some ladies' clinics in Minnesota, Illinois, and eh, California, I think. That's a federal misdemeanor offense.

"The New York Society for the Suppression of Vice came down on her like a ton of bricks, invoking the Comstock Law against mailing printed obscenity. That's *Anthony* Comstock."

"Anthony Comstock?" Noah asked.

"Comstock's a shrewd, old New York demagogue. He was appointed a special agent of the U. S. Postal Service back in the Hayes administration. He's even got police powers that allow the old blue-nose to carry a weapon, which he loves to wave around for the photogs.

"He and his moral dragons were just looking for an excuse to shut the Gallagher woman's operation down. It's the clinical names she uses for parts of the body, and the anatomical diagrams. It gave them just what they wanted.

"Raided her office, arrested her, and confiscated bundles of pamphlets about to be mailed out. Comstock himself showed up, prepared to personally set fire to the kindling being piled at her feet. They'd love to see her burn, and not just figuratively. Gallagher's exactly the kind of bluestocking Comstock and his zealots hate.

"She's looking at a possible five years hard labor in Federal prison, *if* she's got the guts for it."

"What do you mean?"

"She's got a lot of support abroad. If she ducked out of the country she'd be welcomed, celebrated even, in Europe. And free. The law's going to change eventually. Why spend that time in prison?"

"Principles, perhaps?" Noah volunteered.

"We'll see. Some very powerful people have written letters of protest on her behalf. Kahn retrieved a folder from the second level of chaos on top of his desk, and opened it. "Like this," he said holding up a newspaper clipping. "George Bernard Shaw in the *Manchester Guardian*: '*Comstockery is the world's standing joke at the expense of the United States. Europe likes to hear of such things. It confirms the deep-seated conviction of the Old World that America is a provincial place, a second-rate, country-town civilization after all.*'

"Here's another one, talking about Comstock: '*His obsessive efforts to suppress public information on sex education materials and birth control are misguided and medically irresponsible.*' Dr. Albert Schweitzer, no less. Her sentencing is going to draw international attention. That's for certain."

Noah thumbed through Kahn's news clippings. "How long have you been writing about the immigrant killings?" Noah asked.

"Since the third one, Agnes Lombardi. Head chopped off, floating in the river. That made me start asking questions about the Mendoza girl. She was the nursing student from Barcelona. They found her off Broadway near Lispenard Street, stabbed straight through the heart. But there was no blood at the crime scene; she bled to death somewhere else. Then the Profaci girl four months before that. These were *very* grisly murders, my friend. And nobody seemed to be doing much about it.

"Here," Mr. Kahn continued, pushing forward a folder. "I've got a dossier on all the murdered women. And there's probably more, swept under the rug, so to speak. You have to understand something, Goodwin," and now his eyes were flinty. "Mayor Gaynor and his Tammany cronies are literally getting away with murder."

"You don't suggest they're directly responsible?" Noah asked, incredulous but intrigued.

"Listen, if these had been five women from Mayor Gaynor's social set butchered, the entire city would be on alert, and you would see such a manhunt like you can't even think of. Mass arrests, the jails filled to overflow until the killer's ferreted out. Or, made to flee, maybe. But because these are the poor, the immigrant—not *real* Americans, they're voiceless. They're not seen, they are not heard, they are not protected. All so Tammany bosses, like Big Tim Sullivan and Bill Gaynor can maintain the strangle-hold they have on the New York vote come November."

"Well, I know there's some corruption—"

"*Some?* Know what they call Sullivan? *King of the Tenderloin.* The guy has bouts of delusional dementia, they say from late stage syphilis. Our next senator from the great state of New York! Sullivan grew up in Five Points—toddled in those sewers, so he's got this reptilian view of the world. He's dangerous in a way that dwarfs *ordinary* greed. Him, Gaynor and Waldo are the bastards who *make sure* vice, corruption, crime of all sorts gets swept under the rug, while they publicly polish their Knights of Columbus medals."

"Sounds like you hate them," Noah said.

"No, I don't hate them. I just want to expose them, however I can."

"Can Miss Gallagher help?"

"Maybe. I need to find out how she spotted the body. What were the exact circumstances? Did she know the dead woman. *Anything* she can tell me." Abie re-lit his cheroot. I got a job to do between now and November. Anyway, that's my story. Now, what's yours?"

"My story?" Noah asked.

"What's your interest in all this? I've asked you twice now; what can I do for you?"

"Well, you see, I'm employed only a few hours a day, and I have a couple of months before I return to my excavation in India and—"

Kahn sat forward with his elbows on his desk. "Just who the hell did you say you are?"

"Goodwin. Noah Goodwin."

"The big-wig over at New York University?"

"No. That would be my father, Asa Goodwin. He's Dean of Archaeological Studies."

"And you're the son?"

"Yes."

"And you're doing some kind of archeological study of New York?"

"Not exactly. It's underground geological surveying, to update the city's official subterranean map—you don't want to set your next skyscraper on top an underground marsh. But, surveyed with the ability to recognize and preserve any archaeological finds: artifacts of colonial culture, burial grounds, Indian history. That sort of thing. I supervise a team. They do most of the legwork and I do the inspections and chart their findings. Pretty routine stuff."

"I get it. You're bored and on the make for Miss Gallagher," Kahn said conclusively.

"On the *make*?" Noah asked. It was a term he didn't know.

"Never bullshit a bullshitter. It can't be done. You're looking to get laid. Stand up." Resigned to defeat, Noah stood to leave. "You're a pretty big guy, Mr. Goodwin. Ever do any boxing?"

"A little, at Cambridge."

"You got a motorcar?"

"I do. My father's."

"Tell you what." Kahn got unsteadily to his feet. "Let's drop by the offices of the Family Aid Society. See if Miss Gallagher is in."

"Mr. Kahn—"

"My friends call me Abie."

"Abie, you're a prince of a fellow."

"Me, I'm no prince, except maybe to my mother, God rest her. I'm a gimpy reporter, who's tired of trolleys and paying for hacks. I need to do some serious looking around in places where I just might need a strong arm. You've got a strong arm, and legs. You want to drive for me? The first stop is to see Miss Gallagher, where *you* will introduce *me*.

"You've got a deal," Noah said. The two men shook hands.

"O.K., now—Gallagher, I already know, has a brain. And she's pretty."

"Yes, she *is* a pretty woman."

"Yeah, well that could be worth sticking your neck out for, a pretty woman with a good brain. But I gotta tell you; there's a lot of people in this town who don't like me and aren't too crazy about her either. Powerful people, even dangerous."

"In which case, we should hurry," Noah smiled.

"Ya' know, this just might work out. O.K. Onward, Lochinvar." Kahn lifted a spiffy straw boater from a hook on the wall, and with a clunking gait started toward the office door.

"Mr. Kahn. Abie, what about your dossier—"

"Right. Thanks. I might need it. See, you're a big help already." He grabbed his file on the immigrant killings. "O.K., let's go."

Noah followed Abie Kahn out of the *Post's* offices and down two flights of marble stairs. "You know, Abie, you don't talk like you write."

"Yeah, so? You talk like you're from the middle of the Atlantic ocean. You some kind of Limey?"

"Well, my father is. My mother was a Texan."

"Yeah, no kidding? Go figure." When Noah and Mr. Kahn reached the sidewalk they both climbed into Professor

Goodwin's Cadillac 53. "Don't you have to crank this buggy?"
Mr. Kahn asked.

"The latest thing," Noah said pulling a brass key from his
vest pocket. "Self-starting choke valve. Dad's pride and joy."

"Yeah? What'll they think of next!"

"Don't you ever use the IRT?" Noah asked as they pulled
away.

"The subway? What—I should travel in a hole in the
ground? When I'm dead they'll put me in a hole in the ground,
Mr. Goodwin."

"It's perfectly safe. They've had one in London for nearly
fifty years. And, please, call me Noah."

"London, I don't care about. You got a motorcar, Noah.
That's all I care about. That, and making *someone* officially admit
there's a goddamn homicidal maniac on the loose.

THIRTEEN

It was hot and stuffy inside the confessional booth. Two flies buzzed near Father Clarence O'Malley's head, attracted to the sweat in his unkempt hair. He dozed when he could.

He was very old now, and had outlived nearly everyone he'd known in the days when he was the parochial pastor here at St. Stephen's. A younger man, Father Costello, held that rigorous position now. O'Malley assumed few ecclesiastical duties, weekday Confession being the only one of any real interest to him. Even after so many years, he still found the veniality of others fascinating: the adulterers, the blasphemers, the cheats, even the little girls reduced to guilty tears for having eaten meat on Friday. And then there were the schoolboys with their adolescent fantasies. From them he extracted subtle details. The confessional was the perfect cocoon for sins that hatched in darkness.

The Cardinal had placed Father Costello in O'Malley's stead when finally the old priest had been forced into diocesan retirement. Because the decision had come from the Cardinal's office, there was no doubt it was Monsignor Palladin's doing. Very well then.

He could have resisted more strenuously and prevailed if he'd chosen, but the truth was he'd long since tired of his pastoral duties. He felt little kinship toward his Italian parishioners with their endless, Old World, religious festivals, their *Carnevale* and street fairs. He was appalled at the garish costumes, the miles of colored lamps strung everywhere, the brightly painted effigies, and public revelry.

He didn't hate these Italian immigrants, with their *Dago* red wine, garlic stench, and *maccheroni*, any more or less than he hated the rest of humanity. He was merely, supremely indifferent to the promotion of their spiritual welfare.

In the end, O'Malley had welcomed Father Costello for significantly more reasons than one. He'd immediately taken the measure of the man, and happily saw bestowed on him the title of pastor with all the attendant duties. He was an entirely suitable successor.

Father O'Malley himself retained the title of *rector inamovibiles,* meaning he could never be removed from St. Stephen's against his will. He had the right of perpetuity of tenure now. St. Stephen's had been his home for nearly fifty years. It was here he desired to live out his days, and so, here it would be, for as long as there was breath in his body.

If the Cardinal's office had had its way, it would have been St. Fiacre Retreat House in Pennsylvania for Father O'Malley, the retirement home and hospice for the priests of his order. That ramshackle pile of wood and stone where doddering and demented priests who'd outlived their life expectancy were sent to die. *Monastic seclusion* they called it. *A rarified environment in which to live out the fullness of one's spiritual life.*

O'Malley vowed to have none of it. Quick and tough, the old priest was, and determined to cheat the grave for as long as he could, right where he was. He was far more powerful than his station in life might otherwise decree because he was a tomb of secrets: secrets of his own and the secrets of others, confessional secrets and open secrets. Secrets which could pull down the heavens if he chose.

The priest roused himself at the sound of the left enclosure door opening and shutting. O'Malley slide open the wicket in the booth wall, and leaned toward the latticed grille that separated priest from penitent. With two fingers of his right hand raised, he traced a desultory sign of the cross in the air and mumbled: *In nomine Patris, et Filii et Spiritus Sancti*—

He knew just then who had entered. The air in the confessional booth turned static. Flies no longer buzzed, as if they, too, waited expectantly.

"*Bless me, Father, for I confess I have sinned…*" The penitent's breathing was deep and rugged. "It has been a month—no, six months; I can't remember." His whisper became rapid, panicked. "I see hellfire, Father."

"Where?" O'Malley asked sitting up eagerly.

"Before me. At my feet," the voice whimpered. "A great pit of fire everywhere before me. An ocean of molten fire! *All* are aflame. Writhing, screaming. I must—I must save myself! I must *not* burn." His voice was a screeched whisper now. "*Oh, Gawd in Heaven*, don't let me burn."

Suddenly, he was calm again. "He seeks to confuse me with his wiles. To trick me and then I *will* burn."

"Who does this?" O'Malley asked eagerly.

The penitent cupped his hands to his mouth lest the sound escape. "The Serpent."

"The *Sairpent*, y'say?" O'Malley goaded. "Himself?"

"He speaks to me."

"You hear him aloud? What does he say?"

"'*Hell awaits!*' Help me, Father. I—I have sinned again. Twice more." His voice was a frightened, hoarse whisper.

O'Malley's fingers twitched in his lap. "The same as before? Their bodies—" he croaked.

"Worse, Father. Worse this time." Terror glazed his eyes. "I did *such* things that I—I'm afraid. Of the fire. I must atone, must be washed in the sacred blood of the holy martyrs. Give me absolution, Father. Absolve me of my sins!"

His voice was angry now, dangerous and aggressive. "You *must* absolve me!" He rushed on ritually without breathing. "*Oh my God, I am heartily sorry for having offended Thee—*"

O'Malley sat back and cackled softly, "*Dominus noster Jesus Christus te absolvat.*"

"*—and I detest all my sins because I dread the loss of Heaven and the pains of Hell but most of all because I have offended Thee my God who art all good and deserving of all my love—*" as if a child reciting his catechism.

The priest droned on. *"Deinde, ego te absolvo a peccatis tuis in nomine Patris, et Filii, et Spiritus Sancti."* By the time O'Malley finished, he was alone again in the confessional. Alone with a secret he was sworn to take to his grave. *"Amen."*

FOURTEEN

Please explain to her it is a myth. Gin and quinine will
do nothing to relieve her of her pregnancy."

"Es stimmt nicht. Der gin und quinine werden nicht helfen." Cate
waited while Dora Adler, a volunteer social nurse, translated for
the distraught Mrs. Mueller. Mrs. Mueller, however, could
scarcely pay attention to what was being said, so busy was she
attempting to corral her four rambunctious children.

"Here, let me hoist the baby for you," Cate said taking
the infant from Mrs. Mueller's arm. This allowed Mrs. Mueller
to gather the rest of her brood by the back of their collars, two to
a hand, and hold them up until only their toes touched the
hardwood floor of Cate's small office.

That overburdened women, like Mrs. Mueller, found
themselves desperate for help was no longer a surprise to Cate.
She was beginning to feel overwhelmed just watching Mrs.
Mueller juggle her kids from hand to hand.

"Aber was soll ich machen?" Mrs. Mueller pleaded. *"Meine
Mutter sorgt schon füer drei. Sie ist zu alt sich um die Kleinen zu
küemmern."*

"She says she has two older children at home and an
elderly mother," Dora Adler said as she scribbled on a
stenographer's pad.

"What about the pessary she was given? Ask her did she
not use it," Cate said.

"Hast Du das pessary benutzt?"

"Oh, *ja*. But *mein* husband in *Abfall* put. Priest tell *es Verboten*—big *Sünde*."

"Yes, of course he did! Damn it—these meddlesome priests," Cate exploded. "Why doesn't he just crawl into bed with them, and while he's there tell Mister Mueller how to put food on the table for seven children and three adults!"

"Shall I translate that?" asked Dora earnestly.

"No. Of course not." The baby on Cate's lap started to bawl. "Sssh, don't cry—what's the baby's name?"

"Angelika— Geli," Mrs. Mueller beamed.

"Don't cry, Geli," Cate said bouncing the baby awkwardly. She was just beginning to feel a growing dampness through the baby's diaper, when a knock on the door interrupted.

"Yes," Cate called out impatiently.

"There are two gentlemen here to see you."

"From the Prosecutor's office? Again?" Cate asked exasperated. Since her conviction, political pressure had mounted steadily in the form of a very juicy carrot and a very big stick. Just issue a public statement that you're throwing yourself on the mercy of the Court, she'd been urged. Submit to the authority of the State in matters of moral decency, and there's no reason why imposition of sentence shouldn't be suspended. After all, five years is a very long time to spend in a penitentiary just for a stubborn, misguided idea. Of course, she'd have to close her clinic. Leave the care of women's health rightfully to doctors who better understand the complexity of issues bearing upon…

"I don't think so," the young volunteer said. "One of them," she whispered, "is a cripple."

"Where are they?"

"In the waiting room."

"All right. Show them into my parlor, please. I'll be right there." Cate abruptly handed the still bawling Geli over to the startled nurse. "Dora, here—please, hold the baby and explain to Mrs. Mueller all we can do at this point is schedule regular care during the pregnancy, here in the infirmary, and arrange to have the birth in a hospital if she's willing.

Mrs. Mueller reacted as expected, with a rush of unhappy pleading.

"*Es tut mir leid, Frau Mueller,*" Cate managed in her halting high school German. "There's nothing to be done now. And, Dora, please warn her strongly against anymore foolish attempts at ridding herself of this pregnancy." Cate stood and swiped at the damp spot on her skirt with a handkerchief. "You'll have to excuse me now. Do the best you can, Dora."

The office and clinic of the Family Aid Society were located in a brownstone storefront, on Perry Street near Bleecker. Cate's small apartment was to the rear. The vestibule served as a waiting room, which as usual, was filled with a mix of New York's female population. There were immigrant women, uptown middle-class matrons, and several younger women, most likely co-eds or newly married. They were all, at the moment, regarding the two male intruders with hostile apprehension.

To everyone's great relief, the men were presently led away to Cate's sitting room, where she soon joined them.

"May I help you, gentlemen? Why, it's Mr. Goodwin. What a surprise. To what do I owe this pleasure?" Still chaffing from her encounter with Noah at Mrs. Astor's party, and her embarrassing faint, Cate was determined neither her annoyance nor embarrassment show.

Noah proceeded to introduce Mr. Abie Kahn. Cate, who knew his writing from the Post, told him how much she admired his outspoken social views. She was pleased to meet Mr. Kahn, but wondered how he came to be in the company of a wolf like Goodwin.

Noah asked Cate if she'd seen Mr. Kahn's recent editorial in the *Post*. When Cate said it was still on her desk in a stack, Mr. Kahn handed her a copy opened to his piece. Noah took the opportunity, while she read, to ogle, piece-by-piece, the brick wall of rectitude he hoped to dismantle.

"So, you think there is a political cover-up of these crimes?" Cate asked Abie oblivious to Noah's appraisal.

"In a metropolitan city like New York, murder happens on a regular basis, to be sure. But, if there's a lone madman loose in Manhattan, and he's preying on the lower classes, that's a big problem for both the Police Commissioner and the Mayor. A problem they're determined to do without just before an election. The last headline they want to see is *Killer At Large Police Baffled!*"

"They'd much rather see *Catherine Gallagher Imprisoned for Obscenity Conviction,*" Noah piped up. Cate, who'd nearly forgotten Noah was there, allowed him a glance of acknowledgement.

"And are they baffled, Mr. Kahn?"

"There have been several, particularly brutal—grotesque even—killings, over the last year, that I can track. All female, European immigrants in a certain age group, no criminal records, no jealous boyfriends or bad habits or itchy-feet. They just vanish and turn up slaughtered like spring lambs.

"And because the grief-stricken family doesn't speak enough English to ask much of anything beyond *why*, nobody pays much attention. The police are too busy collecting their graft, and the politicians are too busy buying blocks of voters who vote as they're told. City Hall says the deaths are not related. I say they are. All five, a single killer."

"And no arrests have been made." Cate said after a thoughtful moment.

"Not a one. No arrest means no trial, no publicity. What they're afraid of, Miss Gallagher, is a political spotlight on New York slum conditions. National scrutiny. International notoriety. Look at what happened in England with the Whitechapel murders. About twenty-three years ago, five women killed, and suddenly every newspaper in the world is writing about, not just the failure to apprehend a killer, but far worse, the unspeakable living conditions of London's East End. It's the kind of publicity politicians would do anything to avoid. Along with wealthy landlords—certain privileged, land-owning interests, who keep the flock docile and obedient."

"I see," Cate said momentarily enthralled by Mr. Kahn's fervor. "And, Mr. Goodwin has taken advantage of our slight acquaintance to bring you here, so you and I might speak?"

"Yes, exactly," Mr. Kahn said.

"Do you know," she said after a moment's thought, "the police still have not interviewed me, or anyone else who knew Mrs. Nicolosi?"

"Exactly my point. I'll want a list of her acquaintances, if you can help with that."

"Yes, I can do that. You are pursuing a private investigation of these killings?"

"Oh, yes, Miss Gallagher. I am. This story will change New York politics forever. The bloodcurdling demise of Tammany Hall. An ignoble end to the most corrupt political machine in American history. I intend to pursue this story to the furthest extent I'm able, Miss Gallagher. And expose those who have not done their sworn civil duty."

"And you, Mr. Goodwin?"

Abie hurriedly answered for Noah, "Yes, you see, Mr. Goodwin possesses certain abilities and assets which I require."

"How convenient," Cate said with a sidelong glance at Noah. "Well then, please, ask any questions you wish."

"You knew the last victim? Mrs. Nicolosi?" Mr. Kahn asked.

"Yes. She would from time to time help us care for children who needed temporary shelter. Her home was always tidy, well-run. The father is sober and takes care of his family, though recently they've had hard times."

"Tell me how you and the two ladies came to discover the body?"

Cate explained the circumstances of her presence at the Nicolosi home on the morning after the killing. Mr. Kahn took careful notes in a small pocket tablet, interrupting her narrative several times for elaboration.

"You say the daughter slammed the door when you asked to enter the apartment?"

"Well, not slammed, but she didn't allow us in."

"How often had you been in the home before?"

"Several times."

"Was there anyone else in the apartment with her—what's the child's name?"

"Seraphia."

"Serafina Nicol..."

"No, no. *Seraphia*," Cate pronounced. "She has four siblings but there was no way for me to tell who was inside. She barely opened the door a few inches; I couldn't see beyond. I assume the other children were there. The father had gone to the police station."

"And you heard nothing?" Noah interrupted.

"Nothing."

"Five children with no parent at home. And not a sound?"

"Hey, yeah. Kids are noisy," Mr. Kahn said. "You didn't hear anything, Miss Gallagher?"

"No, as I've said. But, I could see from her face, the child was terribly frightened."

"Of you?"

"Well, at the time I thought so. Actually, I'm not sure now what I thought."

"I see. And then what happened?" Mr. Kahn continued.

Cate completed her account up to and including the arrival of the parish priest, Father Costello, and her own departure from the Nicolosi apartment. "That's really all I can tell you."

"One more thing," Abie said. "If I could just ask, was there a funeral?"

"No. But there was a Mass for the dead at St. Stephen's Church. Yesterday."

"Did you attend?" he asked.

"Yes. Father Costello asked me to accompany the family. To calm the children."

Mr. Kahn quickly thumbed backward through his small notepad. "St. Stephen's? Miss Gallagher, do you think I could ask you to take us to the rooftop from which you discovered the body?" he asked.

"Certainly, but I have a roomful of women. I can't just—"

"I don't mean now. What time did the little girl say her mother left to go cool herself on the roof?"

"She just said *last night*."

"Was Mrs. Nicolosi the type to—eh, you know," Mr. Kahn asked.

"No," Cate quickly responded. "Mrs. Nicolosi was not at all the type. When she wasn't caring for a sick neighbor or taking in a foster child, she was praying her rosary or making novenas. If she met someone that night, it certainly wasn't a lover."

"O.K., well that fits. With the other victims, I mean. Good reputations," Mr. Kahn said. "Actually what I was hoping was for you to take us up to that roof, say about ten o'clock tonight?"

"If you think there's anything to be learned."

"It couldn't hurt," Mr. Kahn shrugged.

Cate laughed to cover her concern. "Considering it's a vicious murderer you're looking for, let's hope that's true."

FIFTEEN

Just after ten o'clock, Noah parked his father's Cadillac across the street from St. Stephen's Church. Noah, Cate and Mr. Kahn piled out and stood together on the sidewalk, in the shadow beyond the single electric streetlight. They took a moment to get their bearings, then Cate said, "Here's about where we started that morning. We walked west on Broome."

"That's what we'll do tonight, everything exactly as you ladies did that morning," Mr. Kahn said.

"I have things that might be useful," Noah said. He went to the auto's trunk box and pulled out two flashlights and a handheld, carbide lamp on a lanyard. "My surveyors use them," he explained to Cate.

"Good idea," Mr. Kahn said looking up at the night sky. "There's a nearly full moon but it's cloudy. It could be dark as pitch on the rooftops."

"I suggest the carbide lamp for you, Miss Goodwin. It's not as heavy. It has an on-off toggle here. Mr. Kahn and I will use the flashlights," he said. "They operate with a slide switch here," he said demonstrating for Mr. Kahn.

Cate tested her lamp and was surprised at how bright a beam it produced.

"All right then. Let's get going," Mr. Kahn said.

Cate led the way across Mott Street and turned right at the corner. Shop awnings had been rolled up and stalls stored inside dark storefronts. There were only one or two streetlamps on each block, and most of the foot traffic was from the two brightly lit saloons on either side of the street.

A bit more than half a block in, Cate stopped in front of a brownstone building. "This one," she said. She led the way up the Dutch stoop and they entered. The hallway was lit by a single dim bulb creating more shadows than light.

"Go all the way back," she said. "There's a courtyard at the end, and an open staircase to the left."

Noah switched on his flashlight illuminating the grimy, black and white, mosaic-tile floor. Twice they heard scampering just beyond their arc of light. They stepped quickly into the dark but open courtyard. It was a five-story canyon of apartment windows. Most were open to the passage of whatever feeble breeze might be stirring. A few were still lit-up behind shades yellow as old skin. Muffled words could be heard every few seconds. And coughing. A baby bawling far away. But mostly, it was silent, an oppressive silence, as though this part of the city lay under a mort cloth.

"Don't you think someone would have reported a woman's scream?" Cate whispered.

"That may just mean no one was asked."

"Or perhaps, she was struck down *before* she could scream, perhaps by someone she knew and wasn't afraid of," Noah said.

"That makes pretty good sense, too," Mr. Kahn said.

"Or, maybe she was fighting for her life and *couldn't* scream." Cate took the lead again, directly to and up the wooden stairs. The steps had a decrepit creak she'd never noticed in the daytime.

On the fifth floor landing, she told them they'd reached the Nicolosi's floor.

"Show us the apartment, please" Mr. Kahn said. "We won't knock at this hour, but I'd like to see where it is."

Cate led the way into the building interior and up the hall to the front flat. Mr. Kahn examined the doorknob and lock in the beam of his flashlight. "Is it the usual shotgun apartment; rooms connecting to each other with no hallway?" he asked.

"Yes. This door opens into the first room. It's the kitchen, very small. Two of the children sleep there. That opens onto a tiny room, hardly bigger than a pantry, for the parents. Then there's a larger room. The family does piecework there in the daytime. The other three children sleep there at night."

"Anything else?" Noah asked.

"Not really. Oh, there's a fire escape outside the front window," she added.

Noah seemed lost in thought, caught up in the moment. "So you could see nothing but the kitchen wall behind the daughter?" he asked.

"Right. She opened the door only wide enough to look through the gap," Cate said. Noah nodded.

"Let's get up to the roof," Mr. Kahn said.

"It's this way." Cate turned back the way they'd come and led them out to the rusted metal ladder leading to the roof. Noah was the first up, then Cate who ignored Noah's helping hand.

"Can you manage all right, Abie?" Noah called down to Mr. Kahn.

"Yes, I can make it," Abie said. He tucked the long flashlight securely in his belt and climbed to the roof without aid.

Noah switched off his flashlight and told Cate and Abie to do the same. "If you wait a minute," he said, "your eyes will adjust more than you think."

Clouds momentarily swathed the moon and it was, as Abie predicted, pitch black on the roof, but after several moments, their eyes began to discern the shape of random things against the gray ambience: chimneys, plumbing conduits, air vents, and the roof edge. They could see each other quite well now, too, even their own shadows cast by the moon peeping in and out of cloud cover.

To their rear was the open space of the airshaft and the courtyard below. Beyond that were similar roofs stretching back to Mott Street.

"In what direction was the body found?" Abie asked.

"Straight ahead of us. Over the further edge."

Noah switched on his flashlight, then with the two men on either side of Cate, they made their way across the roof to the edge separating this building from its neighbor.

"You see the bloodstains here on the surface," Cate pointed out in the glare of her carbide light. "Her body was right down there. I don't wish to look again," she said turning away from the edge.

Noah stepped close and pointed his flashlight into the chasm sixty feet below. The flashlight illuminated little down there, but just then, a smuggler's moon slid out from behind a cloudy patch and beamed directly into the depths. It swarmed with rodents, a scampering sea of brown fur. Abie scribbled in his notebook.

"Norwegian rats," Noah said. "There must be two-hundred of them."

"Norwegian?" Cate asked. "Some special kind of—"

"No, not at all," he said. "Just your ordinary brown rat. Not really from Norway."

"How do you know so much about rats?" Cate asked. "They're such disgusting creatures."

"Oh, I don't really know all that much," he shrugged. "Just part of the culture I grew up with. Rats are worshipped in some places in India—where I was raised. They're fed, groomed and housed by the hundreds in certain temples of a particular sect, where they crawl freely over worshipers. But, nothing so big as these," he said looking over the side of the building again. "These are monsters. They must absolutely thrive down there—"

"Please, Mr. Goodwin," Cate shuddered. "You didn't see that poor woman's body."

"Right," he responded. "Sorry. I can imagine how terrible it must have been for you," he said reaching for her in a consoling gesture.

"What now, Mr. Kahn?" Cate asked ignoring Noah.

"We look around some more. What's over there?"

Cate, because of her frequent comings and goings, was the most at ease moving around. She stepped over the gap between the two buildings so quickly that Abie yelped, thinking she'd tumbled off the roof.

"I'm fine. It's just a little jump from there to here. I'm naturally sure-footed, plus I'm wearing these," Cate said shining the light down at her feet. "My youngest brother's old hiking boots."

"Great," Abie said, "but, please don't do it again."

"I'm fine, really," Cate said taking another step back and immediately falling hard on the tar pitch roof.

"*Good God!*" Abie shouted. "What happened?"

Noah leapt across the gap to Cate's side. "Are you all right?" he asked, helping her to her feet. He enjoyed the feel of his hands around her tightly corseted waist. She did not.

"Yes. I'm fine," she snapped. "I tripped on something—"

Noah shone his light down to the thing laying at their feet. It was a mesh cage, like a lobster trap with a long rope attached. Inside was a pale paste smelling of fish and rotten egg.

"Aawh, that's awful," Cate reacted. "What on earth—".

"It's a rat trap, I'll bet. This smelly stuff is the bait. Here are three more," Noah said running the long length of attached ropes through his hand. He swept the area with his flashlight beam. "And, look here," he said holding up several canvas sacks with rope ties. One of the sacks was squirming violently. "Someone's been fishing over the side of the building for rats."

Noah directed the beam of his flashlight slowly across the roof line. Suddenly, a man sprinted from somewhere behind Cate. He leapt across the gap and raced toward the roof ladder forty feet away.

Without a word, Noah made the leap as well, and took off running after the fleeing figure. He caught up with him just as the man cleared the roof edge onto the ladder. Noah might have lost him had the man not misstepped the first rung and fallen several feet to the landing below.

Before he could get up and run away, Noah slid down the iron handrails, and knelt on the man's chest. In the light of his flashlight, Noah saw it wasn't at all a man he'd caught. It was a frightened boy.

"Have you got him?" Abie called sticking his head over the edge of the roof.

"Yes. Stay there. We're coming back up." Noah pulled the boy to his feet.

"Don't hurt me, Mister. I ain't done nothin'."

"Up the steps," Noah said.

Once more on the rooftop they were all able to get a good look at the boy, a young Negro about twelve or thirteen years old, who tried but failed to conceal his fear.

"O.K., kid. No one's gonna hurt you," Abie Kahn said. "What's your name, boy?"

Anger displaced a little of the fear. "I ain't no boy, Mister."

"Yeah, well, you *ain't* no man, either, son. Not yet, you ain't. I suggest you cooperate, so we don't have to haul you around to the Twenty-second Street station, and let the cops hand you over to your parents."

"Ain't got parents."

"I'll bet you got somebody though, who's probably not going to be too happy when the cops lock you up. A grandma, maybe. Or auntie," Mr. Kahn said.

The boy stubbornly looked away from him, as good an admission as any that Abie was right.

"O.K., fine. Come on, Noah, Miss Gallagher. He's a hard case. We won't get anything out of this tough guy. I say we just hand him over to the coppers, and let them make him explain what he's doing up here, in the middle of the night, where a woman was recently murdered. I'll bet the police would be very curious about that."

"All right, all right. Don't do that. Them paddies got it in for me already. Honest, I ain't done nothin'."

"It's O.K.," Cate said. "No one's going to hurt you. You have my word. We just need your help. Please, won't you at least tell us your name?"

The boy considered the three white people a minute, deciding how dangerous to his welfare they might be, then squared his shoulders. He snatched his arm from Noah's grip. "Lemuel," he said.

"Thank you, Lemuel. My name is Miss Cate Gallagher. This is Mr. Noah Goodwin and Mr. Abie Kahn. Please, what were you doing up here at night, all alone? Do you come up here often?"

"Sometimes. I mean, now I do. Didn't used to."

"What does that mean? What do you do up here? This equipment belong to you?" Abie asked.

"Yeah. And, I need it back, too."

"Of course," Cate said. "You may go get it. But, first, tell me, do you catch rats? Are you an exterminator?"

"An extrem—I don't know about that. I catch rats for Dollar Bill. A short bit apiece."

"Dollar Bill?"

"I know who he is," Mr. Kahn said. "Dollar Bill Baylor. He's a Brit; has a couple of aliases: Will Pryor, Wiley Willy... who knows his real name. Owns a saloon down on the waterfront, a bucket-of-blood called The White Rose Sport and Tavern. It has a pit where he stages rat and dog contests. He's a, eh—colorful sort. You name it: gambling, blackmail, shylocking, opium trade, graft, smuggling, 'hoors. Pardon me, Miss Gallagher, I meant—young ladies."

"What you mean is prostitutes," Cate provided. "Unfortunate women with no other means."

"Yes. Well, at any rate. He's a dangerous piece of humanity. Brags he committed his first murder when he was still in short pants. Most people believe him."

"This must be where he gets the rats for his contests," Noah guessed.

"I don't understand. For what exactly does he use the dogs and rats? What kind of contests?" Cate asked.

"Well, it's not very pretty. Are you sure you want to know?"

"Mr. Kahn—"

"O.K., but don't say I didn't warn you. It's got nothing to do with you being a woman, though. I'm not sure even Goodwin here is going to want to hear this. Baylor's got this pit, like a small arena. Sometimes he matches one of his own dogs, sometimes it's another contender for the title."

"Title of what?"

"Champion rat killer. I think the current champ is Baylor's fox terrier. See, they funnel rats into the pit, about a hundred of them, then set the dog in the pit and time him, from the minute his feet hit the sawdust until the last rat is—well, until the frenzy is over. The wagers are on both the time and the dog. The dog disposing of a hundred rats in the shortest time wins."

"How awful."

"Yes, well, that's the dog and rat competition," Kahn finished.

"Then there's the man and rat comp'tition—that's what Dollar Bill wants these here for," Lemuel piped up. "He says they's the biggest rats in the city and they put on the best show. Some fellas pay six bits just to come and look. Ain't everyday you see a man bitin' the head offa hundred rats at a time. Three, four minutes all it takes. Mack Monty, he took the heads off a hundred twenty rats in four minutes, twenty-two seconds last spring. I saw—"

"Thank you, Lemuel, that's probably all we need to know about it," Cate said. "Good lord, can such things be true?" she shuddered.

"Tell me, have you been working for this Dollar Bill very long?" Noah asked.

"About a year."

"And what else do you do for him, Lem?" Abie asked.

"My names not Lem. It's Lemuel." The boy's and Abie's eyes locked in a Mexican standoff.

"Lemuel," Abie finally said.

"He lets me clean up the pit in the mornings. Sweep out the sawdust and sprinkle fresh. Then I haul the dead rats over to the leather fact'ry. Sometimes the city pays a bounty for rats, dead or alive. The ones ain't quite dead get drown in the river in cages. City pays even better than the fact'ry folk does.

"But I just started catchin' these here for Dollar Bill. Before, he wouldn't let nobody know *where* he catches these great big ones from. Trade secret he calls it. But startin', uhm—some days ago, he says I to do the catchin' from this partic'lar spot here, from now on. I think something happened up here."

"He saw something?" Noah asked. "What did he see?"

"I didn't mean *that*. Why, he didn't see *nothin'*. I don't know why I said that—I guess I was just makin' it up."

"He did see something, didn't he," Abie insisted. "Was he here the night the woman got killed?"

"I don't know nothin' about it, Mister. Not nothin', you hear me." The boy was agitated now, shifting his weight nervously from one foot to the other. "I want to go now. I ain't done nothin' wrong, and you got no right to hold on to me. I told you everythin' I know."

"Let him leave, Mr. Goodwin, please. We're frightening him. It's this Baylor person you should be talking to," Cate said.

"O.K.," Noah said drawing the boy off to one side. "Lemuel, I'll make you a deal. We're going to go see your boss. You take your things and get on out of here. I'll even throw in a dollar since we spoiled your revenue for tonight. You don't tell Dollar Bill anything about us, and we won't tell him about you. Is that fair?"

The boy ran to collect his rat-catching equipment without responding. When he returned Noah held up a silver dollar. Lemuel eyed it suspiciously, then quickly snatched it from Noah's fingers.

"O.K., Mister. You got a deal," he said pointing his finger at Noah. "I don't want nobody knowin' I even seen you up here, so no doubt, I'm gonna keep my end of the bargain. Just have to see if you keep yours." With a baleful look in Abie's direction, the boy hung his sacks and traps over his shoulder and hurried over the roof edge, down the steps to the courtyard, and was quickly swallowed by the building.

"Will you go tonight?" Cate asked Mr. Kahn.

"What do you think, Noah?"

"Now's as good a time as any. These are likely his working hours."

"O.K., let's do it now. We'll take Miss Gallagher home and head down to South Street," Abie said.

Single file, they carefully descended to the courtyard unaware of the eyes watching from above.

SIXTEEN

The black figure had seen and heard everything. He watched until the three strangers entered the ground floor hallway; then, moving confidently along the roof edge, he spied as they progressed all the way up Broom Street to Mott. The watcher crossed the roofs to the corniced edge of St. Stephen's church and hid between the concrete figures like some latter-day Quasimodo. He peered down intently at the three interlopers as they crossed Mott Street, got into a fancy car and drove away.

The figure made his way to the rooftop door of the church utility stairwell. He went through and locked the door behind him, then padded down the stairs. Father O'Malley paused at the stair bottom and thought about all he'd just seen and heard.

His nocturnal habits, not for the first time, had added a valuable secret to his store. This time, a secret whose power lay not in keeping but in revealing.

The priest made his way carefully in the dark, through the rectory, to what was now Father Costello's office. He felt his way to the desk, upon which Father Costello, devout soul that he was, kept a little votive candle burning in front of a small statue of Our Lady of Sorrows.

Father O'Malley slid the bright, little flame next to the telephone and picked up the receiver. He flashed the switchhook twice for an open telephone line. The small noise that made cut loudly through the silence.

O'Malley quickly dropped the receiver onto the telephone hook, blew out the candle and stood in the dark listening for movement. He knew there were ears within the walls of St. Stephen's. Amongst those who shared a vow of poverty, secrets were coveted above gold. He must insure absolutely that Father Costello learn nothing of what he'd seen.

In the morning would be soon enough, he decided. Some secrets were best negotiated in the broad light of day when one could be certain of who might be lurking within earshot.

SEVENTEEN

Noah and Abie drove southeast through Chinatown to the harbor area. Along the waterfront the Cadillac's big headlamps cut through fog so thick the river was barely visible. As they passed the Brooklyn Bridge, a foghorn announced its presence to any vessels entering the tidal strait.

"You know your way around the city pretty good," Abie said to break the silence.

"I spent about six months here with my father, two years ago, after my mother died."

Abie nodded. "See this stretch of pier along here," he said. "My brother and our gang used to swim here when we were kids."

Noah glanced sideways at Abie, then to his left at the wooden piers jutting out over the water.

"The streets were so hot in the summer; to us kids this was heaven," Abie continued. "I guess it's pretty hot in India sometimes, too."

"Pretty hot," Noah agreed. "It can reach a hundred and fifteen degrees."

"That's pretty hot." It was a moment before he spoke again. "There's all kinds of stuff floating around in this water. Once, we found a drum, like from a band—just bobbing by. Another time, we found a grandfather clock. It looked brand new, just floating along like a canoe. All kinds of stuff in the water. It was like pirate treasure to us.

"I couldn't dive real well—my leg, you know. But I could swim like a sonafabitch. Strong arms, big shoulders."

Noah nodded to acknowledge he was listening, and wondered where this was leading.

"Now, my brother—he was younger, he could dive. Like a swan he could dive, from the pier. He'd push off with those strong legs of his and kind of hang in the air at the top of a perfect arc, and then down like a knife slicing through the water. It was beautiful.

"One day he dives in; we're all in the water, about five of us, all from the Lower East Side. We're swimming and splashing and suddenly someone notices; Mendel hasn't come up. Where's Mendel?"

Abie squinted through the car window, then pointed. "This is Baylor's place here," he said. Noah slowed in front of a dilapidated brick building then pulled into an adjacent alley and parked.

"Anyway, we start swimming under the water trying to find my brother Mendel. We held our breath as long as we could, then come up for air, expecting Mendel would be there laughing at us for being such scaredy cats. Twenty minutes we must've swum around.

"The harbor authorities—they found him. Had to send in divers. He'd dove in, straight in, and got his head stuck in a milk jug—you know, the big twenty gallon ones they use at the dairies. It was stuck in the mud down there. Eleven-years-old he was. He was a beautiful boy, my brother. I was the big brother and there wasn't anything I could do to save him."

Noah said nothing. After a moment, Abie said, "So, I go in here now and do what I can do."

The two men climbed out of the Cadillac and cautiously walked around to the waterfront entrance. "These old counting houses have been abandoned for probably forty years. There's the fish market over on Fulton, a few seafood eateries, but most of it's brothels, flophouses, and rough joints like this," he said.

The dormer windows were boarded-up. Thin slats of yellow light streamed out through the cracks. The only attempt at décor was a rotted fishing-net draped from a painted sign above the door announcing White Rose Sport and Tavern.

"You know, I'm thinking we shouldn't both go in there," Noah said. "Might scare him off."

"Yeah?"

"I take it you have a certain celebrity in Manhattan. Someone's sure to peg you. And besides, if there're two of us he might—"

"I get it," Abie said. "What do you propose?"

"Let me have a go at this. You wait here."

"O.K., but no heroics. You do what you can do. That's all."

"You have my word on it," Noah said.

Inside the White Rose, salt air mixed with the smell of urine, and tobacco smoke whorled like ectoplasm. Two dozen men of various ages, but all with similar flinty faces and colorless garments, either stood drinking at the bar or sat hunched over a hand of cards with a wary eye on their table stakes.

Several blowsy women, attired in a fashion they must have imagined enticing, looked up at Noah's entrance. One who had stationed herself advantageously near the door immediately wrapped her arms around his waist. Noah stuck his hand in his pocket and grabbed the woman's thin fingers as she lifted his cash.

"Buy us a drink, sugar," she said as though being caught in a felony was entirely unremarkable. "Buy ol' Mae a drink."

Pulling her hand from his pocket, Noah gently propelled the woman toward a space at the noisy bar.

"Two whiskies," he said.

The sour looking barkeeper stared at Noah, stroked his red moustache with the tip of a finger, then shifted his weight impatiently from one foot to the other. "I ain't got all night," the man finally growled. Mae poked Noah's pocket with a boney finger then tapped the bar top. Noah put down several coins and the barman finally stepped away to fetch a bottle and two shot glasses.

"So, Mae, my dear," Noah said as she tossed back her shot. "You can do me a great favor."

"Sure, sugar. We can just step over to the corner there for a quick'en. Or go 'round out back if you're the shy—"

"Aah, I can't imagine anything more delightful," he said pushing his own shot glass and the remaining coins on the bar toward her. "But I actually had something simpler in mind."

"You mean you just want I should—"

"Dollar Bill Baylor," Noah hastened to say before ol' Mae could suggest any additional proposals. "Could you point him out for me?"

Mae quickly tossed back Noah's whisky shot and scooped the remaining coins from the bar to her fist. "I could," she said pointedly. "Yup, I surely could." When Noah realized she could, but she wasn't going to, he pulled a dollar from his pocket and waved it at the barkeep.

"For the bottle," he said.

"Whatcha want Bill for?" Mae asked suspiciously.

"Well, I heard he's a man who can arrange certain things."

Mae ogled the near-full bottle. She cleared her throat roughly then spat on the sawdust floor. "Well, yes he can, honey, but I'd watch out, if I was you. See the guy in the black derby at the end of the bar? That's him."

"Much obliged, Mae," Noah said stepping away.

He walked to the opposite end of the room ignoring the curious, unfriendly attention of the room's trade. These were hard men, mostly merchant seamen and stevedores, but none who would have looked out of place on a wanted poster.

Baylor had a face gnarled as a tree trunk. He stood at the end of the bar, beneath a life-size oil portrait of a black and tan Fell Terrier and a plaque, which read *Sporny 1903-1911.*

"'Evening," Noah said, insinuating himself next to the wall where the portrait hung. He tossed coins on the bar and raised a hand to the barkeep. "Can I buy you a drink?" he asked. Bill Baylor turned from his drinking companions and gave Noah his full attention.

"Na then', why would ye be wantin' to do that fer?" Baylor replied.

"Are you the one they call Dollar Bill Baylor?" Noah asked.

"Aye, there may be a few calls me that, but nay to ma face. William Baylor's ma name and a right good sort I be to them wot calls me such, and best y'do, too."

"Yes, of course," Noah said trying to keep up with the man's Yorkshire dialect. "William it is."

"Naw then, young'en, what can I do fer ye since ye canna hardly buy an auld man a drink in his own house, naw can ye?"

The old man cackled at his own rejoin, along with the men standing nearest him.

"Well, I suppose not. I'll just have my own then," Noah said tossing back the shot the barkeep had set before him. He tried not to wince as the rotgut seared his throat. "And, maybe a little something stronger I've heard you can provide."

"A little sumthin stronger, ye say? By 'eck! That be a queer phrase! I wonder, can ye mean it best be spoke 'bout with pri'vacy?"

"Yes," Noah agreed. "In private, if we could."

"Well, wh'int ye say so? Come along, young'en. Look 'ere, lads, this feller needs the loan of ma lug'ole, so I'm gone away a bit, but I'm back by the by." Baylor doffed his hat comically to his patrons and headed to the back of the room. Noah could see he was a showman who enjoyed the approbation of his cronies. A bit stooped in the shoulders perhaps, Baylor was still spare and only an inch or two shorter than Noah.

"We'll just go right up t' stairs," Baylor said affably. "I've an office of sorts, not room enough to swing a cat in, and a bit of a middin, but least not 'alf dozen buggers staring down ma pie 'ole," the old man chortled.

Noah climbed upstairs behind Baylor who moved slowly on legs that seemed to ache. Angled up the stairway wall was a gallery of framed, autographed photos of champion prizefighters, each with a polished brass plaque, like the dog's, beginning with John L. Sullivan, Jim Corbett and Bob FitzSimmons. Not surprisingly, missing from the title-holders was the current

Heavyweight Champion of the World for the last four years, the black boxer Jack Johnson—the most famous, and by many, the most despised black man in America.

At the top of the stairs, Baylor stopped to catch his breath, then with a sigh turned the doorknob and stepped aside as he swung open the door to his office.

"Thank you," Noah said to his host, who responded with a small, polite nod before stepping in behind Noah and shutting the door.

Instantly, Baylor had Noah in a headlock with a blade eight inches long and three inches wide against his throat.

"Now, ya' lying bastard," Baylor said with a diction many years Americanized. "What do you and your nosey pals want?"

"Information. That's all."

"You ain't the goddamn police, I know that much. Oh yeah, you didn't really think that little Sambo, Lemuel could keep a secret from me did you? When he got back here with empty traps, and a bright shiny dollar he couldn't help showing off, it didn't take much to get the story out of the little pissant."

"You didn't hurt h—"

"You've your own sorry arse to worry about, Goodwin. That's the name ain't it?"

"Yes," Noah said calmly. "And if you'll let me go, I'll tell you the rest of the story. What the boy didn't tell you."

After a moment of indecision, Baylor released Noah and quickly jumped back, putting himself just out of reach. He held his Bowie knife at the ready in a tight, underhand grip.

"Talk," the old man said.

"The woman who was with us tonight knew the woman who was killed on that roof. The other man is a newspaper writer—"

"Kahn?"

"Yes. You know who he is?"

"I've heard of him. Go on."

"We found the boy on the roof, put two and two together and figured you must have seen something on the roof that frightened you off. We want to know what."

"Nothing; you get me? I seen nothing. Know nothing. You tell your newspaper friend to write that. William Baylor don't know nothing about any murders."

"You said murders. Plural."

"I'm not stupid, Sunny Jim. I read the newspapers, and I know that guy Kahn is tryin' to make a case of some kind of cover up going on."

"That's right."

"Well, leave me outa it. You get me?"

"Sure. But what are you so afraid of? You're scared to death, aren't you?"

"You know what? The best thing for me would be if you was to be found in an alley somewhere with your throat cut. You *and* the hymie."

"You going to kill me? Is that your plan?" Noah squared his weight. The old guy was tough and armed but Noah still had him by thirty years.

"Not right now, I'm not. Too many goddamn people saw you walk in here. And all those same goddamn people are gonna see you walk your arse outa here again, safe and healthy like. But after that, I'd stay outa places I didn't belong if I was you, Mr. Goodwin."

"Is that it? Can I go now?"

"Yeah," Baylor said straightening from his crouched fighting stance.

"Allow me," he said opening the door. "I suggest you go down the stairs, right through the room, so all those nice people can see you walk straight out the front door."

Baylor tipped his derby again as Noah started for the stairs, then hollered after him sardonically, "*I'll see ye, lad, and s'long,* you sodding sonofabitch!"

Outside, Noah made his way quickly back to the alley where Abie waited in the car. He wondered what could be so awful as to thoroughly frighten an old reprobate like Baylor. In an ocean where the big fish ate the little fish, it must be a pretty big fish indeed that Baylor feared. As he drew closer, Noah could make out a dark outline on the ground and someone kneeling. It was Lemuel leaning over Abie's body. The boy sported a cut lip and a bulging eye swollen shut. He was crying but not for himself.

"They beat him. They beat him bad," Lemuel whispered as Noah knelt down. "I didn't mean to tell on you, Mister. Honest. I tried to warn him, but it was too late. They beat your friend bad, Mister. I think he's dead."

EIGHTEEN

Cate was sound asleep when urgent banging woke her from a vivid dream.

For weeks now, her unconscious mind had been conjuring visions of imprisonment. She tried to stop it but could not. Tonight she'd resorted, as she had quite a bit lately, to a dose of Teasdale's Tincture of Chlorodyne. Teasdale's was advertised widely for use as a calmative—and a treatment for everything from cholera to diarrhea, neuralgia, migraines, and ladies' ailments. It was, in fact, a patented mixture of capsicum, cannabis, opium, and chloroform.

Startled awake from a turbulent dream, Cate fearing the pounding on her door meant a fire alarm ran barefoot in her nightgown to answer. When she opened the door, it was something just as alarming. One look at the amount of blood on Mr. Kahn and Cate said, "You have to take him to a hospital!"

"No hospital," Abie said sounding stronger than he looked. He was leaning on Noah who held him up with an arm around his back. The boy Lemuel was with them carrying Abie's battered boater. "And no police. They would not be helpful."

"I need to lay him down," Noah said.

Cate led the way into her infirmary. Lemuel helped Noah deposit Abie on the examination table while Cate ran quickly to her bedroom for slippers and a dressing gown then back again.

She lathered her hands with carbolic soap and steamy hot water and dried them on a clean towel. "I'll do what I can," she said, and set about putting seven stitches in the scalp wound that had bled profusely enough to convince Lemuel that Abie was dead.

Mr. Kahn bore the mercurochrome and stitching gamely, wincing through gritted teeth. The taping of his ribs, on the other hand, produced a bellow that unnerved Cate and renewed her insistence he ought to be seen at a hospital.

"Nonsense, Miss Gallagher," Abie insisted between shallow breaths. "I understand that you have a diploma in nursing. Waste of time and money if you can't handle a little scalp cut and a bruised rib."

"You might very well have a concussion and the rib is probably broken," she retorted.

"I've had a broken rib before. This ain't that," Abie insisted.

Cate finished taping his ribs, then cleaned and dressed half a dozen other scrapes on Abie's battered body before turning her attention to Lemuel's swollen eye and lip, all the while listening to a recount of events at the White Rose.

It was sometime around three A.M. when they moved to Cate's parlor. She poured them milk and served up slices of cold chicken on slabs of buttered bread, which they ate as if they were starving.

Cate was the first to pose the pertinent question, "What now?"

"Well, this much we know; Baylor is involved," Noah said between mouthfuls.

"Do you think he could have killed Mrs. Nicolosi?" Cate asked.

"He could have. He's capable," Noah said.

"But the other four women as well? I doubt it," Abie said. "A murderer, he surely is, but only if there's a profit in it for him."

"I agree," Noah said. "He's an old man, comfortable in his little kingdom. Maybe a bit crazy, but crazy like a fox. My impression is what we thought at first; he saw something that frightened him. He's scared. In fact, he even said—his exact words, *'I seen nothing, know nothing. Tell... eh, your newspaper friend to write that.'* I think he's afraid the killer saw him and might come after him to shut him up."

"That makes sense," Abie said. "But Baylor's a pretty dangerous fellow. Think about it: someone kills a defenseless woman, and one of the biggest cutthroats in the borough is running scared? Not too many people could scare a guy like Bill Baylor."

"I know," a voice piped up from a chair in the corner of the room. They turned to look at Lemuel whom they'd all but forgotten was still with them.

"I know who's he scared of," the boy said wiping butter from his chin.

"Who, Lemuel? Tell us," Abie pressed.

"Well, that night, when ol' Dollar Bill comes back, he got drunk. I mean fallin' down, babblin' drunk. And, he said it."

They stared at the boy, waiting for him to continue.

"Well?" Abie blurted. "What did Baylor say?"

"He said he knew somethin' that was worth its weight in gold—gonna make him rich as he oughta be. He was real happy."

"Make him rich?" Noah asked.

"He said all kinds a crazy things."

"Like what else?" Abie asked.

"I can't remember, honest. Just crazy drunk stuff."

"Well, what happened after that?" Cate asked gently.

"Nothin'. He just drank and drank and then he fell asleep on the floor like he always does. All curled up, like a big ol' baby. A big ol' mean baby, that is. So, I just drag him upstairs like I always do, onto that divan in his office."

"That's it?" Abie asked.

"Lemme finish, if you want the whole story. So, as I was sayin'—the next day, in the afternoon a big ol' car pulls up out front. Sit'n in the back is Big Tim Sullivan, the Tam'ny Boss hisself. But he don't get out. He says 'tell him I'm here.' Just that. 'Course I know who he means and who he is. So, I fetch Dollar Bill to the car and he gets in with Big Tim. They pull the shade down so you couldn't see and musta talked real low.

"They talked a long time. Then finally, Big Tim yells at him to get out! Ol' Bill looked as white as this piece of bread here. He musta said somethin' to make Big Tim real mad. That's when ol' Bill said he's never goin' back to that rattin' place again, and that I was to go do the trappin' there for now on."

"And what about his plan to get rich?" Cate asked. "Did anything come of it?"

"No, ma'am. In fact, I asked him about it once't and he put his knife on me; said if I ever mention anything about that again I was one dead nigger. That's what he said. He's the most mean man I guess I ever did see. Ask me, I think ol' Dollar Bill just as soon kill everyone here, if he had to. That's 'cluding you, too, Miss Cate. Do it and like it, too. That's what I think."

NINETEEN

S he was disoriented and couldn't comprehend the utter darkness engulfing her. It was as though her mind had fled her body and floated now in some dimensionless void. A stab of fear jolted her alert.

She tried to move her hand to her face only to find her wrists were restrained. Panic set in now as she strained and pulled against iron.

"Omigod," she whimpered. "What's happening?" The sound of her own hollow voice, alone in the silence, was more frightening than the silence itself. She clamped her lips shut, barely daring to breath.

Think, think—what's happened? I can't *think. What did I do? I have to think. Where am I? I can't remember— My name, what is my name? Think of that—my name—is Apollonia; my name is Apollonia, and—where was I? With my brother. I was visiting my brother—Vincenzo, and I was near the church—near St. Cecilia's.*

As she formed cohesive thoughts her fright lessened slightly, and her breathing began to relax.

I was walking home—after dinner with my brother. I remember—I was walking near the subway construction. On Delancey. I remember now! The street is ripped open where they're building the subway. I must have fallen, that's it. I fell into the excavation and—but that can't be right, why would I be chained? And why is it so airless?

Oh, dear Mother of God, help me. Someone help me, please. Apollonia fell to quiet sobbing while mentally she began a recitation of the Rosary. Over and over, she repeated the *Our Father*, which began each decade of *Hail Marys*. She counted her fingers for beads, and concluded with *Glory be to the Father and to the Son and to the Holy Ghost who was in the beginning, is now, and ever shall be, world without end.*

"Amen," she whimpered.

Over and over, she prayed through the five Sorrowful Mysteries of the rosary. Then she began again, this time reciting the five Joyful Mysteries, which gave her hope, then the five Glorious Mysteries, which gave her courage.

Again and again mentally, the complete recitation of the Rosary, blessedly giving her mind something on which to anchor sanity.

Apollonia was so fervently immersed in her prayer she didn't at first hear the sound of nearby footsteps. When she did, she realized that despite the profound blackness all around she'd squeezed her eyes shut while she prayed. Opening them, she saw that a faint glow of gray ambient light had replaced the pitch-blackness.

She could at least see her hands chained in front of her now and some detail of the wall to which she was shackled. It was hard rock. She heard movement behind her somewhere. Something heavy being banged across the ground.

Thank you, God. Thank you. It's morning. The workmen are starting to arrive! Oh, thank God—

"Help! Help me. Over here!" she screamed. Apollonia waited for an answering call. When she heard none, she yelled louder. She strained her neck to see behind her, who was there, and why she couldn't be heard. But she couldn't see anything beyond gray rock wall.

Then she heard a distinct *whoosh* and the entire chamber lit up in the bright glow of fire. She could smell it, too, the hearth smell of wood burning. Her heart raced inside a body petrified by fear. In front of her, the dancing light cast her shadow on the cave wall, like a magic lantern show. A dark silhouette of herself pranced and flickered about the chamber. Apollonia was horrified by the dancing image. Another joined it now. This other carried a long pole. She could see it clearly in black relief on the wall, the pole at least as long as she was tall.

Apollonia watched the dancing shadow as it fastened two manacled wrists to a bolt in the metal pole, then a chain at the waist and at the ankles. Her own? She could no longer tell. For a minute she thought it must be; then her frantic, gentle heart stopped and she woke as a sleeper does from a nightmare marveling at how real it had all once seemed.

The fire made a roaring sound she didn't hear and bits of ash floated in the air like snowflakes. There was still work to be done, to make it exact. The shadow form picked up a short hammer, and swung it. Twice. Clumsy, grimy fingers rummaged in her mouth, plucking and pulling out teeth.

Then he lifted the iron pole, and plunged the girl into the roaring fire pit. A greasy glow filled the chamber washing away the shadows on the wall.

TWENTY

It was no secret His Eminence Timothy Cardinal Bernard believed he could one day be the first American Pope. In his church, all aisles led to the altar of this ambition. A flaw which, in fact, made it easier for Monsignor Palladin, Bernard's chancellor, to control him, not for his own ends but for the sake of the Church, which he loved above all else, and therefore, its living master, Pius X, Bishop of Rome and Vicar of Christ. Pius was the *Pontifex Maximus,* the highest priest, the Pope. Moreover, he was bankrupt.

One by one, the governments of nineteenth century Europe had confiscated the Church's enormous wealth and land holdings. The last of the eighteen Papal States, of which the Pope was the monarch, was the Patrimony of St. Peter: Rome. It had been seized by armed troops in 1870 when the Italian government declared war on Rome. Now, the Pope *leased* the land on which the Vatican stood from the Italian government.

Pius X was all but an impoverished, stateless refugee within the Vatican compound. Uppermost in the minds of Pontiff, Cardinal and Monsignor was the absolute necessity of keeping the Church in America not just solvent, but lucrative, insuring American dollars would continue to finance the diminishing Roman Catholic Church.

Ultimately, Palladin served that Church by allowing Bernard to be the public face of what he himself arranged in private. Monsignor Palladin was the one with whom the politicians and industrial barons negotiated; and while it was Cardinal Bernard's ring they kissed on public occasions of high religious or civic pomp, it was the Monsignor whom they respected. And feared.

This morning Monsignor Palladin sat on a horsehair-stuffed chair in the Cardinal's study and waited for His Eminence to arrive.

Father Sebastian, the Cardinal's secretary, a man whose phlegmatic mien would have served him well in a Trappist cloister, sat at a small table answering telephone calls, receiving dispatches and fussing with his note-taking. He never showed, by even so much as a glance, the slightest acknowledgment of His Eminence's habitual tardiness. Palladin was hard pressed to control his irritation at this pointless waste of time. But control himself he did, for a solid hour.

The Cardinal arrived accompanied by his chamberlain Father Elbi. An unabashed woman hater, Elbi considered even the consecrated sisters of his religious order loathsome creatures. The consummate toady, when in the presence of the Cardinal, Father Elbi preened like a fox that knows its agility keeps it safe from the lion's jaw. Palladin intensely disliked Father Elbi. The feeling was mutual but unspoken.

Elbi held His Eminence's chair, and only when settled comfortably, with his hands folded on the desktop, did the Cardinal speak.

"Good morning, Monsignor."

"Good morning, Your Eminence. May we begin?"

For the next half-hour, Monsignor Palladin explained the many details of a particular revenue proposal. Four rundown city blocks of housing in the Polish section of Brooklyn had been condemned by the Kings County building department. Eminent domain was to be invoked to force the sale of the real estate, so that a new fire station and a public library can be built, Palladin explained. A considerable amount of the remaining real estate will be proffered to developers for bidding.

"Certain officials," the Monsignor continued, "have suggested a new parochial school would fit in with the civic redevelopment envisioned by the Mayor for this predominantly Catholic neighborhood.

"We have been invited to bid on any or all of the remaining available real estate; our bid, of course, having some foregone assurance of success.

"Contracts for demolition, hauling, architecture and new construction will be available to Church laity. Knights of Columbus business members and other organizations, such as the Catholic Layman's Association, will have full access to participation.

"There are labor considerations to our advantage, as well. And, of course, the tax exempt status which makes it all feasible.

"In five years time, the Archdiocese stands to see a net profit seven-fold the initial investment over the following ten year period. The Church will have a new school in Brooklyn, a creeping blight in the Polish community will be eradicated, and there will be many good jobs for Church faithful."

His Eminence waggled a finger and Father Elbi stepped forward to pour tea for the Cardinal alone. They sat in silence while the Cardinal sipped as reposed and silent as a jack of diamonds, his attention fixed in vacant mid-space. Finally the Cardinal said, continue.

"In return, His Honor the Mayor has asked me to mention to you the name of Charles Wojciechowski," Palladin said.

"Who is—?"

"Who is running for a district seat on the City Council."

"I see. And it would be appreciated if Mr. Wojciechowski, a good Catholic I assume, had the approval of the Catholic community."

"Not exactly, Your Eminence. A good Catholic? Who can know the secret conscience of a man?" Monsignor Palladin shrugged. "Many of his social ideas are radically reformist, bordering on extreme."

"Well, that doesn't sound like a candidate this office could support," Cardinal Bernard said.

"No, Your Eminence. The Mayor is of the same opinion. I've prepared a file on the entire proposal. If Your Eminence would look at it in the next few days, initial your approval and give me any notes of concern or improvement you may have," he said closing the velour folder.

The Cardinal waggled his finger again, and Father Elbi stepped forward. Palladin ignored Elbi's outstretched hand and carelessly pushed the folder a few inches in his direction; a petty gesture that successfully irked the smug Elbi.

"Anything else, Monsignor?" the Cardinal asked.

"Yes, with your permission. We've promised Mayor Gaynor and Police Commissioner Waldo a response in their support against the false and fomentive editorials appearing in the *Post*. You'll recall we spoke of it recently."

"Oh, yes—the Kahn person. I've given it some thought. Arrange with Father Campion to have something published in *The Morning Messenger* denouncing the propagandistic policies of a certain type of newspaper. Then get off a letter to the *Post's* publisher, what's-his-name?" Cardinal Bernard asked.

"Villard."

"Make Mr. Villard aware of the financial consequences if the Catholic population of this city were to stop buying his rag."

"Very good, Your Eminence. However, that step has already been taken, to no avail. Mr. Kahn's attacks against Mayor Gaynor and Police Commissioner Waldo continue unabated. Therefore, I've taken the liberty of contacting the *New York Evening Journal*, a paper with a somewhat larger circulation than *The Morning Messenger*."

"*The Journal*. Mr. Hearst?"

"Yes, Your Eminence."

"And why should Mr. Hearst take an interest in this issue on behalf of Mayor Gaynor? Gaynor trounced him in his last run for mayor. Besides, Hearst is a Methodist, I believe."

"True, Your Eminence. However, who better to defend against the creeping plague of Bolshevism in American journalism. Mr. Hearst is very concerned that the tide be stemmed before it gets further out of hand; just as concerned as the Church naturally is. Mr. Abraham Kahn's anti-establishment opinions have struck Mr. Hearst as essentially un-American. Pitting the classes against each other, he says; and he assures me he is prepared for his own newspaper chain to respond accordingly."

"Well, I'm very happy to hear it. Well done, Monsignor. If this were Europe, however, a good public thrashing would easily serve the same purpose.

"Yes, Your Eminence."

"You seem to finally be out of folders," the Cardinal said.

"I am, Your Eminence," Palladin said with a self-deprecating smile.

"Good. Just time enough for a nap before luncheon. I slept very little last night."

TWENTY-ONE

T hey've found another one," Abie said, slamming the telephone on its hook.

He and Noah piled into the Cadillac and headed across town from the Post Building on Vesey Street to the corner of Delancey and Essex where the Brooklyn subway loop through Manhattan was being dug.

They parked near a gaping rip in the street. For more than a block, the earth had been excavated, a tunnel dug, infrastructure built and track laid. Once done, it would again be covered and the street re-paved, before the process was repeated block after block. This system of cut and cover worked well in those areas where the substrata consisted of dirt and gravel. In other areas, where nearly impenetrable schist rock formed Manhattan's base, tunnels had to be bored underground by heavy equipment. This section of the borough was a patchwork of both types of excavation.

"Come on," Abie said. They descended, via open elevator, twenty-five feet to the excavation floor, where Abie's police contact Sgt. Simonov met them. The policeman led them into the excavated tunnel which stretched a hundred feet further in. At a spot where a tributary led off from the main excavation, a by-passage brought them to a honeycomb of adjacent tunnels already in use by IRT trains. Some tunnels merely dead-ended after a few dozen feet where the original excavators made course corrections.

It was in a tunnel like this that the body, or rather the charred remains of a woman had been discovered early that morning by a workman who'd taken a wrong turn.

Sgt. Simonov, in his high domed hat and perennial woolen tunic, stood by while Abie and Noah examined the crime scene. The remains had been removed, but police light bulbs strung overhead were still in place like Christmas trim in July. There was a fire pit and an empty can smelling of kerosene nearby. Chunks of charred rail ties and at least three-feet of ash at the bottom of the pit, attested to the ferocity of the fire it had contained. The victim had been nearly consumed by fire, Sgt. Simonov said; only a brittle, blackened skeleton fused at charcoal joints. Noah spent quite a bit of time just standing and staring at the fire pit.

After a while, he stooped to examine something in the ash. Just below the top layer of flake, he found a small object, a tooth, an incisor, yellow and fossilized by the flames. Noah walked silently around the chamber itself, careful not to disturb anything which hadn't already been trampled by the authorities. He knelt to brush away a bit of dirt revealing another broken tooth, which had escaped the fire, a mandibular third molar.

Noah knew this was not a recent murder. From the amount of dust and settled ash that rested in a layer over every undisturbed surface, he was sure the murder had to have gone undiscovered for at least some months. Abie questioned the sergeant who described what the police had found at the scene. As they left Noah pressed the two dental findings into Sgt. Simonov's hand.

On returning to Abie's office their spirits were low, buoyed only by Cate's unexpected presence. She'd followed through on her promise of a list of people who knew Mrs. Nicolosi, and was just leaving when Abie and Noah arrived. She was horrified to hear the news they had to tell.

"At least," Noah observed, "the authorities can no longer deny there's a deranged killer at large. This wasn't murder merely for the sake of extinguishing a life. Handcuffs, chains, the rail ties and kerosene. The digging of that deep pit in hard packed earth. This took effort, planning, and then the specific execution of that plan. For what purpose?

"That's what the police will have to discover in order to catch him. The why of it," Noah added.

"Perhaps he's too cleaver for the police to ever catch him. Like the Ripper killer," Cate said frightened.

Abie angrily inserted paper into his typewriter. "Then maybe citizen vigilantes will have to do it," he said.

"Is that what you intend to print?" Noah asked a little startled.

Abie pounded with two fingers on the keys of his Oliver faster than one would have thought possible. He grunted something indecipherable and continued punching keys.

Cate and Noah exchanged glances. After a moment more of being ignored, Cate reluctantly stood to go and bid Noah her usual curt good-bye. She was about to leave Abie to his work and Noah to his own devices, when a man appeared at the office door. It was a priest wishing to speak with Mr. Kahn regarding the remains of the woman found in the subway tunnel that morning. Anxious to hear what this priest might have to say, Cate and Noah crowded back into the small office.

"My name," the priest began softly, "is Father Leoni. Vincenzo Leoni. I am the pastor of St. Cecilia's Church on Essex Street. I have a sister, Apollonia whom I've not heard from since February." The little man swallowed hard and pursed his lips it seemed to restrain his grief.

"You think the dead woman may be your sister?" Cate asked gently. "What makes you think so?"

The priest seemed anxious to tell his story but unsure how. Abie urged him to sit down and just speak.

"Thank you, thank you," he said relieved to have listeners. He perched on the edge of his chair like a carelessly placed cup and saucer. "Last February, on the 9th, her birthday, we dined together at the rectory," Father Vincenzo said. "Always, on that day, we celebrate the feast of her namesake."

"And have you reported her to the police as missing?" Abie asked. He absently peeled a piece of Dentyne gum from its wrapper.

"I have not. Concern for my sister's safety was communicated to my diocesan vicar, who in turn consulted with his superior. I was informed a police report would be made on my behalf through official channels, and I would be told the outcome of the investigation."

"And what was the outcome?" Abie asked between chews.

"I was told the police had concluded my sister most probably eloped with a young man who was known to have affections for Apollonia. And, who they say, disappeared at about the same time. The police were certain I would have word from my sister in due time, and perhaps she was even in a certain condition which required such an elopement."

"And is that not possible?" Cate asked Father Vincenzo.

"I do not know who has started such a rumor about my sister," he said, "but it is *not* true. The circumstance, which the police describe, is just not possible!" Father Vincenzo quickly subdued a flash of painful ire.

"You see, my sister and I are quite close," he continued almost whispering. "Our parents died when she was very young. We are all that is left of our family. Apollonia is of marriageable age now; if she had a suitor there was no need to keep it a secret from me. But, I have an even better reason for being convinced she did not elope with any young man. You see, the last night we dined together, Apollonia told me of her decision in a matter she'd contemplated since she was a little girl. Apollonia intended to take the veil. She wished to become a Missionary Sister of the Sacred Heart and serve the poor."

"A Cabrini nun. I've seen them in the slums," Cate said.

Father Vincenzo continued with a sweet smile. "My little sister was a saint, wishing only to serve the helpless. Apollonia had applied for admission as a postulant."

"Tell me, did your vicar know your sister's intentions?" Noah asked.

"Only later, when several weeks had passed, and I expressed my grave doubts about the police investigation of my sister's disappearance."

"And what happened?"

"I received a telephone call from Cardinal Bernard's chancellor, Monsignor Palladin. He called, he said, to offer me his personal support. And because the situation directly involved the Church—a priest and his sister, a girl about to be consecrated to the Church—His Eminence was going to personally have the matter looked into, so no scandal could attach itself to the Church, should the *rumor* prove true. He begged my forbearance, on behalf of Holy Mother Church."

"And I take it you've heard nothing more of the matter?"

"You are correct, Mr. Kahn. I read your editorial a few days ago. I wanted to contact you then, but it's been a difficult decision to make. Then this morning, when word from my parishioners reached me, a young woman had been killed, so nearby—I knew I had to speak up, although I fear it may be too late now for my dear Apollonia." Father Vincenzo pulled a handkerchief from his pocket and unselfconsciously wiped his eyes.

"Father," Noah asked, "this may sound odd, but do you know if your sister had all her teeth?"

"Her teeth? Why, yes, I believe so. I remember once she complained of an ache in a wisdom tooth, but she refused to have it out. Why do you ask?"

"I found something at the crime scene, a tooth, a bottom, back tooth. If your sister had had hers out, before her disappearance, then perhaps she is not the victim. But, as you say—"

"I'm sorry, Father," Mr. Kahn spoke up. "I wish there was some hope we could offer you—"

"But you can, Mr. Kahn. You can offer me hope that the person who has done this will never be able to do it again. The police are doing nothing. So, you must write the truth. Make them admit the truth and do something about it before it is too late for some other poor girl."

TWENTY-TWO

Standing on the sidewalk in front of the *Post's* offices, Noah offered both Cate and Father Vincenzo a lift.

"Very kind of you," the priest said climbing into the back.

"You look peaked, Father," Cate said. "Are you all right?"

"I'm in the Lord's keeping. He sees fit to occasionally visit headaches on me. This seems to be one of those occasions." The priest attempted a small smile but it was wan and forced.

"I'm sorry to hear it, Father. We'll have you back at your residence in no time," Noah said. "And you Miss Gallagher?" Sensing a quick refusal on her lips, he added, "Actually, I want to go back to the Broome Street rooftop. I think the daylight may give a fresh perspective, and I could use your help."

Cate was still suspicious of Noah's character and wanted to decline, but she didn't see how she could after promising to help.

"All right, Mr. Goodwin, if I can be of assistance," she said. In the backseat, Father Vincenzo appeared to doze except for a barely perceptible movement of his lips. They rode the distance to St. Cecelia's in silence.

On the sidewalk in front of his rectory the priest said goodbye. Cate and Noah assured him they'd do all they could to help. It felt flat and devoid of hope even to their own ears. They thanked him for having the courage to come forward and the good Father seemed satisfied with that.

Noah and Cate were alone now in the Cadillac. In front of them the unregulated New York traffic was barely controlled mayhem.

"Terrible way to die," Noah said.

"Unimaginable."

A gloomy pall settled on top of the awkward gulf already between them. After several more minutes silence, Noah pulled the motorcar to the curb, shut off the engine and set the brake. A Bull Moose-candidate brass band, which had been marching along behind them, passed noisily by.

"Thank you," Cate said. "They were giving me such a headache."

"Miss Gallagher, there's something I want to say to you—"

"Not necessary, Mr. Goodwin, truly. I said I would lend my assistance to Mr. Kahn's investigation, and I meant it."

"That's not it. Miss Gallagher, hear me out. There is something which needs to be said."

"No, really there is not."

"There really *is*, Miss Gallagher." Noah turned in his seat to face her.

"Could you look at me, please," he asked.

Cate turn and faced him in the front seat like a hanging judge about to pronounce sentence. "You have something you wish to say?"

"I'm quite aware," Noah began earnestly, "that I offended you with my brash behavior at our first meeting and I do apologize. That I was drunk is no excuse. Actually, it makes it worse, I'm sure.

"And, I admit my initial motivation in approaching Mr. Kahn was self-serving. I'd be a liar if I said I didn't, and still do, find you remarkably pretty. And, *interesting*. In other ways. As well as—interesting. Nevertheless, I must also admit I am, by nature a bit of a—"

"—a womanizer?" Cate provided.

"Well, not—"

"A cad?"

"Go on, get it out—"

"A wolf?"

"*A thrill-seeker*, I was going to say, Miss Gallagher. An explorer—"

"—of women?"

"Miss Gallagher, this isn't going to get us anywhere."

"But I don't wish to *get anywhere* with you, Mr. Goodwin, except to Broome Street, if you actually need my assistance. Otherwise, I'll be happy to get out now and take the trolley home."

"Very well, Miss Gallagher, I'll leave you right here if you like. But first," he said reaching across to latch her door, "you're going to hear me out. Then you may do as you please with no interference from me. That's a promise. Now, will you agree to listen or not?"

"Just get on with it, please, Mr. Goodwin."

Noah seemed to search for a place to start. "It *was* a terrible way for that girl to die. And all the others as well. At first, when I approached Mr. Kahn, it was simply a lark. A way to impress you and perhaps enjoy a summer fling—"

"With me? You really are too much—"

"I'm trying to be honest with you. Now, however, knowing what I know," he hurried on, "and understanding what's at stake, I feel differently. I'm telling you this because I'd like to make a fresh start.

"Am I a womanizer? That's a fair accusation. And did you seem a woman I wanted to... know, before getting back to my work in India? Yes, I fully admit it. But, Miss Gallagher, despite what you think of me, and perhaps rightly so, if I may be an aide to Mr. Kahn or to yourself, then I'm at your service."

Cate exhaled. "Thank you, Mr. Goodwin," she said, not sure yet how she really wanted to respond to this overture. "Maybe you could start the engine now, so we can proceed to Broome Street?"

Noah pulled the starter, shifted and turned into the free-for-all traffic. After a moment he ventured, "Could we at least dispense with the formalities, and use our Christian names? If you don't find that too forward."

"I've no objection," Cate said coolly. "In fact, since we're having this confessional moment, what exactly has changed your motives?"

"The crimes are dreadful."

"Well, that's given," she said.

"What about you, Noah asked abruptly. " Why stick *your* neck out?"

"It's what I do," Cate said. "I stick my neck out for the women of my community."

"Including prison?"

"I hope not. But if necessary—" Cate said solemnly. "However, we've good reason to believe Judge Hand will levy a lenient sentence and allow me my freedom during the appeals process. It will take some time to reach the Supreme Court where we hope to make new law—"

"Where you fervently hope to see a woman seated one day," Noah smiled at her.

"Aah, dawns the light," Cate said. "In the meantime, not even the exclusively male, high court will fail to strike down as unconstitutional laws clearly violating first and fourth amendment rights."

"I understand your concerns for—I guess you could call it womankind—more than I've allowed you to know." Noah concentrated on the traffic. "In India," he said, "among the Hindu, there's a practice called *suttee*. Part of their tradition. The British authorities have outlawed it but still it continues. Widows, either voluntarily or by coercion, are placed on their husband's funeral pyre and immolated. Burned alive. Like we said, a terrible way to die." Noah took a long breath. "Shall I tell you?"

Cate looked to Noah and questioned for the first time who was he really; and what had he to teach her. "Tell me," she said.

Noah shifted gears smoothly and settled into the flow of Fifth Avenue traffic. "Before being lead to the pyre, the widow dips her hand in red dye and leaves a palm print on the arch wall of the village square. Indian women are tiny. You see these walls in many places, covered with red palm prints. They look like the handprints of children; many times they *are* still children, married off to older men." Noah paused to allow Cate to end the narrative there, if she wished.

"Go on," she said.

"The widow sits next to the body of her husband on the pyre, perhaps eight or nine feet high. The heat from the fire below catches her hair first, and then she can no longer just sit. Her sari flames up. She tries to escape, but men with long poles prevent her. The pyre, saturated with butter fat, roars upward and the girl falls screaming into the center of it with her husband's remains. The screams are something you never forget.

"You've no idea the emotions aroused in me seeing that fire pit today. You see, I had an *ayah* once, a sort of nursemaid. She was my first love I guess, when I was just a tot. Later, when I was eight, my little ayah was married off by her father to a man thirty years older. She was widowed young.

"Whether you believe me or not, Cate, I want to help."

There was the long silence of something understood between them. If they had looked at each other they'd have discovered something exceptional in its wondrous simplicity. But the moment passed. The traffic flowed. A trolley clanged its bell and they moved on. Beyond the windshield, ordinary people went about their ordinary business in New York City, the horror of immolation the furthest thing from their minds; except for one amongst them, who awaited his next opportunity.

TWENTY-THREE

Noah parked where they'd parked before, across the street from St. Stephen's. When they alighted, he was surprisingly taken with Cate's hat. She, too, thought it attractive, black-lacquered straw, but didn't understand Noah's fascination, until he said, "Your hatpin. I need it."

"What the devil for?" she asked pulling the pearl-headed pin free.

"And do you also have a hairpin?" She pulled one from several anchoring her mound of hair, and handed it over as well. "I have something of a plan," he said. "I'm going to the roof, and what would be helpful is if you would go sit in the church."

"But, for how long?"

"Until I come get you," he said already dodging traffic of all sorts crossing Mott to Broome.

"All right. But I really don't understand. What am I to do?"

"Just sit. Wait there for me," he hollered back above the swarm of population that quickly absorbed him.

Cate maneuvered more carefully across the street than Noah had and entered St. Stephen's Church. Inside was open, empty and quiet space in utter contrast to the heated turmoil outside. As she walked up the aisle, the gentle tap tap of her footsteps sounded loud and intrusive to her own ears, a violation of sacred silence. She slipped into a front pew, exactly where she'd sat for Felicita Nicolosi's funeral Mass, the memory still vivid: Father Costello in a black chasuble and the choirboys singing the *Requiem* as sweetly as welcoming angels.

There was something comforting to Cate about the familiarity of every Catholic church: the dramatic Stations of the Cross, the sweet-pungent smell, the ritual burning of candles, the serene, blue-clad figure of the Virgin. It had a paganism that fascinated Cate still. Ironic, since it was the Church's leadership which most wished to see her sent to federal prison.

Cate stood in direct opposition to Church dogma regarding birth control and the right of the male hierarchy to make this secular decision. Yet, sitting here in its confines, she willingly submitted to the seductive appeal of church as sanctuary. Like so many others, she felt safe here and she realized, more than anything else, it was what she most yearned for. To feel safe.

Cate opened her handbag and pulled out the letter she'd carried all week. It was part of the ongoing correspondence she was having with several notables who wished to assist her. This from Dr. Havelock Ellis, a defender and personal admirer, who addressed her as his *beloved colleague.* He'd found a small house for her in Dartmoor to which she could flee while there was still opportunity. Members of the Fabian Society had raised funds to support her until the American law that convicted her could be overturned. If the Progressive Party prevailed in November, that could be as little as a year or two. He wanted her to collaborate with him on a book, which *The Manchester Guardian* promised to publish in a daily serial. It was a rosy picture he painted.

More pragmatically, to Cate it was an extraordinary opportunity to win allies among the medical profession. She couldn't imagine the irresponsibility of letting this prospect come to nil.

But the dishonor of flight would break her father's heart. Her cowardice would kill him; she was sure of it. Never had a father been so proud of a daughter marching off to prison.

Flee to freedom and safety. No, you cannot do that, her conscience replied. Cate slumped under the weight of her own hypocrisy and indecision.

Then, from nowhere, Noah appeared on the priests' side of the chancel. He opened the gate in the communion rail and passed through to the nave of the church signaling Cate to follow him out. Cate followed aghast, expecting at any moment a hew and cry to thunder down the aisle after them.

On the sidewalk, Noah took her elbow and silently led her around the corner of the church exterior, where he set about searching for something.

"Here's what I'm looking for," he announced. It was a small, hinged grate, shuttered on the inside, covering a coal chute at ground level. Satisfying whatever was his curiosity, he grabbed her hand and they dashed across the street dodging pushcarts and horse drays. Noah started the Cadillac, and they sped off like bank robbers.

"So, tell me, please," she said panting. "Just what did you need me for?"

"Back there? Maybe moral support."

"But, you told me you needed me to go sit in the church—"

"I couldn't just leave you standing outside in the hot sun. It must be a hundred degrees already," he said clutching and shifting in the stop and go traffic.

"Why—you didn't really need me at all," she protested.

"I need you *now*, to help figure out what we actually know," he said flashing a ridiculously charming smile.

Cate's first reaction was that he'd wasted her time duping her into coming along for the ride, then realized, well, what if he had? He was obviously trying very hard to help Mr. Kahn's investigation; perhaps she did owe him her moral support. And, he was currently one of the few men she knew not trying to put her in prison.

"For instance," he continued, interrupting her confusion, "the victims—I'd be willing to bet, of the five—now six known victims, there's not a Protestant or Jew among them."

"O.K. Well, yes, southern Europeans. It's likely they all were Catholic," Cate agreed.

"Is that just coincidence? And today, a priest, with reason to believe someone in the Cardinal's office is—obscuring the facts."

"Perhaps, but we have only Father Vincenzo's fervent belief that his sister could not *possibly* have eloped with a young man."

"Do you believe that's what happened to her? About to become a nun?"

"It happens."

"Well, let's hope for the good father's sake it did," Noah said. "But two women killed within a stone's throw of two churches?"

"The woman killed in the tunnel might have nothing whatever to do with St. Cecilia's Church. In fact, there're so many churches in Manhattan, one would be hard pressed to get killed anywhere *but* near a church," Cate said.

"Maybe," Noah said. "Nevertheless, there's a vicious killer loose in New York, preying on *Catholic* girls and young women. We know why the politicians don't want it splashed all over the newspapers. But, why isn't the Cardinal's office raising an alarm—?"

"They're protecting the professional reputations of the city's three most prominent Catholic politicians. Mayor Gaynor, Police Commissioner Waldo and Tammany Boss Sullivan. That's why."

"But, wouldn't you think they'd put their own interests first?" Noah puzzled.

Cate was quick to respond. "They are. The one thing the Church hates more than sin is scandal. The greater the offense, the greater the need for secrecy."

"Institutionalized secrecy," Noah agreed.

"How do you mean?" Cate asked.

"Well, a religion born in an age of persecution—say, first century Rome—survives by mastering the art of secrecy. It becomes an essential part of the institution."

"That's it. That's it exactly!" Cate said.

Noah slowed for a long team of sweat-shiny, black mules hauling a mountain of bricks on a flatbed. "So, did you at least find out anything useful roaming around inside there? What exactly *did* you do?"

Noah down shifted smoothly just as the last mule lifted its tail and let loose a pile of greenish muck in its wake.

"Yes, well, I went to the Broome Street rooftop and walked across the roofs to St. Stephen's, just to make sure it was possible. Had a quick look around, and at the base of the church belfry, I found a locked door leading into the church. Oh, by the way, thank you for these," he said. He pulled her pins from his lapel. "Very useful."

"You pried the lock?" she sputtered.

"You'd be surprised how many archaeological finds are discovered in locked chambers."

"With *these*?"

"Tumbler locks have been around for four thousand years, Cate, and the principle is still the same. So, yes, I picked the lock. With those. Shall I show you how to do it sometime? Anyway, inside there's a staircase into the interior of the living quarters, the rectory I guess. There're three bedrooms on the second floor: two are priests' and one is a nun's."

"How do you know?" she asked astonished at his boldness.

"I looked in dresser drawers."

"You didn't!"

"Of course I did. Cleric collars, a shaving brush and razor in two rooms. A nun's habit in the closet of the third bedroom."

"Wait— A nun's? That's odd."

"It's all odd."

"You might have been caught—"

"I figured I had the element of surprise and could have raced back up the stairs and disappeared in the tenements faster than anyone could summon the police."

"But this is amazing. And criminal. What else did you do?"

"I went down to the ground floor and luckily missed an old nun who passed right by where I was standing—eyeglasses thick as Coca-Cola bottles. I stayed hidden until I heard the banging of kitchen pots and pans and was about to leave when I had another bit of luck. A priest exited a door down the hall. It looked to lead to another staircase down to a basement."

"A lot of these old buildings have large subfloors and basements."

"This door has a double-deadbolt lock."

"I don't understand. What is it?"

"It's a precision lock, on both sides of the door. Costly and unusual.

"Why is it unusual?"

"Why lock the door from the outside, except to prevent entry to the basement while it's occupied? It's usually the other way around, lock the door from inside the house, to prevent entry to the house from the basement."

"Well, there could be lots of reasons," she said.

"Name one."

Cate was silent a little too long. "And here's something odder, at least it looked odd to me. The priest I saw had a bunch of keys on a ring clipped to his belt. But he used a key on a chain around his neck, from under his shirt, to lock the basement door. There was just something furtive about the way he did it."

"I've met him a few times. Father Costello. He was at Mrs. Nicolosi's apartment the day after she was killed."

"An old man, probably in his eighties?"

"No. Father Costello is a younger man. Father O'Malley is the old one. A retiree, I think."

"Then Costello must have been the one I saw working at a desk in a room up the hall."

"Rather average and nondescript?" Cate asked.

"Maybe. His back to me, fortunately."

"Father Costello is the pastor now."

"An old man, a blind nun, and a mousey cleric."

"Well, the nun, probably their housekeeper, wouldn't actually live in the rectory. She'd live next door in the convent. Nuns teach at the parochial school on the far corner, at Kenmare Street."

Cate noticed they were pulling up in front of City Hall. Noah parked at the curb under a tree where a jug-eared man was nailing a poster for an A.F. of L. rally in Union Square. The police were already on stand-by alert; violence was expected.

"What are we doing here?" Cate asked.

"The City Engineer's office is here."

"Where you work?" she asked as Noah got out.

"Yup," he said sounding like a Texan. "Right now, what I need is a map. I've got plenty of those in there," he said pointing toward the building's marble facade. "And a crowbar. I've got one of those in there, too."

TWENTY-FOUR

A few minutes later, Noah emerged from City Hall's columned portico, with a haversack slung over his shoulder, a leather knife sheath on his belt, a crowbar and small pickaxe in hand. He trotted quickly down the long flight of steps to the sidewalk.

At the car, he handed over the tools and haversack. He handed over something else, too.

"A pink slip?" Cate asked. Noah shrugged and stuffed a pay envelope in his back pocket. "Let me see that— You've been sacked?"

"Poking around with you and Abie has stepped on someone's toes."

"Oh, Noah, I'm so sorry."

"Don't be. The mayor's office is not a happy place right now. Outside looking in is better." Noah put the idling engine in gear, pulled into traffic, and drove to the *Post's* art nouveau building. When they entered Abie's office, he was putting on his jacket.

"Oh, good. You're here. I need to talk to you, Noah," he said.

"How's your newspaper piece coming?" Cate asked.

"Done. Mr. Villard—he's the owner—is giving it a three-line, four-column, bold, front-page head.

"That's good, isn't it?" Cate asked.

"By this afternoon, every paper in town will have picked it up," Abie said.

"The Mayor and the Police Commissioner will *have* to respond, and the public will at least know there's a killer on the loose," Noah added.

"Bulls-eye! But, eh—listen, there's one thing, Noah," Abie said. "I guaranteed Villard the victim found this morning fits within the time frame of the other killings. So now, you've got to assure *me*—we're right about this. Right?"

"Look," Noah said. "I didn't see the remains of the body, so all I can say for certain is the crime *scene* is less than a year old."

"O.K.," Abie said. He moved with his ungainly gait to the window behind his desk and opened it wide. The roar of modern urban life, two stories below, filled the room.

"Coroner Hellenstein could still claim the remains are years older, maybe even primitive," Abie said.

"I think he'd be deliberately lying if he did, or unbelievably inept," Noah said.

"Still, it could be disastrous. Cast a huge shadow on the newspaper's credibility," Abie said.

"They're certain the bones are a woman's?" Cate asked.

"Sgt. Simonov saw the remains carried out on a stretcher. He was pretty certain. Something about the wide pelvic bones and small brow bone. Even charred as they were, he said he could tell."

Cate nodded her head.

"Oh, and you were right, Noah, about the teeth. Simonov says he asked a morgue orderly to look. Most of the teeth had been broken. Some where yanked. What you found matched the stub of one in the mouth. The sergeant says a lot of the information is being hushed for now.

"Anyway, Coroner Hellenstein is supposed to issue a statement late this afternoon."

"Today? That's fast."

"Well, its just a preliminary report. But word is the Mayor is starting to sweat. He told Hellenstein to speed it up."

"Well, I can tell you this much with certainty," Noah said. "If *that* woman died in *that* fire, then it happened less than a year ago," Noah said.

"Would you stake your reputation on it?" Abie asked.

"Me? I have no reputation. But, my father does."

"Yeah, that's right. He probably knows all about old bones, and what're *not* old bones. If Hellenstein tries to pull a fast one, the *Post* can challenge his findings; subpoena the remains and have an independent examination done," Abie said. "Bring in a slew of bone experts—your old man, and maybe a couple of medical big wigs. What a headline that would make! The papers could easily drag it out 'til election day. As long as you're certain about the age of the crime scene."

"I'm *reasonably* certain."

"O.K.. Good enough for me. I'm going to tell Villard the story is solid. We go with it. The crime scene fits within the time frame of Apollonia Leoni's disappearance. Nobody else has *that* story." Abie grabbed his hat.

"Take a look at this," Cate said, showing him Noah's pink slip.

"Hah! Well, I told you some people weren't going to like you paling around with the likes of me and the infamous Miss Gallagher," Abie said. He lit a cheroot with his pocket flint lighter.

Noah shrugged his shoulders dismissively. "Where are you off to now?" he asked.

"Coroner's office. When the paper hits the street, I want to be there for Hellenstein's reaction. See how a little public pressure effects his statement."

"I'll drive you," Noah said.

"I'll catch a taxi. Villard's got me on an expense account for this."

"In that case, could we use your office. I want to plot all the crime scenes on a map or at least the points where bodies were found. See if it indicates some kind of physical pattern."

"Say, good idea!" Abie said snapping his fingers. "You two stay here and work on that. The dossier is on my desk somewhere. I'll head over to Hellenstein's office and telephone you when he gives his press statement."

When he'd left, Noah looked thoughtful. "Do you ever think maybe Abie's got a dog in this fight we don't know about?"

Cate took off her hat and gloves. "What do you mean?"

"I mean— I'm not sure what I mean, really. Just sometimes, he's a little *too* passionate. There's a fervor that's almost—obsessive."

"I think you're wrong. Abie's just very good at his job. And dedicated to a good cause."

"O.K. sure. Forget I said anything. Come on, let's look at this map." They put their heads together over a map of Manhattan and twenty minutes later Cate sat back and stared at what they'd plotted: Alice Lombardi in the water below Bowling Green, Susanna Profaci at the Municipal Building construction site, Lucy Mendoza in an alley off Broadway, Engratia Ricci in the Bowery, Felicita Nicolosi on Broome Street and finally Apollonia Leoni near Delancey and Essex.

"Do you see a pattern?" Cate asked.

"It's scattershot, but not random. He organizes his killing."

"It certainly isn't the proximity of a church, unless you count Trinity several blocks from Bowling Green. But, Trinity is Episcopalian, not Roman Catholic. And look here," Cate said pointing to the map. "Eldridge Street Synagogue near the Ricci woman's flat. What do we make of that?"

Noah was thoughtful a minute then said, "Think you're up to another excursion?" he asked.

"You're going back to St. Stephen's, aren't you?"

"Yes. I am."

"With a crowbar?"

"With a crowbar."

"And you want me to go with you?"

"I could use a lookout," he said.

Cate huffed a sigh, not bothering to argue. Her sense was that a reasonable argument would avail nothing.

"What time?"

Noah looked at his pocket watch. "It's three-thirty now. I should go back to the University and check on my father. See if he needs his car. I'll drop you off and come back for you about ten o'clock tonight. How's that?"

"All right," Cate said unenthusiastically.

Noah was looking at her with a blank intensity that told Cate his thoughts were weighty.

"Are you O.K.?" Cate asked.

"What—? Yes. I'm fine."

"Good." Cate gathered her hat, gloves, and purse and faced Noah who seemed distracted by something on her lip. He bent closer. Uncomfortably close. When he kissed her briefly but firmly on the mouth Cate realized she wasn't as angry as she ought to be.

TWENTY-FIVE

Word of the body found near St. Cecelia's had spread quickly among the parishioners of Manhattan's fifty-eight Catholic churches. A whispered rumor had it that the victim was a nun. Some said the nun had run away with a young man. Still others heard it was a young girl in a family way, perhaps disposed of by the baby's father. A few even said there was a maniac on the prowl, an idea most of the God-fearing considered an overreaction. Father O'Malley knew it was not an overreaction.

It occurred to nearly no one to connect that death with the mother who'd fallen from the rooftop near St. Stephen's. There'd been rumors about her death as well. She was robbed of her wedding ring chopped from her hand; she'd received a note summoning her to the roof where she was attacked; it was an assignation; she'd fallen while cooling herself and rats the size of cats had torn her to pieces. As in the old countries, gossip was the common news outlet.

Father O'Malley concerned himself with none of it. The parishioners' fears were Father Costello's responsibility. O'Malley was concerned only with what effected his own splendid isolation. Right now what disturbed him was his garden patch of onions behind the rectory. It had been trampled again by the stray dog the nuns insisted on feeding scraps. O'Malley had a scrap for him today. A juicy bit of pork fat he'd saved for the occasion. He spread a napkin holding the gobbet on the ground in the patch of Timothy grass, which the dog trampled his onions to get to, and waited.

The little beagle lay dozing under the convent's back steps. The hot afternoon air wafted a scent in his direction that roused him. He was a young beagle and constantly hungry. In less than three minutes he'd followed his nose to Father O'Malley. The pup was cautious of the man, but his food drive urged him on. Even as O'Malley grabbed him by his scruff he pawed at the greasy morsel just out of reach.

"You little pest," O'Malley said with a small chuckle. "Gotcha' now." He stroked the animal so it wouldn't struggle and carried it to a pile of discarded broken bricks. Squatting down, he set the beagle on the ground and stroked it's head. It curled and licked O'Malley's hand, then rolled on its back, belly up, paws dancing in the air.

O'Malley lifted a brick and tested its heft, dropped it and chose a larger brick. He stroked the pup's belly until it lay supine and passive. The old man tightened his grip on the brick and raised it high overhead. The puppy's eyes closed as he surrendered to the pleasurable petting. O'Malley reared back and bent his elbow to strike with all his might.

"You will *not!*" a voice behind him thundered. O'Malley, startled, froze. A firm hand pried the brick from O'Malley's fist. Father Costello pushed his brother priest aside and scooped-up the bewildered beagle. "Poor soulless creature," he said kindly.

"He's been trampling my garden!" O'Malley said petulantly.

"Then I shall find him a home." Father Costello's voice rang with an authority that momentarily cowered O'Malley.

"Who? Where?" he sulked.

"Mrs. Hartley may take him. She's just lost her child and can have no more."

"Well, make it your business if you choose. Just keep that nuisance out of my garden."

"Or you'll do what?" Costello asked grimly.

Father O'Malley retreated a step like a cur dog on the verge of flight. "Never mind," he said over his shoulder as he slunk away. "Just keep it out of my garden."

Father Costello nuzzled the small dog under his chin and wondered was he going to have to do something about Father O'Malley.

TWENTY-SIX

When Noah arrived to pick Cate up at ten o'clock, they were both elated, for more reasons than one. Coroner Hellenstein had announced, without comment, that the charred remains of a female had been found in an excavated tunnel on Essex Street. His preliminary finding was that the unidentified female had met death at the hands of another, within the last twelve months. With Mayor Gaynor standing behind him on the steps of City Hall, a vociferous Police Commissioner Rhinlander Waldo announced a swift investigation into the *Fire Pit Murder*. The press scattered like jackrabbits to file the story.

The *Post* scooped them all by printing that the most likely identity of the victim was Miss Apollonia Leoni, first reported to the police as missing in February. *Post* newsies hollered their headlines on every city corner:

WHERE IS APPOLONIA?
MISSING GIRL MAY BE FIRE PIT VICTIM!
Police Bungle Missing Person Search
Sixth Female Victim of City Hall Incompetence

That sent the other twelve New York dailies into a fervor of extra editions. By midnight, morning presses, from Portland, Maine to Portland, Oregon, were setting type announcing something was rotten in the Big Apple.

Abie Kahn led the stampede of journalists demanding access to police records for every unsolved female murder and every unsolved disappearance over the last two years.

Reports by distraught relatives of missing or murdered females were coming in to every newspaper office and police station in the state. Twenty-two missing person reports were brought to Mr. Kahn personally. Finally, the alarm had been rung.

Abie had to somehow conform the influx of new reports with what he already knew of the six known victims. What was known of them would be the criteria: eliminate anyone not of the European immigrant class; exclude any females missing outside lower Manhattan; those over the age of forty; those engaged in prostitution or other crime; those missing from mental hospitals.

That winnowed it down to three possible, additional victims over the last eighteen months. It was these police records Abie most wanted to examine.

Police Commissioner Waldo knew full well the *Post's* attorneys were eager to get a court order, if necessary, for police records, or any document, which *is required by law to be created or maintained*, so the law read. And they'd get it, too. With the state and federal elections so near, the *Post* was winding-up to take a good, hard crack at Tammany Hall. The timing was critical; if Tammany Hall looked vulnerable, their Democratic candidates up for election in Albany and in Washington would be the first to disavow and condemn the New York machine.

The *Post* gave the Commissioner's office twenty-four hours to comply with Abie's request for police reports.

"It's all very good news, isn't it," Cate said smiling as she climbed into the Cadillac. She and Noah drove to St. Stephen's and parked where they had before. Armed with his flashlight and a small crowbar, Noah and Cate slipped into the shadow of the elm trees flanking the church.

At the coal chute on the side of the church, Noah dropped to his knees and lifted the chute's rusty iron grate, while Cate nervously kept watch. He applied the crowbar to the wooden shutter inside until it creaked open on old hinges. Noah cupped the beam of his flashlight then aimed it around the dark interior.

"Hold this," he said handing her the crowbar. "I'm going in for a little look around."

"Have you taken leave of your senses?" Cate knew it was no use but said it anyway.

"Listen to me," he said. "Can you drive?"

"Yes. My father taught all of us to drive."

"Good—"

"But I'm not licensed."

"That's O. K.; neither am I," he said. "Stand with your back against the wall, so no one can sneak up on you." Cate was positioning herself as he said, when he slipped, smooth as an eel, into the dark chute.

"What are you doing!" she whispered as loudly as she dared. She tried to bend and see into the chute while keeping her back against the church wall but could only see the beam of his light sweeping about inside. In a moment, however, his face reappeared at ground level.

"All right," he said. "Listen to me. I think there's a sub-basement. The entrance is covered by a cement slab in the floor. But there's a handle; I can move it."

"You're going *down* there?!" Cate was incredulous.

"It could be important. The slab has no lock. It's an escape hatch, both coming and going. Like a rat hole."

"Well, if you know that already, why do you have to go in there?" she protested.

"Because it could also just be the root cellar."

"But what if it's not?"

"Then we'll have learned something important."

"What?" Cate asked eagerly.

"I won't know *what* until I go in there. Please—I want you to go sit in the car. Count to one hundred. If you don't see me coming back by a hundred and *one*, leave," he said. "Go home. If I'm not there in an hour, telephone Abie. Tell him everything."

"You are scaring me half to death."

"Don't be afraid. Really. Just, follow the plan. Now, go on to the car. Here, take the ignition key."

"No," she said.

"What do you mean *no?*"

"I mean, no, I'm not leaving until you've moved the slab. Maybe there's just dirt underneath and you can come out of there right away." She could tell she was exasperating him, but one of them had to behave responsibly.

"I tell you what," he said. "Wait right here. When I have the slab opened, I'll whistle. That's your signal to get back to the car because I'm going in."

"Awh, Jesus," she sighed. "All right, you'll whistle. O.K. go!

She could hear the sound of the cement slab scraping on the floor, then, his whistle and the sound of the slab being pulled back in place, followed by awful silence.

Suddenly, the basement lit up like a Christmas tree. She heard footsteps come down the creaky staircase then stop abruptly. Whoever was in there had to see the open shutter. She heard a rush across the cement floor to the open chute.

"Who's there?" someone hissed.

What would happen if Noah suddenly emerged from the sub-basement? Fear made her nauseous. And, what would happen if she were found lurking outside this coal chute with a crowbar in her hand? She'd be arrested and jailed for burglarizing a Catholic church, that's what. The scandal would not only ruin her name and legal cause, but would leave the Family Aid Society a shamble. Why had she ever gone along with this reckless criminal adventure? It was that goddamn kiss. She knew entirely well that romance addled the brain and this was the most addle-brained thing she'd ever done.

Cate broke and ran for the Cadillac. She started the engine immediately, and drove home as fast as possible.

TWENTY-SEVEN

Cate heard the banging on her front door and raced to open it.

"Thank you for coming so quickly."

She hadn't waited the hour Noah had asked for when she got home. Instead, she'd immediately telephoned Mr. Kahn at home. Unable to make much sense of her disjointed and excited speech, he told her he was catching a taxi and coming right over.

While she waited she paced. When that proved intolerable she made herself a cup of tea and added a dose of Teasdale's Tincture. Cate blew on her tea, then downed as much as she could in three big swallows. Teasdale's readily lived up to its calmative claims.

She led Mr. Kahn into the sitting room where he asked exactly what had happened, and she was able now to give a calm, clear account of Noah's two forays into St. Stephen's.

The moment she'd finished, there was another banging on her door.

Cate and Mr. Kahn shared an apprehensive glance as they went to answer. To their relief, it was Noah, covered in grime. Cate brought him a glass of water and then sat to hear what had happened.

"The chink around the slab lit up when someone—I couldn't see who—turned on the basement lights, so, I knew I couldn't return that way," he said.

"Well, what was under there?" Cate asked impatient to know the whole story.

"Hang on. I'm going to tell you everything," Noah said with a smile. He seemed pleased she was *so* concerned. She made a mental note of it, and reminded herself he'd just put her at great legal risk.

"The sub-basement is open at the far end where it looks like it's been tunneled into: maybe an engineering mistake or maybe intentionally dug. It's difficult to say, but I suspect the latter. It leads to a warren which connects with the subway tunnels. It's how I got here, actually."

"How exactly?" Abie asked.

"Subway. I picked a direction underground and started walking until I came to subway train tracks. I was followed, by the way."

"You didn't see who it was?"

"No. But I heard someone a couple of times. I did *not* slow down to see who. With trains passing at fairly high speeds, it wouldn't have been the safest place for an unfriendly confrontation."

"It may have been one of the priests from St. Stephen's. I think he may have seen me," Cate told Noah.

"Maybe," he said. "At any rate, I followed the subway tracks to the closest station, which turned out to be south of St. Stephen's, at Centre and Canal. I climbed up onto the platform and caught the uptown express to Sheridan Square. Then walked the two blocks here," he said with a shrug. "How'd *you* get here so soon?" he asked Abie.

"I couldn't wait," Cate confessed. "I mean, after the lights went on in the basement. I was supposed to give Noah an hour to get back here before I telephoned you," she explained to Abie. "But I was too frightened to wait. We could have both been arrested," she added emphatically looking at Noah.

"Well, you did the right thing," Abie said. "The next time you two decide on a little breaking and entering, could you let me know before hand. So I can stop you!"

"I didn't want to expose you to the liability," Noah explained to Abie.

"But you exposed *her*."

"You're right. I should have left her out of it as well."

"Excuse me," Cate said. "Do you mind not discussing *her* as though I weren't capable of speaking for myself. It was foolhardy but it's done now, so let's move on. After all, you've discovered something valuable."

Both men looked at her quizzically. "Aren't you thinking the same thing I am?" Cate asked. "The killer could be using the subway tunnel system to move about unseen. I mean, he's kidnapping women; he has to be able to move about secretively."

"The thought did occur to me as I was walking. But maybe he has an automobile."

"Then, wouldn't he need an accomplice?" Cate questioned. "Someone to drive while he——"

Abie perked up, "Wait a minute—the Ricci woman killed in the Bowery—isn't that along the route being excavated for the Brooklyn loop line? And not only that, the loop line connects with the excavation where the fire pit is."

"I think we're on to something important," Noah said.

"We are," Abie replied. "But, listen, now that the mayor has been goaded into some kind of action, it's time we gave all this information to the police, and let the coppers take it from here. It's too dangerous to continue poking around."

"I think Abie's right," Noah said. "Getting you involved tonight was a big mistake."

"Yes, it was," she said. "We won't be doing any more illegal trespassing."

"So, we're agreed. We let the police handle the whole thing," Noah said.

"Just a moment, Noah. That's easy for you to say. In a few weeks it's back to India for you. But this is my community," Cate said. "I can't just pretend I don't know what I know, and do nothing. Besides, we've discovered nothing the police couldn't also have easily discovered had they mounted any investigation at all. There's no reason to believe, this close to the election, they're not going to just minimize the threat to the public, and whitewash themselves." Cate was working herself up now.

"I know how these politicians operate. Oh, they'll put on a good political show, round up a lot of so-called suspects, make arrests, likely find some scapegoat, preferably a dead one, and call the case solved. And, you know I'm right, Mr. Kahn. Nothing is as important to them as November's election."

"Yes. That's likely what will happen. Nevertheless, it's dangerous, Miss Gallagher. More dangerous than you know," Abie insisted.

"Are *you* going to stop writing about the murders now? Because it's dangerous?" Cate asked.

"Absolutely not. In fact, my piece in tomorrow's paper is going to name names, including Dollar Bill Baylor's. I promise to get to the whole rotten bottom of it. Gaynor and Waldo aren't alone in this. Nothing happens at Tammany Hall without Big Tim Sullivan's O.K. and he'd serve his own grandmother to wolves to save his bid for the Senate."

"Then why—?"

"It's what *I do*, Miss Gallagher. My job. I'm *accustomed* to death threats. But I won't keep involving you two in this."

"Death threats? What are you talking about?" Cate asked.

Abie reached into his inside pocket and pulled out several pieces of paper. He handed them to Cate and Noah, one at a time.

"One was smeared with excrement, so I burned it," Abie said.

It was shocking, the language vile and beyond merely vulgar. Some of the words Cate had never in her life seen actually written down on paper. The anti-Semitic epithets were unnerving in the hatred conveyed.

"These," Mr. Kahn said, "have been arriving at the newspaper since the first piece I wrote confronting Gaynor and Waldo."

"They are unsigned," Cate observed.

"They always are." Mr. Kahn lit a cheroot with his flint-lighter. He was angry, but not at Cate and Noah.

Cate finally looked up at him. "And you expect us to just withdraw our support while you carry on alone, is that it?" she asked.

"Look. *I'm* the—" he snatched the letters back and pointed, "—*the filthy Jew, Godless kike, Jewish spawn of Lucifer.* Shall I go on? And here—I saved the most frightening of them. The one which shows what we're really up against." Mr. Kahn handed over a small, gilt-edged card from his pocket.

"This hate is institutionalized; it's culturally and socially bred into people who think Heaven holds a special place for anyone putting a bullet in my head, right between my horns."

Noah and Cate inspected the printed card. On the front side, there is a pastel painting of a small, blond boy gagged, his arms held out in a pose of crucifixion. He is surrounded by evil looking men wielding sharp bits of metal. In the painting, the boy stands in a basin into which his blood flows. A white circle haloes his head. Cherubs await him in clouds above.

"What is this?" Noah asked.

"It's a Catholic holy card. They're passed out to parochial school children. I found it on my chair when I got back from the coroner's office. Read it."

Noah turned the holy card over and read aloud the hagiography on the back.

'*St. Simon, Infant Martyr. In 1472, the Jews in the city of Trent determined to vent their hate against the crucified Lord by slaying a Christian child at the coming of Passover. Tobias, one of their number, was deputed to trap a victim. He found a bright, smiling boy named Simon playing outside his home, and with no one guarding him, coaxed the child to take his hand. The boy, who was not yet two years old, did so; but he began to cry and call for his mother when he found himself being led from home. Tobias with many caresses silenced the boy's grief and conducted the child away. At midnight on Holy Thursday, the work of butchery began. Having gagged the child's mouth, they held his arms in the form of a cross, while they pierced his tender body with awls and bodkins in blasphemous mockery of the suffering of Jesus Christ. After an hour of torture, the little martyr lifted his eyes to heaven and gave up his innocent soul. The Jews cast his body into the river but their crime was discovered. Simon's holy relics were enshrined in the church there, where they have worked many miracles.*'

Abie pulled one more sheet from his pocket. "*This* was with it. On my chair, in my office. It was placed there personally, by God knows who. Someone who wants us to know they're nearby."

"Someone at your newspaper?" Cate asked naively.

Abie shrugged and handed the piece of paper to Noah. Over his shoulder Cate could see writing: *Death to the Christ killer and the whores who do his bidding. 66773*

"What's 66773?" Cate asked. "A Biblical verse?"

Abie and Noah exchanged a worried look. "No," Noah said. "It's the license plate number on the Cadillac."

TWENTY-EIGHT

Seraphia Nicolosi led her father up the front steps of the Family Aid office at eight o'clock the next morning as arranged. Seraphia had to coax her father the last few steps, tugging on his empty sleeve when he balked at the entrance.

"For your new hand, Papa. You promised to me today," she pleaded.

"*Quanto costerà?*" he asked again.

"I told you—in English, Papa. Now listen." Seraphia spoke slowly, distinguishing each word. "Miss Gallagher, she says you don't hava to pay nothing. Now, you please come on."

Cate had been watching for Seraphia and her father through a window, and was relieved to see the girl had managed to convince him to come. At their approach, she waved through the open window, encouraging them on.

When Mrs. Pankhurst's two hundred dollar draft on the Bank of England was received, Cate had immediately arranged through the artificial limb program at Bellevue Hospital, for Mr. Nicolosi to be fit with the latest achievement in prosthetics.

Made of wood and nickel steel, the device had a leather shoulder harness with small pulleys that allowed strong pinchers to open and close—to *articulate*. It was an ingenious leap in technology over the primitive hooks thousands of wounded soldiers had been fitted with after the Civil War.

Mr. Nicolosi was fortunate to have lost only his hand to the nitroglycerine, which had sweat through a stick of dynamite he grabbed the day of his accident. New York was a city ripped apart by the subway construction. Utility cables and chunks of sidewalk pavement were littered everywhere. Street signs and lamp posts toppled like saplings. Great gaping holes appeared daily as if hell were clawing its way up from below. Emergency vehicles were a constant sight in the snarled traffic.

The sound of dynamite blasts caused horses and pedestrians alike to rear in terror at the unexpected, underground explosions. Facades crumbled, cornices fell. The reverberations showered sudden, malevolent hailstorms of broken window-glass onto the sidewalks of Manhattan.

But the most terrible calamities of all were the fate of workmen crushed under falling boulders or blown apart by miscalculated charges. For the sum of $3.75 a day, twice the wage of the average unskilled laborer, men like Mr. Nicolosi faced the specter of gruesome death in the bowels of the city, ten hours a day, six days a week. Mr. Nicolosi was lucky to be alive.

"I'm so glad you're here," Cate assured him now.

"Me, too," he responded bowing politely. "I thanka you for you help me and me *famiglia*."

"Why, your English is so much improved, Mr. Nicolosi. It's my pleasure to help," Cate said. She led Mr. Nicolosi, whose head turned everywhere at once, as if expecting a bogeyman to leap from behind each door, into the examination room where the sight of so much clinical whiteness and the smell of disinfectant clearly caused him serious hesitation.

Further startling him was the limb specialist from Bellevue Hospital who'd come to take measurements for his prosthesis. Cate introduced Dr. Juanita Crump, who'd been kind enough to give them her Saturday morning. Cate reassured Mr. Nicolosi and the astonished Seraphia that Dr. Crump was a medical doctor graduated from the New England Female Medical College.

Cate could not tell if their incredulity was caused by Dr. Crump's gender, or her skin, which happened to be the brown of burnished copper. Cate suspected it was their first sighting of either attribute in a *dottore*.

Nevertheless, so gentle and appealing was Dr. Crump's professional manner, soon both father and daughter were relaxed and making game attempts at conversational English, as measurements were taken and a plaster mold of his wrist stump was cast.

The Nicolosies were exuberant with plans for the balance of Mrs. Pankhurst's money gift, and the likelihood that the children would be able to stop piece-working and return to school.

Seraphia, the oldest, would be entering the eighth-grade at St. Stephen's Parochial School. By next June, she could be the first in her family to be graduated from elementary school. There was even the great possibility she might be able to continue on to a four-year high school.

Mr. Nicolosi beamed approval at his daughter. What could a young woman with so great an education not accomplish in this new country. Cate was relieved in some measure to see hope replace the terrible sorrow that had been his face since the brutal loss of his wife.

While the plaster set, and seeing all was going well, Cate excused herself. Saturday was cleaning day at the clinic when she and her volunteer nurse, Dora Adler, cleaned, did laundry and inventoried supplies. Cate slipped into her apron and pulled on sleeve protectors. She returned to sweeping her office but her wheels were spinning too fast to focus on dust balls. Feeling edgy, she emptied the dust pan, then went to the dispensary to see how Dora Adler was getting on.

"Oh, good timing; I'm just about done here," Dora said. "The floors are mopped and disinfected, I boiled the laundry and hung it to dry, and I have a list of supplies I'll pick up Monday morning.

"I've got to dash now, though. We're going to Coney Island tonight," Dora grinned. "I want to get my hair done up. My fella likes my curls." Cate nodded and opened the medicine cabinet. She pulled out the little bottle of Teasdale's Tincture.

"Feeling jumpy, Cate?" Dora asked.

"A little." Cate pressed her finger tips against the smooth surface of the cupboard to stop their slight tremble.

"It's a lot," Dora said coming to Cate's side. "The sentencing coming up, these terrible deaths, all the work you do." She looked at the Teasdale's bottle then at Cate. "We've gone through two bottles already just this month."

Cate quickly put the bottle of Teasdale's back in the cupboard. "I just—" She threw her hands up. "I'm tense. I'm tired and scared; sometimes I'm not sure if I shouldn't just chuck it all. Run away. To Europe!"

"And do what?" Dora countered.

"I don't know. Anything. Tour museums." Cate stared blankly at Dora who gave her such a horrified look that Cate had to laugh.

"You wouldn't!" Dora said incredulously.

"No, of course not," Cate said quickly. "But really, I need..."

"You *need* a respite. Get out of here; go have some fun. That Goodwin fella likes you. I can tell."

"*Him*—he's trouble. He could have got us arrested. He scares me, Dora."

"What scares you, Cate? Huh?" When she looked close to tears and couldn't answer Dora put her arm around Cate's shoulders. "You like him; that's what scares you. But you don't have to marry the man."

"Did I tell you, he said he thought I'd be his summer fling? A *fling*, Dora!"

"Well, and what's wrong with that?" Dora lowered her voice. "And whose to know anyway?" she giggled. "You of all people needn't worry about getting in a family way."

Cate smiled at the absurdity. The scandalously infamous Cate Gallagher nervous as a schoolgirl because a boy liked her. "He did ask me out," she said.

"For when?"

"Tonight. Birthday celebration."

"Oh, it's your birthday! Many happy returns."

"—*and* his father's. Same date."

Dora looked completely exasperated. "And the reason you're not going?"

"He is *such* a masher..." Cate muttered.

"Look," Dora said. "You've got twenty-five dollars stashed in the Folgers can. Bonwit's is open 'til five. Go buy something really smart. Curl your hair and go. You never know what could happen; you could even have a good time for a change."

"But he..."

"You don't have to jump into bed with the man, just because he asks—and he probably will. You just go get your mind off your troubles awhile," she smiled. "Or do I need to order extra bottles of Teasdales?" she asked her voice now quite serious.

"You're right, Dora. Of course you're right. I'll do it. I don't know why I'm so skittish."

"You've a lot on your shoulders, but things will work out; you'll see. And happy birthday, for goodness sake. See you Monday." That settled, Dora Adler hung her apron on a peg, grabbed her gloves and handbag, and headed out the door.

She checked her coin purse for subway fare as she rushed down the building's front steps, brushing right past the madman who'd been watching the Family Aid entrance all morning.

TWENTY-NINE

Cate was happy with the dress she bought. It had a narrow, lilac skirt embroidered with silver thread. She wore white evening gloves past the elbow and a string of pearls, which had been her grandmother's, and her décolletage was fashionably low and exaggerated. After their second round of gin rickeys, she was not at all concerned about it and felt decidedly empowered by the admiring attention all around her, especially from Noah who seemed mesmerized by her glamour. She found she enjoyed seeing him a bit agog and not quite so cocksure of himself, for once. She decided to ignore him as much as possible without being rude.

"Something is different about you, I think," she said addressing herself to Professor Goodwin.

"Oh, you noticed."

"I'm not quite sure, but your face has changed—" she said.

"It's the beard," Noah interjected.

"He doesn't have a beard," Cate said.

"Precisely."

"Oh, that's what it is," she said. "You wore a beard when we first met. A sort of goatee."

"I'm flattered you remember," Professor Goodwin said.

"Your son is certainly the spitting image of his father. He should take that as a compliment."

"Yes, he should," the professor preen. "Are you enjoying yourself, my dear?"

Cate told the elder Goodwin it was her first visit to the Madison Square Garden rooftop. She said she'd dined at Delmonico's with an aunt once, which in no way compared to this newer supper club. Delmonico's was over-wrought with pillars, Victorian gilt, and dusty velvet, she said.

Here the walls and ceiling were covered in chalk silk. Lalique chandeliers hung like celestial bodies. The marble floor was stepped, so the view of the floorshow was everywhere excellent. The terrace beyond the bandstand was open to the sky, and beyond that, the nightlights of Manhattan competed with the stars for attention.

Supper, served by waiters in white aprons to their shins, began with a *consommé*, followed by a fish aspic and the entrée: thick porterhouse steaks with *pommes frit* and a bottle of Bordeaux. The dessert was Peach Melba, in which the chef inserted a sparkler, and presented his birthday compliments with a bottle of *Veuve Clicquot*. Professor Goodwin assured Cate it was an excellent Champagne.

The mood turned a bit glum when the after-dinner conversation brought up Abie's latest newspaper piece. As promised, he hadn't spared Dollar Bill Baylor, doing exactly what Baylor hadn't wanted, naming him as a possible witness the night of Felicita Nicolosi's death.

Abie also stated his intent, if all else failed, to call for a federal investigation of constitutional violations of the first amendment by Mayor Gaynor, Commissioner Waldo, Boss Tim Sullivan and as many of their deputies and associates as could be implicated. That covered a lot of territory. Abie was playing with fire. Even Noah felt he had stopped just short of calling for a witch hunt. There were now mighty and implacable forces arrayed against Abie.

"Perhaps the publicity itself will serve to protect him," Cate suggested. "After all, any violent action against him now would only lend credence to his allegations, and draw more press attention."

"If I may say," Professor Goodwin interjected. "I've never met the man, but I've been closely following his editorials in the *Post*. He's not at all reticent about presenting himself publicly as a sacrificial lamb. A martyr for the cause."

"That's what frightens me," Cate said. "He *knows* his position at the forefront marks him for retaliation by the irrational."

"Well, there's an old saying, which seems to apply here: Don't feel sorry for the martyr; he loves his job."

"Enough," Noah said. "Tonight you have nothing to be frightened of. Come on," he insisted, and led Cate onto the dance floor. He tucked her into his right arm and they slid into a slow two-step.

"Now, you see; this isn't so awful," he said. "We could have done this weeks ago when we first met."

Cate stalled on the dance floor. "The day we met, you were pie-eyed drunk. Do you actually want to talk about it?"

Noah refused to feel chagrined. Instead, he wordlessly pulled her close again and they both felt the *frisson* of their bodies. The narrow gap between their torsos was as charged as a thunderbolt at rest. It was something primordial: the way sea creatures confer through electrical impulse; the thing which causes a flock of birds to turn in a single instant on a current. Cate had to remind herself to breath, and when she did, she slid into the crevasses of his body as easily as snow falling on the tops of trees.

When the band played livelier music, it was the Professor who took to the floor to show off his Turkey Trot and then a sultry tango with the tall brunette at the next table.

With the final abrupt note of the *Paso Doble*, everyone returned to their chairs for the floorshow. A line of pretty chorines wearing silver sequins and patent leather tap shoes sang and danced up a storm.

Then Miss Sophie Tucker played piano and joked with the audience, belting out several songs, which Professor Goodwin had on phonograph recordings. He promised to share them with Cate.

He told her how much he loved Harlem, that beautiful section of Manhattan between 110th Street and 145th Street, and the culturally rich, colored people who had steadily been migrating there from San Juan Hill and Hell's Kitchen, along with a burgeoning influx of southern Negroes. He said America was on the verge of a cultural naissance of astounding importance and suggested another outing to acquaint her with jazz music.

When the evening was over and everyone was tipsy, Professor Goodwin drove while Noah sprawled in the backseat. Through sly smiles and tilting of the head, Noah gestured for Cate to join him in the back, which, of course, she would not do. It nevertheless caused them both suppressed, giddy laughter, which the Professor was polite enough to ignore.

As they drove south on Madison Avenue, Professor Goodwin taught them a new song, *Melancholy Baby* and after about the fifth harmonized repetition they'd finally exhausted themselves.

Professor Goodwin stopped at the curb across the street from NYU and Noah replaced his father in the driver's seat. "I'm so glad to have met you and have this time with you," he said. They said cheery good-nights and for the sake of propriety Noah assured Professor Goodwin he'd deliver Cate home, and return within the hour.

They left the professor smiling and bobbing in his cups. He waved a dismissive hand as he weaved across Washington Square toward his university apartment.

As for Noah, he was behaving like a man on a mission. Alone now with Cate, his conversation was reduced to quick monosyllabic responses as he drove much too fast through the near empty streets. There was little doubt as to how he hoped to spend the rest of the night.

Cate was not so sure.

THIRTY

Cate couldn't tell how many times the telephone had rung by the time she heard it. She wasn't sound asleep in her bed, but was just drifting off. Noah was passed out cold on the sofa where Cate had covered him with a blanket, and left him to sleep it off.

He hadn't persisted his entreaties too much, a respectful regard on his part that surprised even himself. After he promised to behave, Cate allowed him to stretched out on the sofa with his head on a cushion in her lap, from whence he mesmerized her with stories about India and the village where his dig was: the battle the Great Alexander had fought at that *very* river against King Porous and his three-hundred war elephants. Huge creatures, monsters the Macedonians had never seen before, charging out of a violent thunderstorm.

"It was a fierce, eight-hour slaughter of men and beasts. Alexander fell in that battle; an arrow pierced his breastplate, possibly his lung. But he survived. And the Macedonians won the day.

"Beucephalus, Alexander's mighty warhorse, the one he'd ridden in every battle across his Eastern Empire, did not survive. Alexander's great black stallion, with a heart like a thunderbolt, was trampled by an elephant.

"Alexander raised a shrine to his horse and buried with him all his golden harnesses and armor, silver bits, ceremonial ornaments embedded with a king's ransom in jewels—" Cate listened closely as he droned dreamily on. Noah fell asleep, his head beneath her chin, muttering about *shabds* that chimed like silver…

…*bells.* It was the shrilling of the telephone. Cate climbed from bed and ran up the hall to answer. She heard Abie's voice and knew immediately something was wrong. He tried to be nonchalant in his inquiry if, by any chance, Noah was with her, as he wasn't at the University. His careful nonchalance signaled urgency to Cate. Otherwise, he would never have telephoned Noah here, at this hour.

She called Noah to the telephone, and stood by apprehensively while he spoke with Abie. Noah's face turned ashen, and when he hung up he continued to grip the telephone tightly in his two hands. "My father has been run over by a motorcar," he said incredulously. "It happened this morning, right after we left him." Cate felt her heart drop in her chest like ballast.

"Is he—" She had no idea how to even ask it.

"That police sergeant telephoned Abie and told him. The driver didn't stop. Some students called for an ambulance. They've taken him to Bellevue hospital. The university staff have been trying to locate me." Noah ticked off the bits of information like a list of completed errands.

"Oh, Noah, I'm so sorry." She put her arms around him and held him tight. He was much bigger than Cate, but she held him like he was her child. When shuddering tears flowed, she said nothing. There was nothing to say.

"He's not expected to live. Abie said I should hurry."

"Come on," Cate said leading him by the hand to the bedroom. She slipped on a dress over her chemise and stepped into shoes, grabbed a comb, her purse, and rushed out the door with Noah. He insisted on driving, and as he seemed in better shape than a few moments ago, Cate hurried into the passenger seat. At the same moment, some forty blocks away, someone else was also reacting to the news that Professor Asa Goodwin had been run down by a motorcar during the night.

THIRTY-ONE

Monsignor Palladin was not without his own contacts in the police department. "Thank you, Chaplain," he said. "You were quite right to alert me. Keep me posted."

Palladin hung up and was livid, his reaction instant. He telephoned the Police Commissioner's home waking him.

"What do you know about this Goodwin business?" Palladin demanded.

"What's happened?" Commissioner Waldo asked cautiously.

"Asa Goodwin's been mowed down by an automobile. I thought you had men keeping an eye on that situation."

"I do—"

"Then explain how this happened under your very nose. Do you know the possible repercussions of this? He is a prominent citizen, and his son is a known associate of Abraham Kahn's—"

Police Commissioner Waldo swore he knew nothing of an automobile accident involving Professor Goodwin. "I'm as much in the dark about this as you are, Monsignor," he sputtered. "When did it happen?"

"Sometime after midnight I'm told. The driver left the scene. What do you think will happen when the press gets news of another unsolved crime? You've got to get a handle on this, now. Find that driver. And God help us all if this was anything but a terrible, random accident."

Mollifying the irate prelate for the moment, Waldo promised to find out what had happened and telephone him back.

The Commissioner hung up and slipped quietly from bed. What irritated him most was that the priest had word of it before he had. Likely, none of his own men had the balls to wake him with such colossal bad news.

Morning light was beginning to filter around the edges of drawn drapes. Waldo wrapped himself in a paisley dressing gown and fumbled under the bed for his carpet slippers. It's nothing, Virginia, he said to the newly wed, and immensely wealthy, Mrs. Waldo.

Waldo padded down the staircase to his personal office. His first call was to Detective Lt. Dermot O'Keeffe, in charge of the so-called *fire pit murder* investigation. He would know whatever facts were available.

"For shit's sake, what's happened, O'Keeffe?" In private, the genteel Waldo cursed like the former army commander he was.

O'Keeffe told him the elder Goodwin was undergoing surgery at Bellevue Hospital, but the prospects weren't good. Students found him but didn't see anything else. There's no evidence from the scene, except a bit of glass from a headlamp. And that, Boss, I have safely in my pocket, he said.

"*Boss*, my aunt's ass!" Waldo said. "Why wasn't I called?"

"You wouldn't of wanted me wakin' you up, would you, sir? The middle of the night and all?"

"Look, you bog-brained Mick. Next time I hear about something I need to know, from someone other than you, you'll wish you were back in the potato field where your father buggered the sheep that birthed you! Now, get out there and make sure the kids that found him don't do any talking to the press."

Waldo slammed the telephone onto its hook, and plucked a cigar from a humidor. He fumed as he cut the cap of a Robusto and shoved it in his mouth. His next call was to his own deputy commissioner George Dougherty, bagman for the ailing "Big Tim" Sullivan.

"You idiot!" he shouted into the mouthpiece. "How did this happen? It's not even the right man, you goddamn numbskull. It's his father! And who authorized a rubout? That was never discussed. These people were to be scared off, not killed off! Do you realize the kind of goddamn press this is going to get?"

The response from the other end of the telephone was a hodgepodge excuse of mistaken identity, an inexperienced hireling, and a drunk old man who didn't move out of the way fast enough.

"It was an accident," came the final feeble word.

"Goddamnit! You should have handled it yourself," Waldo barked hanging up.

This would have to be managed carefully now. He was pretty sure nothing tying any of his associates to this screw-up would be discovered, but *Jesus jumped down!* Any hint to the press that this wasn't just an unfortunate accident would be a political Krakatoa.

Waldo hated having to deal with moronic scum and their blundering. Now, Dougherty would have to come up with a couple of witnesses willing to testify the old man had staggered and stumbled in front of an on-rushing car. A hundred bucks would cover that expense. And, they'd need a fall guy, which shouldn't be a problem.

His immediate concern was to convince the good churchman this was just a late-night, random auto accident—in which alcohol had probably played a part. His men already had a lead on the driver and an arrest would be made shortly. Because it was what the Monsignor would *want* to believe, it would be a simple matter convincing him it was so.

Waldo chomped his cigar, softening the end in his mouth with saliva. "Father," he began between puffs. "It's Rhinlander. I've spoken with the lieutenant in charge of the case and, certain other people. Someone was keeping tabs on Goodwin, the girl and Kahn, but it's not a twenty-four hour surveillance, you know. We're using a lot of manpower to track down this fire pit killer, but I expect word of an arrest at any time now. In both cases.

"As for anything—eh, untoward, I'm assured neither we, nor ours, played any part in this terrible accident. We can, with clean conscious, pray earnestly for the recovery of the good professor, though I'm told it doesn't look good."

Monsignor Palladin sat stiffly in his chair wondering why the police commissioner's assurances brought no sense of relief.

"Thank you, Rhinlander," the Monsignor said precisely. "Would you be good enough to keep me informed."

Perhaps it was the phrase *clean conscience* which niggled at the Monsignor's own conscience when he hung up. What did it mean? To protect Church interests the Monsignor had to work with these Tammany politicos, hand in glove, in fact. But sometimes the Monsignor wondered which of them was the hand and which the glove.

Monsignor Palladin felt something dark and apprehensive unfurl within him. Naturally, he had agreed in private with the mayor and police commissioner when the gruesome deaths were discovered that their public position be that the deaths are unrelated until proven otherwise. Alarming the community at a time when the police needed to focus all their attention on finding the killer would serve no one well. Particularly since nearly a year had now passed and the killer or killers were not yet apprehended.

Not that he doubted Rhinlander Waldo's sincerity, but he was beginning to wonder at his competency. If these controversial killings *were* the work of a single lunatic, surely his lunacy would have betrayed him by now. Bellevue Asylum and Matteawan were full of such homicidal creatures. Just how hard was the commissioner actually looking for the murderer of these women?

He stared for a moment longer, then telephoned his police chaplain. There was something, for the sake of his soul, which required his immediate attention.

"Aloysius? It's Monsignor Palladin. I'd like you to do something for me. Will you *unofficially* get me the police report on the motor accident this morning. Yes. And, eh, one other, a missing persons report. The last name is Leoni." This was something, Palladin realized miserably, he should perhaps have done before personally assuring Father Vincenzo of his sister's safety.

"The first name is—let me think—the one the newspapers are calling the *Fire Pit Murder*. Yes, that's it—Apollonia. You're right—burned to death like the martyrdom of Saint Apollonia. A sad coincidence. Terrible thing. As soon as you can. I appreciate it. Yes, dinner together soon."

Monsignor Palladin hung up the telephone, pleased to have taken some step toward assuring himself his hands were clean and there was no threat of Church wrongdoing. The dark thing inside him retreated a bit and was momentarily still. Still and quiet, like a thing laying in wait.

THIRTY-TWO

It was the week after the graveside service for Noah's father. The burial of the dead had been recited from the *Book of Common Prayer.* Cate had been struck by it's hopeful, easter energy. But there was still a jagged tear in Noah, like a scarf ripped from a thorn bush. It was terrible to see the pain in his eyes. She stayed physically close to him, trying, in whatever way she could, to staunch his wound.

It was a beautiful spot in Trinity Cemetery near a splendid White Oak. The sod had been laid, and a granite tombstone, identical to his mother's, had been put in place this morning.

This final duty observed, the two of them just stood there for a while. It was quite still except for the mad cack of a jay.

Cate saw the animal anguish in Noah's eyes, and cupped his hand in hers. They walked slowly among the mossy graves, silently reading epitaphs and examining the faces of marble effigies.

They passed a family plot in which six children of various ages, named Vandervoort, all died on a single day in 1892. Cate puzzled over what would have been the cause. Not even an epidemic could have been so efficient in a single day. A house fire, perhaps, Noah said, unasked.

Not far away was the grave of Clement Moore, and Cate wondered if the Vandervoort children had ever recited: *T'was the night before Christmas and all through the house—* It was a sadness she and Noah had no additional tolerance for, and so, walked abruptly away.

At last, they reached the block of stone steps leading down to Broadway near 155th Street. It was a relief to again be in the pedestrian bustle.

When they climbed into the Cadillac, Noah just sat there behind the wheel. Her greatest fear for him was he might attach some blame for his father's death to himself. She was about to gently question him about it when he started the motor and abruptly announced he wanted to go see Abie.

When they arrived at his office, Abie was out. A woman with a pencil behind her ear said she thought he'd be back shortly. He's on deadline, she told them and said they could have a seat in his office. Ten minutes later Abie burst through the door.

"Copy," he shouted down the hall, to which, of all people, young Lemuel responded on the run. The boy grabbed the pages from Abie's hand and, with a fast *hey there* to Cate and Noah, ran on down the corridor.

Abie slumped in his desk chair. "Gonna make a newspaperman out of that kid. Maybe a really good one. Glad you're here. I've been expecting you, actually" Abie said.

Noah stood up. "My father's dead; I'm not staying out of it," he said simply.

"That's why I've been expecting you."

Noah nodded his head slightly then sat back down in the chair across from Abie's desk as though something had clearly been settled.

"They've made a positive identification of the body in the fire pit," Abie announced.

"Is it Father Vincenzo's sister?" Noah asked.

"Yeah. There was a ring with an inscription in the ashes. A wedding ring. Mostly melted but enough there to read part of a name. Their mother's. Father Vincenzo said the girl always wore it on a ribbon around her neck.

"And, another thing. Dollar Bill Baylor's dead," Abie said. "Fell in front of a subway. They identified him by his tattoos."

"Where?" Noah asked.

"The platform of the Brooklyn Bridge Station."

"How?"

"Dunno. But I'm going to find out. Look, according to Lemuel, Baylor may have seen the killer, or someone, on the roof, right? He was scared and now he's dead. My police contacts have nothing. I'm going to do some digging. Want a drink?"

"Don't mind if I do," Noah said. "Maybe two or three."

It wasn't what Cate expected, but then, she thought, why wouldn't he want a good, stiff drink under the circumstances. A little bottled courage against the onslaught of grief.

Abie reached into a bottom desk drawer and pulled out a bottle of rye. It was empty and he tossed it into the wastebasket. "However, be not alarmed," he said. "I do know where others are to be had. Follow me."

On the sidewalk, Abie hemmed and hawed a moment, long enough for Cate to take the hint.

"Actually," she said turning to Noah, "my attorney needs to see me. I wonder if you two would excuse me?"

"Yes, yes, of course," Noah said holding open the front passenger door for her. "We'll drop you off and then—Abie, where exactly are we going?"

"To see a man about a dog," was all Abie would say.

THIRTY-THREE

After dropping Cate off, Noah and Abie drove straight to the White Rose Sport and Tavern. Noah noticed Abie tense as soon as they were in sight of the ramshackle building, no doubt reacting to the shellacking he'd taken on their last visit. Abie grunted as he stepped out of the motorcar, and spit his chewing gum on the ground.

Inside, it was so dark they at first thought the joint was closed for business until they saw the handful of patrons leaning against the bar. The barkeeper wore a black armband and a sour expression. He abruptly stopped wiping down the bar as they approached.

Abie ordered two shots of rye with beer chasers. The barkeep poured the whiskey then drew two drafts which he slid like a strike down the bar.

"Forty cents," he said inflating the price.
Noah shot his whiskey, then the beer in two big sudsy gulps. He banged down his mug and signaled for another.

"Feel better?" Abie asked.

"Not really," Noah said. "But at least I'm not thirsty anymore." Abie nodded. The bartender poured again for Noah, and Abie slid a ten dollar bill onto the bar.

"I can't change that this early in the day," the barkeep groused, wiping peanut shells from the bar with a filthy slop rag. "Ain't you got nothin' smaller?"

"I don't want change," Abie said. "I want information."

"I dunno nothin'." The bartender's jaws snapped shut like a bulldog's.

"Mind if we take a look around upstairs?" Noah asked.

"I don't mind if you kiss me arse, bucko. How's that suit you?"

Abie slowly picked up the money on the bar, and a small flash of regret glinted in the bartender's eyes as Abie pocketed it. He drained his mug then reached in his pocket again. This time his hand came out holding a gold double eagle. Abie bounced it on the bar top.

Twenty dollars was as much money as the redheaded bartender was likely to see in a month. He snapped up the coin then quickly turned his back on Abie and Noah.

The two of them climbed the stairs to the late Dollar Bill's office and closed the door behind them. The room was as Noah remembered it, except now desk drawers were pulled out and papers were strewn on the floor. In a corner of the room an iron safe stood gaping open.

"The police?" Noah wondered.

"Maybe. Maybe the bartender—after cash, not evidence I'll bet."

"So what specifically are *we* looking for?" Noah asked.

"We'll know it when we see it."

They began picking up the papers, mostly bills and receipts, and dumped everything in a single pile. For the next ten minutes Noah and Abie sat cross-legged on the floor sorting and examining each item carefully.

"Look here," Abie said. "Must have come from the safe. Looks like the deed to this property." Abie read. "He owned the land as well as the building. I'll bet there's a will."

"There is," Noah said holding up an onionskin document.

"So, who inherits? It's possible it could be a motive for killing him. I mean, I don't for a minute think Bill Baylor just happened to fall off a train platform. Even if he was drunk at four in the afternoon. That was the time of death by the way," Abie said.

"Listen to this." Noah read, '*Upon my death I give and bequeath all my property and goods to St. Clare's Charitable Hospital, in exchange for the continued board and care of my orphan grandson, Alfie Baylor, a feeble-minded invalid, for the balance of his natural life.* It's dated nineteen years ago."

"St. Clare's? That's in Brooklyn," Abie said.

"No motive there. Unless you think the nuns killed him to get their hands on this dump."

"The riverfront will bring a pretty penny."

"I still say whoever Dollar Bill recognized on the roof that night saw a chance to shut him up permanently, and took it. It's what Baylor was afraid of, I'd say."

Noah stood and took one last look around.

Abie struggled to his feet. "Let's get out of here," he said sticking the deed and the will back in the open safe.

"O.K.," Noah said. "You going to leave those here?"

"Yeah. I'll give Sgt. Simonov a telephone call. Tip him off there's a next of kin." Abie pulled a piece of gum from his pocket and peeled off the wrapper. He righted a toppled wastebasket and dropped the wrapper in.

"Hold on a second," he said to Noah. Abie leaned over the wastebasket and picked out a wad of yellow paper at the bottom. He flattened the paper and saw it was a telegram, sent to William Baylor. "Listen to this," Abie said.

ALFIE GRAVELY ILL COME AT ONCE
SR MARY ALICE ST CLARES HOSPITAL

"Five'll get you ten the good sister didn't send this. We can telephone there from my office."

What's the date on it?" Noah asked.

"August fifteenth, the day Baylor went under the subway wheels." Abie folded the telegram and retrieved the will and deed from the open safe. "Think I'll hand these over to the Sergeant personally."

He shook his head looking at the shabby room and chaotic disarray. "Poor bastard. Someone dangled the right bait and he was lured out. Guess old Billy wasn't quite scared enough."

THIRTY-FOUR

Cate's attorney needed to see her because disaster had struck. The judge in Cate's case, the Honorable Learned Hand had come down with chicken pox. The district supervising judge was adamant sentencing would proceed as scheduled, and had denied Cate's motion to stay sentencing until Judge Hand resumed the bench. That settled Cate's decision.

She wrote Dr. Havelock Ellis in reply to his offer of refuge overseas. The day was at hand and she would be upstanding in court to face it.

The United States District Courthouse on Pearl Street was typical of the architecture of the day: that is, the same neo-classical style affected by nearly every government building, bank, and library built in the last hundred and fifty years.

Its ornate Greek-revival façade, supported by twelve columns, abutted a limestone box of a building. It was to a courtroom on the third floor of this building that Noah, Cate and her august attorney Alistair Knox, Esq. now glumly headed.

Mr. Knox had requested and received two delays in the earlier trial process, hoping the amount of accumulated letters favorable to Cate's cause would bring to bear some favorable influence on the court. This hope, however, was dashed when Attorney Knox learned the judge now about to hand down sentence was the Honorable Hieronymus Thomas Knickerbocker.

Judge Knickerbocker's judicial findings were generally considered to be only slightly less severe than Torquemada's. That this lifelong bachelor was an avowed misogynist was no secret. Her attorney, when informing Cate of this unfortunate turn of events, repeated to her remarks Judge Knickerbocker had recently made in a speech to members of the New York State Bar Association—remarks which received hardy applause, to wit: *'Like the late, great philosopher Otto Weininger, I believe that just as children, imbeciles and criminals are correctly prevented from taking any part in public affairs, so women must in the same way be kept from having a share in anything which concerns the public welfare.'*

This was not good news. Mr. Knox had prepared Cate for the likelihood Judge Knickerbocker would hand down the severest penalty in his power, and order her into immediate custody.

Cate was stiff with fear. And determination.

Noah's strong right arm got her through the maze of corridors to Courtroom F where Cate took her seat at the defense table next to Mr. Knox. A dozen reporters stood lining the walls. There were many familiar and supportive faces in the visitors seats, including Abie and Lemuel. Cate's father sat with two of her brothers, his lapel festooned, exhibiting support for universal suffrage, the IWW, and the presidential candidacy of Eugene V. Debs.

Who Cate didn't see was Mrs. Stanton Blatch. She'd said she might be late and made Knox promise to save two seats directly behind the defense table.

They all stood as Judge Knickerbocker entered the court and took his seat. At just about that moment, there was a ruffle in the visitors section. Cate turned to see Mrs. Stanton Blatch entering with a handsome, middle-aged woman.

The woman had golden brown hair, and eyes of an arresting green. Her traveling suit was elegant and her carriage confident.

Cate could not tell if the ripple of attention was for Mrs. Stanton Blatch, who was well known and respected, particularly in these circles, or for the woman with her. Mr. Knox turned to see as well, and a quizzical look crossed his face. In response to

Cate's own quizzical look Knox wrote the words *Nelly Taft* in the margin of his legal folio. Cate still had no idea who the woman was.

Mr. Knox proceeded with his request for leniency in the sentencing of his client citing the numerous letters of support received, but he seemed to have a good deal of difficulty holding Judge Knickerbocker's attention, which was fixed just beyond Cate's head.

He didn't think the judge had heard a single word of it, but he must have, because the next words from the judge's mouth were spit out like curdled milk: Catherine Gallagher, the United States District Court for the Southern District of New York, having found you guilty of violating *section 211* of the Postal Law, sentences you to *thirty days in jail and a one-hundred dollar fine. Sentence is suspended pending appeal. This court is adjourned.*

Knickerbocker banged his gavel and exited the court with the alacrity of a man badly needing either a drink or the toilet. Cate was dumbfounded. Mr. Knox looked again at the woman seated next to Mrs. Stanton Blatch and smiled slightly.

"It seems you have friends in high places. And your friends in high places have spoken with those in even higher places."

"I don't understand," Cate protested. "What just happened? Who is she?"

"Nelly—that is, Helen Herron Taft, the president's wife. You know, Knickerbocker was appointed to the bench by Taft. Perhaps what you've just received is a political favor come full circle."

Cate was floored but got her wits about her quickly enough to thank Mrs. Stanton Blatch, though not Mrs. Taft who was already exiting the court on the arm of Mrs. Stanton Blatch's chauffeur.

"I so wanted to thank her," Cate said to Mrs. Stanton Blatch.

"Another time perhaps,"

"However did she manage it? The judge left like a scalded cat."

"And well he should, the old hypocrite," Mrs. Stanton Blatch preened. "I guess I may share this with you, dear, but only in strictest confidence."

"Why, of course," Cate said.

"You see, Nelly—Mrs. Taft, and Judge Knickerbocker were once engaged to be married, oh, many years ago, when she was Helen Herron. She was *the* debutant of the season.

"Anyway, my dear, Nelly—such a sweet girl—was completely swept off her feet by *Hy* Knickerbocker. He was older than her you know, and he was desperately in love with her. Well, it seems a few months after they met—there was to be a baby. All very hush-hush, no one knew except the families. Their engagement was announced immediately, but three weeks later beautiful little Nell Herron apparently told her mother she'd had a miscarriage; although, there are those who knew, who say it was not a miscarriage at all.

"At any rate, freed from the burden of impending motherhood, Nell chose to break the engagement. Knickerbocker was devastated. In rather short order, Nell married William Howard Taft and left with him for the Philippines where he served as Governor-General. The rest is, as they say, history.

"Except for this," Mrs. Stanton Blatch said pulling Cate closer. "Hieronymus Knickerbocker, Esq. continued to bombard poor Helen Taft for an entire year with letters entreating her to leave her husband and elope with him. They were love letters of a particularly torrid nature. The man must have been raving mad. Not only the most inappropriate language—I've seen the letters myself—but addressed to a married woman! Completely depraved. Nell has kept every one. Well, my dear, I guess that's that."

THIRTY-FIVE

Noah and Abie appeared in the courtroom throng of well-wishers. Noah put his arm around Cate's shoulders and propelled her, with Abie limping in tow, sideways through the crowd, all the way to the courthouse steps, where she made a brief statement to the press. She was adamant: a woman's right to birth control is a public policy issue and therefore cannot, under First Amendment free speech protections, be suppressed by the government.

And then down to the Cadillac they ran.

"But my father—I have to say goodbye, at least," she protested.

"Gone. While you were making your press statement. Your father said to tell you how proud of you he is. Your brother Pat is taking him straight to the train and home so he can rest. He was beaming, I assure you."

"If you're game, I suggest we go to my office," Abie said. "There's something I want to show you."

It was still morning and traffic was light, so they covered the short distance to the *Post* quickly. Cate and Noah pulled chairs up to Abie's desk and waited while he fished around in his dossier until he found what he wanted. He untied a brown folder and began pulling out sheets of paper.

"These are some of the police records we've been demanding," he explained. "I finally got them yesterday, but I didn't want to distract you, you know, until after the sentencing. So, I spent a little time by myself going over it all. And look here.

"These death certificates are for the six murders we believe are connected. Now, look at these certificates for three additional murdered women in the same time frame. Look at the certificates, carefully. Notice anything unusual?"

Noah and Cate looked closely at the different documents issued by the coroner's office. At the top of the page was a space filled in with the decedent's name, followed by the gender, race and date of birth, if known. Following was space for address, marital status and next of kin.

And lastly, was a day, date and time at which the coroner fixed the occurrence and manner of death, as closely as possible.

At first their eyes just skimmed the surface of each page, but when Abie said to look at the dates, they saw what he was referring to. In each case, the month and even the day, on which the women were killed, was the same as their day of birth. Born and then murdered on the same calendar day.

Cate said as random events she would have thought it statistically impossible.

"There it is. The conclusive link between all the victims," Abie said. "They were killed on their birthdays. If the coroner knew, then the Mayor's office and the Police Commissioner had to have known as well. They knew all along the murders were connected! And more than just the six we know about. We can prove it was a cover-up conspiracy."

Cate was reading the death certificates over and over. "I wish we had the coroner's original notes."

"Can you subpoena those?" Noah asked.

"I'll see to it." Abie made a note.

"I wonder. Why would someone do that? Choose to kill women on their birthdays?" Cate's brow wrinkled. "Something someone said—was it about Apollonia? Noah, why did Father Vincenzo say they were having dinner?"

"So, she could tell him about joining the convent," Abie said.

"He said, they had dinner, every year, on her birthday," Noah said.

"And look it fits," Abie said. "Nobody saw her again after her birthday."

"No, *not* her birthday," Cate interrupted. "That's not what he said. Father Vincenzo said it was her namesake *feast* day."

"What feast? What's that mean? It was still her birthday, wasn't it" Abie asked.

"Yes, it was, but look," Cate said, "he called it her *feast* day. Among very religious Catholics, children are often named for the saint whose feast day they're born on. Like me. Every Catholic saint has a day in the calendar. I was born on the feast day of Saint Susanna."

"So, your mother named you Catherine. I don't get it," said Abie.

"Catherine Susanna," she told him. "Lots of times the first or middle name is given in honor of the saint of the day."

"O.K., let me see if I follow: we know for sure these women were killed on their birthdays. And depending on what their mothers named them, it could also be some saint's feast day?"

"Yes, Abie," Cate said really thinking about it. "Suppose it does mean that?"

"Some kind of Catholic religious fanatic....?"

"Maybe," Noah said.

"Why do you say that, Noah? Why such a decided maybe," Cate asked him.

"Because we shouldn't rule out *any* possibilities, yet. Suppose it's someone with a grudge against Catholics? An outsider with a grudge against the Church. Some kind of deep-seated hatred."

"That is possible," Cate said to Abie. She decided to let it go for the moment. "Why just women and girls, do you think? Were they violated? The reports don't mention it. Could it be an omission? A number of the wo-men were found nude.

"We don't need the autopsy reports to answer that," Abie said. "My police contact already told me he'd heard none of them were dishonored, he said."

"That rules out sex as the motive," Cate said.

"Females are just easier to subdue. Especially if the killer isn't a big man," Noah said.

"So, how do we figure out for certain?" Abie asked. "I mean about the names and the feast days? What it means."

They were quiet for a moment then Cate said, "Abie, telephone Father Vincenzo. See if he can come right over. And tell him to bring his Butler's *Lives of the Saints*."

THIRTY-SIX

Monsignor Palladin walked quickly through the halls, from his office to the dining room in the residential mansion, behind Saint Patrick's Cathedral. His serene face was a far cry from his inner turmoil.

He was long accustomed to frankincense permeating the entire structure, so much so, he could no longer smell it even when coming in from out-of-doors; he never, however, failed to notice the bottom note of fish announcing supper every Friday night.

Father Elbi and Father Sebastian were already seated at the dining table. Frequently, one or the other of them would be absent, usually because one or the other of them, or both, would be invited to eat with His Eminence in the Cardinal's personal dining room. But, not tonight. The other half-dozen priests and deacons in residence, took their meals in silence, in the refectory abutting the kitchen. Such was the dining hierarchy.

Tonight Cardinal Bernard had elected a solitary tray served in his bedroom. He'd left instructions he was not to be disturbed, as he intended to pass the night in prayer and contemplation. His devotions were not to be interrupted. Elbi and Sebastian were both happy to have the night off whenever His Eminence was struck with these periodic bouts of piety. It allowed them the opportunity to indulge their personal interests.

Protocol required supper not be served until the Monsignor had taken his seat, even as tonight, when he was late coming to table. He'd been delayed by one of the altar boys; a matter Palladin intended to take up with Father Elbi.

He slid open the polished mahogany doors and entered the dining room to find Elbi and Sebastian with their heads together over a sheet of paper, which Father Sebastian quickly hid under the table.

With a nod and a congenial smile, Monsignor Palladin took his seat and said grace, then rang a small dinner bell. A moment later their housekeeper, Sister Amelia ladled brimming bowls of a hearty fish and potato chowder from a steaming tureen.

"Father Sebastian," the Monsignor said affably. "Might the instrument you've so discretely disposed of under the table be an example of your latest astrological inquiries?"

Sebastian carefully took two more mouthfuls of his soup before lowering his spoon. "Monsignor, with all due respect, we've had this conversation before and have agreed, since astrology has been relied upon by numerous Popes throughout the history of the Church, and as His Eminence himself takes a certain interest in the aspect of his planets, *you* are hardly in a position to forbid it's practice."

"It's practice, no, I cannot forbid. It's presence at the dinner table I can."

"Very well, Monsignor," Father Sebastian said tersely.

"Actually, Monsignor," Father Elbi piped in. "You might find this particular horoscope quite interesting as it is your own. After all, since the birth of the Holy Infant Himself was foreseen in the heavens by the Magi, why shouldn't the portents of your own birth be valid?" he asked smugly.

Monsignor Palladin refused to rise to the bait, not just because he considered the whole of astrology to be sacrilegious rubbish, but because he realized they'd had the impertinence to locate and inspect his baptismal certificate for his date of birth. He refused, now, to give them the satisfaction of goading him to temper.

"Need I remind you, Father," Monsignor Palladin said coolly, "the Star of Bethlehem led the Magi, not directly to Christ but to King Herod, who used that astrological prediction as an excuse for the slaughter of the Innocents. Hardly a recommendation in it's favor."

"Monsignor," Sebastian cut in; he never wanted to be the pathetic bone Palladin and Elbi quibbled over. "You are correct," he said equitably. "The dinner table is not the place for such pursuits. I do beg your pardon; it won't happen again."

Not to be tactically outdone, Father Elbi raised the stakes. "Quite so. I will *personally* consign your natal chart to the fireplace. I assure you, it holds nothing which would either cheer or comfort you. Some fates are perhaps best met unwittingly."

Monsignor Palladin tilted his soup dish slightly forward and gave his focused attention to the last of his supper. "Delicious," he said. "I think I'll have another." The Monsignor tinkled the dinner bell that summoned Sister Amelia from the kitchen. While he waited for her to refill his dish, he carefully buttered the remainder of his dinner roll.

"Well, I see you came to table both late *and* hungry," Father Elbi said.

"Ah, yes, I was late, wasn't I," Palladin said. "I was speaking with young Michael Weaver earlier this evening. He's one of our altar boys."

"Yes, I know that rascal. What's he been saying?" Elbi asked.

"He says you boxed his ears several days ago. He's apparently been having a ringing in his ear ever since and is afraid to tell his mother."

"He should well be afraid."

"May I remind you, the discipline of the altar boys does not fall within your concern, Father Elbi."

"It most certainly does when the lack of *proper* discipline results in careless and negligent error."

"And what careless negligence might you be referring to," Palladin asked patiently, "as regards Michael Weaver?"

"Yes, let me see, what exactly was it?" Father Elbi said thoughtfully. "Can you remember, Sebastian? It was a week or so ago."

"Didn't you mention something about His Eminence having worn the wrong liturgical color for Mass—oh, when was it? Sunday before last, I think?"

"Yes, that was it," Father Elbi said smiling as though he had a mouthful of feathers. "It's the Weaver boy you've been instructing—correct, Monsignor? Well, he laid out the wrong chasuble for His Eminence; *green*, when the liturgical color for the day should have been *red*. You're so meticulous Monsignor Palladin; I'm surprised you, yourself, didn't notice the error right away."

Palladin was now thoroughly irritated with Father Elbi's condescension, particularly so if a mistake *had* been made. He finished his second bowl of soup, then held his tongue as Sister Amelia entered with their dessert platter of fruit and cheese.

"I will bid you good evening, Fathers," Palladin said standing. "I've work still to attend to at my desk. As for the matter of the Weaver boy, Father Elbi, it's good of you to take such an earnest interest. If, as you say, an error was made—a glaring error at that, the offence, one of inattention, was still minor. In future, you'll be kind enough to bring any such mistakes to *my* notice.

"As it is now, I've the boy's mother to inform and must make arrangements to have his ear examined by a physician. I certainly hope, for your sake, Father Elbi, that in your zeal, the boy's hearing hasn't been damaged. That would be unfortunate, very unfortunate, indeed."

Elbi shrugged his shoulders dismissively as he cut into a wedge of cheese. "Oh, and I'd be careful of that Provolone," Palladin said. "Smelt a bit off to me."

THIRTY-SEVEN

Monsignor Palladin sat again to the task he'd been occupied with before being interrupted by the Weaver boy. He switched on the desk lamp and donned the spectacles he needed for reading.

The reports he'd finagled from the police department chaplain had shaken him. The file on Asa Goodwin's death was as inept and careless a document as ever produced by any bureaucracy. Furthermore, it was obvious *no* police investigation was being done to find the car and fleeing driver.

The missing person file on Apollonia Leoni was disgraceful, nothing but speculation in no way borne out by any sort of investigation. Palladin was livid. He stared at the clippings, files and reports spread before him as he'd been doing for the several days. He bent over some *Post* clippings and examined the details again.

His head ached with the effort to make the facts other than they appeared to be. It was one thing to be discrete regarding information released to the public during an investigation; that was only prudent. It was quite another matter to feign an investigation, which, in fact, was not taking place.

One thought tumbled after another like the crumbling stones of an old ruin. He was too tired to make emotional sense of the situation. He would sleep on it and in the morning would pray, earnestly and humbly for some inner-self to see the sense of it. For now, he wanted nothing so much as the unburdening of sleep.

Palladin removed his spectacles and snapped off his desk lamp, then quickly turned it on again. There was still that other thing which rankled, a minor thing by comparison, but Palladin knew sleep would not come until *that*, at least, was settled.

It irked him terribly that Father Elbi had been the one to note an error in the liturgical color at Mass. Perhaps Elbi was right; perhaps he *had* become negligent in his duties. Certainly, if the Cardinal had worn the wrong color chasuble, and he himself had not noticed, then he was guilty of being unobservant. He'd been careless and he deplored carelessness, most of all, in himself.

As diocesan Dean of Altar Boys, Palladin personally drilled the boys of Saint Patrick's in their ceremonial duties during Mass: the Latin prayers, antiphons and liturgical responses, when to pour from the cruets of water and wine, the points during the Eucharistic Prayer at which they were to tinkle bells, when to genuflect, when to bow, how even to move about in ankle-length cassocks without tripping over their own clumsy feet. And certainly the boys had been taught the appropriate liturgical colors of the Mass.

It was a small mistake but it should not have happened. Palladin hoped Father Elbi was mistaken.

Putting on his spectacles again, Monsignor Palladin opened his breviary and turned impatiently to the section containing the *Proprium Sanctorum*—the formularies for saints' festivals dependant on the day of the year. Father Elbi had said the color should have been red, indicating the feast of one of the Holy Martyrs.

Palladin looked at his calendar for the day in question; Sunday before last or perhaps the Sunday before that. He noted the previous Sunday had been ordinary as had the Sunday before. But the Sunday before that, August 9th was the feast of two martyred saints; Tiburtius, beaten to death outside Rome in the third century, and Susanna, a noblewoman executed by the Emperor Diocletian at about the same time.

Elbi was correct. It was another bit of crow he'd have to summon the humility to swallow. With a sigh of resignation Palladin began to gather the clippings and reports spread out on his desk when a bit of newsprint caught his eye; '—*the decomposed remains of Mrs. Susanna Profaci, aged twenty-five, an Italian immigrant mother, were discovered on August 11th of last year.'*

Something icy snapped at the edge of the priest's consciousness. What was it? He quickly shuffled through the papers on his desk until he found what he was looking for. It was the police statement given by Father Vincenzo regarding his sister's disappearance. '...*I last saw my sister the evening of February 9th. It was the feast of St. Apollonia and we dined together*...'

Palladin bolted straight in his chair. His thoughts raced for a moment. Then he grabbed a clean sheet of paper and began a list of names: the names of dead women; the dates on which they were most likely believed killed; and then most difficult of all, the manner in which each had been—*martyred* was the word which came unbidden to his mind.

Monsignor Palladin stood and crossed to his bookcase, and returned to his desk with Butler's *Lives of the Saints* in hand. He began with the first suspected victim, fifteen year old Agnes Lombardi discovered naked and beheaded, in the East River on January 22nd. Already knowing what he would find, Palladin opened the *Lives of the Saints* to Saint Agnes, virgin martyr. He read slowly the recounting of her trial and the tribulation which followed, wherein the adolescent Agnes was paraded through the streets of Rome, and was made to stand naked before a pagan crowd at the altar of Minerva. There, by the river Tiber, she was beheaded.

Palladin closed the book and clenched his hands together. His stomach lurched, threatening to bring up the two hearty bowls of his chowder supper. The priest willed himself to calm, then opened the book again. One-by-one he matched names, confirmed dates, read the histories of torture and death well into the night.

When finally he'd fit the pieces together on paper, the enormity of the evil he'd unearthed lurked physically in the shadows around him. Blinded by what he so powerfully believed in, the survival of Christ's true Church on earth, he'd turned a zealot's blind eye to what he believed couldn't *possibly* be true. Now, the same zeal impelled him like a terrier down a rat hole.

The priest picked up the telephone again. It was the middle of the night, perfect for the alley cat hours "Big Tim" Sullivan kept in his Tammany office.

"This is Monsignor Palladin. I wish to speak with Mr. Sullivan."

Big Tim wasn't surprised. Commissioner Waldo had warned him the Chancellor was disturbed. Sullivan's crew always made sure he knew what to expect.

"What can I do for you, Monsignor."

He got right to the point demanding to know what Sullivan knew about the investigation into the fire pit murders.

"Calm down, Father," Sullivan said confidently. "Everything is under control. I know about everything. And I promise you, not a word will leak out. There'll be no scandal. You've my word on that."

"What are you talking about? What is it you know?"

Sullivan put the speaker close to his full lips. "Why— who's responsible, of course." The Monsignor fumed at Sullivan's glib, casual tone, the implied threat of *scandal*. He held his tongue and listened. Big Tim told him exactly what a late associate of his had witnessed, on a certain rooftop, one certain night.

"But, don't worry. The guy's dead. An unfortunate subway accident."

"I don't believe a word of it," Palladin said emphatically. "You'll not intimidate me with your lies!"

"You're right, Monsignor. There's not a word of truth to it. Just vicious anti-Catholic rumor mongering. I promise, you won't hear another word of it. It's our little secret. Like confession, Father. You can't tell. I can't tell. Let certain friends of the Church in City Hall handle *things*, in due course, Father. No muss, no fuss. You have my word on it."

"This is monstrous," the priest said slamming down the telephone hookswitch. It's a lie, he told himself. Just Sullivan's attempt to cower him.

Palladin prayed on his knees like a penitent until dawn, then washed and changed into his layman's suit, shirt, collar and tie. He stuffed papers and clippings into a briefcase, then flagged down a taxicab in front of the cathedral and rushed to do the unthinkable.

THIRTY-EIGHT

The priest stretched out on his bed that night the way he imagined one day he'd be laid out in his casket: legs together at the ankles, forearms neatly folded on his chest, slender fingers interlaced in a gesture of supplication. He lay as still as his own stone edifice.

Asmodeus! He could feel the weight of the demon sitting heavily on his chest. Its breath came in small gasping heaves rousing urges he abhorred.

Be gone. Depraved minion of Satan leave me, he demanded, even as his mind filled with unbidden images of sexual debauchery: horrifying images of plump, smooth flesh and languid limbs entwined in all manner of rutting congress.

He was as impervious as an effigy. Over years he'd learned the forbearance of silence. And stillness. A perfect physical stillness which contained him like the hardened crust of a baker's loaf. Beneath that, he ached in every sinew of his body.

As he'd grown from boy to man, the Enemy had stalked him relentlessly, seeking to foil his piety and drag him down to the bottomless pit as a great prize for his master Beelzebub. Oh, how the demonic legion rejoiced at the falling of one of God's holy anointed of the priesthood.

While the great God Jehovah secluded Himself in the highest Holy of Holies, the Evil One had become the man's constant confidant, ever ready to betray him.

The priest stiffened and prayed to John the Baptist,

Asmodeus's natural adversary. His cry pierced black, inner silence like sonar. He listened as it disappeared into the hollow, the intolerable, silent evidence of his isolation in the universe.

Tonight would end as it had before: a vile and violent crescendo of lust, stupefying and incandescent. That was Asmodeus's way of it.

He sat up abruptly and swung his legs over the side of the bed. He pulled on a watchman's cap, snug flannel clothes and shoes with crepe soles. Then slipped from his quarters, down the back staircase, and cat-like into the Manhattan night.

Father Elbi watched from nearby shadows behind a painted statue of a winged St. Michael with sword high, his foot on the head of the fallen angel. It was not the first time Elbi had witnessed His Eminence slip out of the cathedral residence in the middle of the night. But this evening, when the Cardinal had announced he was not to be disturbed, Elbi determined to keep watch, and to follow this Prince of the Church on his nighttime excursion. Elbi stepped out from behind St. Michael and quickly through the door. Here was a secret worth the risk of getting.

THIRTY-NINE

God spoke to Father Vincenzo Leoni. Every morning at three, he rose for the liturgical hour of *Vigils*. He sat and listened. Then he got up and did what he was impelled to do.

Some years before, God told Father Vincenzo, he must live his beliefs. So, Father Vincenzo gave away everything he owned to the parish poor box, except the one black suit he was constantly mending, and a battered fedora he wore in winter.

The poor of Father Vincenzo's parish were his only regard. This morning he would take a dozen tomatoes from the church vegetable garden, and four of the loaves of bread Mrs. Sousa donated from her husband's bakery, to Mr. and Mrs. Levi's delicatessen where he would barter for a chicken, which he would take to Mrs. Washington to make soup for her boy sick with measles, just as Rabbi Hillel often made the same sort of barter in reverse for his congregation.

This was Father Vincenzo's intention when Monsignor Palladin, in a business suit, appeared at his door. Vincenzo was startled but not surprised. He'd prayed his Church superior—this good man—would finally come and speak to him. It had broken his heart to think Holy Mother Church would allow the reputation of its child, Apollonia, to be stained by indifferent government officials.

"I must speak with you," Monsignor Palladin said. "About many things."

Father Vincenzo sat with the Monsignor in his rectory's small parlor. "Will Your Reverence have a cup of tea? I'm afraid we have no sugar."

"Thank you, Father, no. What I wish to say is urgent—I must beg your forgiveness for having failed you in the matter of your sister's whereabouts. Listen to me.

"I have seen the police file. There *is* *nothing* there to suggest an elopement, or *any* kind of romantic involvement. In fact, there is nothing there indicating a proper investigation at all. Nothing," Palladin said.

"And," he hurried on, "I'm now convinced there is a single murderer who has killed many young, Catholic women. Many, including your sister. I must help do something about it now. I beg your forgiveness for acting too late to save Apollonia."

Monsignor Palladin felt more than heard a ringing in his ears at these last words. The enormity of his failure was overwhelming. Now, like Saul rising from the ground as Paul, Palladin was appalled by his own blindness.

"I'm going to see Mr. Abraham Kahn. Personally. Relying on the police has been pointless. I'm going to show Mr. Kahn what I've discovered. We must all know the truth!"

"Then perhaps we can go there together," Vincenzo said quietly. "There was a telephone call yesterday from Mr. Kahn, asking me to come. But a parishioner's baby has pneumonia, so I did not get the message until late. Mr. Kahn asks that I bring my Butler's *Lives of the Saints*."

"Exactly. Yes, they begin to see," Palladin said. "Come. We should hurry. I have a taxicab waiting."

"Most convenient," Father Vincenzo said rising. "I'll just get my *Butler's* from the shelf—"

"—Never mind; I have mine."

"—and this basket. Could Your Reverence ask the driver if he would first stop at Levi's delicatessen, please? It's not far out of the way."

FORTY

It took Lemuel two long trolley rides to reach *The Post* building from his grandmother's apartment on west 139th Street. He, nevertheless, routinely arrived an hour earlier than any of the other five copyboys working at the *Post*.

It was the time of morning when drunks and newsies were hitting the street. Most of them liked Lemuel well enough. They showed, if not admiration, a grudging sense of respect for the gangly, hard-working colored boy.

A couple of the newsies, though, resented his rise in the world. Uppity as far as they were concerned; he walked the streets as if he was as good as any of them.

But for his grandmother's constantly teaching the biblical lesson of humility, Lemuel would have known he was not just as good as, but better than most.

Of *The New York Evening Post's* one-hundred and seven editorial, advertising and publication employees—not all of whom shared Mr. Oswald Villard's championing of civil liberties—Lemuel was the first Negro. He was the fly in their buttermilk. He knew intuitively he had to do everything the other boys did and do it quicker, better and longer. Consequently, by the time the other copy boys arrived, Lemuel had already raised all the window shades, dumped a dozen ashtrays, emptied two dozen wastebaskets, sharpened a forest of pencils, watered the city editor's philodendron and hied himself to the refuge of the *Post's* morgue.

Abie was the first to see the problems inherent in Lemuel's position at the paper. He was largely ignored by the adult staffers, except for an isolated few for whom Lemuel's presence was an affront to their sense of the natural order. They'd regularly send him on the most menial of tasks—*take these down to the lobby and have George shine them up*—while saving the task of handing over their news copy for the white youngsters, the task copyboys lived for.

Worst of all, the other copyboys quickly picked up on it, and mimicked not the best of their elders but the worst, assigning Lemuel to the cruelest rung of hell—the hazing of adolescent boys.

So, Abie had offered Lemuel the sanctuary of the newspaper's morgue. Inside were archived *The Post's* news clippings dating back to the paper's founding by Alexander Hamilton in 1801. It would prove to be a fateful decision for Abie.

There were volumes of clippings which needed to be transferred or they would be lost: the entire collection photographed for preservation. It would be Lemuel's job to précis every word of it. It was a hands-on education that couldn't be had anywhere else in the world.

"But it still ain't right," Lemuel complained. "That ofay Winslow call my grandma a stupid, nigger whore again, he's getting a fat lip to match his fat white ass. Sorry, Mr. Abie, but he got it comin'."

"Tell me something, where are the other boys right now?" Abie had asked. "I'll tell you where... They're out in the alley, in the hot sun, polishing spittoons, while you're in here working on an important project. So, just spike it, kid. Do your job and forget about them.

"Back to work. I want the indices for 1820 to 1825 on my desk by tonight. And don't ever let me hear you say *ain't* again, 'cause *ain't* ain't in the dictionary."

FORTY-ONE

W here have you two been?" Abie barked.

"Did Father Vincenzo arrive?" Cate asked pulling off her gloves. Abie limped from his desk to the door, shutting it quickly behind Cate and Noah.

"I don't want this to leak before I have more information."

"What's happened?" Cate asked.

"I just got a police tip," Abie said excitedly. "A man has reported his daughter missing since early this morning. Sgt. Simonov got wind of it and thinks there may be a connection with our killer."

"Oh, no—who is the girl?" Cate asked.

"I don't know yet."

"What's the connection?" Noah asked.

"Simonov heard that the cop who took the report from the father was the beat cop where the family lives. Broome Street. That's all he knows, second-hand. No name or address, nothing else yet. Just a police rumor about *goings on*, as he put it, near St. Stephen's."

"We should go down there, shouldn't we?" Cate said.

"Sgt. Simonov is on his way there now. He'll find out what we need to know." Abie leaned back in his chair, and its cracked leather sighed and enveloped him. He opened the bottom drawer of his desk and propped his afflicted leg on its edge.

"You okay?" Noah asked.

"Just fine," Abie said reaching into the drawer. He pulled out a fresh bottle of rye and a glass. "For medicinal purposes," he said as Noah and Cate watched him pour three fingers.

He knocked back the drink avoiding their eyes. "It catches up with me sometimes," he said.

Abie capped the bottle and put it back where he'd gotten it. "Now," he said sitting up and stomping his leg a little. He lit a cheroot and looked a bit more like himself. "I never thought I'd hear myself say it, but we need a priest."

What they got in the next five minutes was not one priest but two.

Abie recognized the second priest immediately despite his business suit. Cate also thought the man with Father Vincenzo looked familiar. Noah had no idea who he was, or why the cheroot fell out of Abie's mouth when the man with Father Vincenzo walked in. It came clear when Father Vincenzo introduced the Cardinal's chancellor, Monsignor Palladin.

Cate remembered she'd glanced the Monsignor at Mrs. Astor's party. She also reminded herself, his was one of the subtle hands behind her recent prosecution. Cate looked from the Monsignor to Father Vincenzo for some hint of explanation.

"May we all sit down?" Father Vincenzo asked gently.

No one spoke as they arranged themselves around Abie's office.

"Monsignor Palladin has brought his Butler's *Lives of the Saints*, as you requested," Father Vincenzo began.

"*And* I have prepared information you must look at," the Monsignor said.

"Why must we?" Abie asked pointedly.

"Of course, you must have an explanation." Palladin waved his hand decisively in the air. "The truth is, I have the gravest concern that I have been wrong. About a great many things. And it puts Holy Mother Church at risk of compromise because of *my* failings."

"Compromise?" Abie scoffed. "There's a good word for it."

"Hear me out. Please," the Monsignor insisted. "I am now thoroughly convinced a killer is preying, specifically, on the Catholic women and girls of New York City. I also believe these events, and others," he said turning to Noah, "have not been competently, or honestly, investigated by the New York police department. Nor, do I think eight weeks before a state and national election, certain officials are going to allow the kind of alert to the community the situation requires. I've come to tell you these things."

"Wait a minute, Padre," Abie said sitting forward. "I've got a couple of questions. *You* could put out an alert, couldn't you? By tonight's six o'clock Mass you could have every priest in the city announce whatever you want, from the pulpit. The way it's been done for centuries. Why are you coming here to make your, waddaya call it, *mea culpa*?"

"Mr. Kahn, you are entirely correct. And I completely understand your mistrust. I do not ask you to act alone. I, too, shall act. But what would happen if any such grotesque announcements as these," he said indicating his briefcase, "were made by parish priests? People would be terribly frightened. They would look to their pastors for physical protection. Something the Church in this regard, cannot provide. *Civil* action is required.

"I, certainly, will personally speak out demanding civil action. Tomorrow, on the front page of *The Morning Messenger,* I will publish a letter, from me to the Catholic Archdiocese of New York, putting forth everything I have said here today. I'm going to publicly call on city officials to take immediate action and reveal information I believe they are hiding. The killer must be identified and caught. God willing," he said crossing himself, "before he strikes again."

Monsignor Palladin, in his brown suit, divested of all the signature of his office, reminded Cate of a weary Saint Francis.

"Show us what you've brought, Monsignor," Cate said gently.

Monsignor Palladin opened his brief case and withdrew a stack of paper. "I have here, police reports, which you will want to inspect.

"I also have autopsy reports. One thing, which does not appear on the death certificates is the fact each victim, that is, the body of each young woman seems to have been, how can I put it, the bodies were not complete. There were pieces—.

"Pieces of what?" Abie demanded.

"You mean, there are body parts missing?" Noah asked.

"Yes. I've created a list, you see here. On this document are the names of each known victim. The date of birth. The approximate date of death."

"Yeah, yeah, we already figured that. The dates match up," Abie said.

"They were each named for the saint on whose feast they were born," Palladin said.

"We thought that might be the case," Cate said. "It's why we asked Father Vincenzo to come with his *Lives of the Saints*."

"Then you would have noticed one more thing. The saints for whom each victim was named, were all holy martyrs. Listen," he said picking up the book.

"*Saint Agnes, Virgin, Martyr. January 21 But twelve years old, she was led naked to the altar of Minerva on the Tiber river and beheaded by sword.* Now, Agnes Lombardi, according to police, an accidental drowning—a headless, naked body. Head and clothes chewed away by snapping turtles police claim."

"That's right. That's what the police claim," said Abie.

"Now, look here. The very *first* police notes. These pencil notes here: body found on dry dock *near* water. Not in the river but on dry dock."

"So?" Abie asked.

"It was only in the final police report that it was changed to say she'd been found floating *in* the river, to explain away the violent, headless condition of the body. But I believe she was killed on land, on the dry dock, as the initial report says, and the head was carried away, not by the tide or turtles, but by the killer."

"Who would do such a thing?" Cate shuddered.

"The Ripper did that, too. Took pieces. The cops said they were like trophies." Abie sat forward.

"I believe this killer may have a specific use for his so-called trophies . If I may continue, the next victim—*Saint Susanna, a noble virgin. Celebrated on August 11th*. It says Susanna was flayed alive, then sealed in the walls of Diocletian's municipal palace under construction in Rome.

"Miss Susanna Profaci was found sealed in an oil-drum at the construction site for the new Manhattan Municipal Building, August 11th, one year ago. It was reported her body was severely decomposed, but according to *this*—Mr. Hellenstein's actual autopsy notes—the body had been skinned; the flesh not *decomposed*, but missing.

"The list goes on and on. Saint Apollonia, thrust into a fire pit. Saint Lucy, stabbed. But here is what you did not know about Lucy Mendoza's death because it is only in the coroner's notes: She, like St. Lucy in the third century, before being stabbed in the heart, had had her eyeballs removed. It's all of it in the autopsy notes. They knew all along."

There was a stunned silence in the room. Cate had read all these martyrdom stories as a Catholic schoolgirl, but now they took on a horrifying, visceral reality.

"If I may ask, Your Reverence. My sister—is there something else I have not been told. St. Apollonia, in her martyrdom, her teeth were first torn out."

Monsignor Palladin looked stricken. "Yes," he said simply.

Cate stood up and walked to the window to compose herself. While the Monsignor had been speaking, Noah looked through the pile of autopsy reports. He got up and took them to Cate and questioned her quietly about something.

"My entire document must be published," Palladin continued quietly. "Someone with a deep seated hatred of the Church has resurrected the two thousand-year-old horrors of Roman Christian martyrdom. Will you do it, Mr. Kahn?"

"May we interrupt for a moment," Noah said. "Monsignor Palladin's theory about Agnes being killed not where she was found is correct."

"In fact," Cate added, "when I look at the Monsignor's autopsy reports all but one of the victims were killed someplace other than where they were found."

"You are certain? How do you know?" Monsignor Palladin asked.

"The amount of body fluids recorded at autopsy indicates the victims were nearly exsanguinated," Cate responded.

"Yet, no massive amounts of blood were apparent at the crime scenes. You noted it yourself, Abie, about Lucy Mendoza," Noah stated. "He kills them, the bodies bleed out, and then he disposes them where they're found."

"If I may say, Mr. Kahn," Father Vincenzo spoke up, "there *is* some immediate urgency."

"What do you mean, Father?" Noah asked.

"Well, this information gives us a timetable. It has been four days since the feast of a holy martyr, Saint John the Baptist on August 29th. The martyr before that was Saint Susanna on August 11th. The next feast of a martyred saint is on September 3rd. Tomorrow—the feast of Saint Seraphia."

FORTY-TWO

Cate gasped and turned back to stare out the window. "Seraphia?" she whispered."

"What, Cate?" Noah said. "What is it?"

"Seraphia Nicolosi. The daughter of Felicita Nicolosi. We went to their apartment door the night we found Lemuel on the roof of their building," Cate said.

"What has happened?" the Monsignor demanded.

"There's a police rumor that a girl has been reported missing from the area near Mott and Broome Street."

"Mott and Broome?" Palladin asked.

"Yes. The daughter of one of the murder victims still lives there—Seraphia Nicolosi," Cate explained.

"O.K.," Abie said, getting up. "We won't wait on Simonov to call. Let's get over there."

As they got to their feet, Abie's telephone rang. He lunged to answer it, nodding his head when he heard Sgt. Simonov's voice. The others sat back down in uneasy silence, watching Abie as he listened. It was long-winded and they seemed to hold their breath as they waited what felt like forever. Finally, Abie hung up.

"It *is* the Nicolosi girl."

"Oh, no," Cate cried. "Are they sure?"

"The father says early this morning a nun from the school shows up at their apartment. Says she's come to fetch his children so they can get sized for their school uniforms. For

Monday, first day of school. The kids came back a couple of hours later but no Seraphia," Abie said.

"But what did they say? Where did she go?" Cate asked.

"They said, the nun took them to the rectory and sat them all down in the parlor while she took Seraphia to the back to be fitted for her school uniform. They never came back. Not Seraphia—not the nun.

"The kids sat there two hours, then the priest, Father Costello came in and asked what they were doing there. He looked all over the rectory but found no sign of the girl. So, he took the children back to their father. Said there must be some confusion and he'd speak to the Mother Superior at the convent right away.

"The girl's father didn't wait. He went to the beat cop who called it in to the Twenty-third Street station. That's where Simonov got wind of it. He says, so far, no one's doing much of anything about it. The cops are calling it just another runaway."

Father Vincenzo immediately crossed himself and clenched his hands in a silent prayer. Monsignor Palladin looked ashen. "St. Stephen's," he said weakly.

"Yes, Your Reverence," Noah said picking up on the priest's apprehension. "Tell us about St. Stephen's. Who lives there? Father Costello and who else? Who's the other priest?"

"Father Costello," Palladin said starting to regain himself. "Father Fergus Costello."

"We know that," Abie said. "Who else?"

"An old priest. Retired there. Father Kieran O'Malley. That's all."

"No. There's a nun living there too. I saw her room, her closet," Noah insisted.

"You saw her closet? Inside the rectory?" Palladin asked. "How could you have?"

"So, there *is* a nun?" Noah asked.

"No. I tell you there's not. Just the two of them."

"We have to get to Mr. Nicolosi," Cate insisted. She stood and gathered her gloves and handbag.

"Yes. Yes, you should," Monsignor Palladin said thoughtfully. "And I must get to Saint Stephen's."

"No. *We'll* go to Saint Stephen's," Abie insisted.

Monsignor Palladin stopped mid-way to the door. "And how far do you think you'll get on your own?"

"You'll come with us, Monsignor," Cate said hopefully.

"Yes, I'll meet you there. You have my word." He hesitated. "There is one thing more I must share with you. An accusation has been made, in private, to a certain city official. There was a witness who says he saw something the night of one of the murders. The witness is dead now, but he said he heard a woman scream. Then he saw a priest, bloodstained. Running across the rooftops to St. Stephen's. But I do not believe it for a minute!" Palladin insisted. "Tim Sullivan lies! To intimidate me."

Abie turned to face the Monsignor. "Would this dead witness by any chance be Bill Baylor? If so, you better start believing it, Padre. He went under the wheels of a train to keep that secret from getting out. We just couldn't have all those good Catholic voters mistrusting their authority figures right before an election, huh, Monsignor.

"Let's get out of here," Abie said to the others heading out the door. "Are you coming, Your Holiness?" Abie tossed back in disgust.

"Yes," Palladin said quietly. "But first, I must retrieve something from my quarters. It's very important. Something I should have taken care of long before now."

FORTY-THREE

At St. Patrick's Cathedral, Palladin slipped into the residence and, lugging his briefcase, climbed the back stairs to his quarters. Something moved in the corner of his eye and he turned on the third step, startled by a figure lurking in the shadow.

"What are you doing there?" he demanded to know. "Oh, it's you, Father Elbi."

Elbi lifted a handkerchief from his pocket and fluffed it across the dusty feet of St. Michael's statue. The Monsignor managed a gruff harrumph. "Has His Eminence nothing more productive for you to do?" he said. He turned away wearily and climbed another step.

"I spend my time productively enough," Elbi said. "Observing the comings and goings of priests not in their cassocks."

Palladin looked down at his brown suit. "I had personal business to attend."

"Yes, it always is *personal* business when a priest takes off his collar. Perhaps you were busy, like His Eminence."

"What the devil are you talking about?"

"Why, the Cardinal. Didn't you know? He goes foot racing, in the middle of the night. Imagine such a thing. You're his chancellor and you didn't know?"

"And just where does His Eminence race to—in the middle of the night? If you've something to say, out with it,"

Palladin demanded.

"Why, nowhere. He doesn't race *to* anywhere. He just runs and runs, as though the devil himself were chasing him. Plastered in sweat. I certainly couldn't keep up with him. I lost him entirely somewhere inside the park. Near the pond. And by the time I returned here," Father Elbi said with a small downward flourish of his hands, "His Eminence was already returned ahead of me. In his bed and apparently, from the snoring, in a deep sleep. I believe he's sleeping still.

"Now, I've told you my secret; you tell me yours. I'll bet yours is more interesting, Monsignor. Huum?"

Not until that moment did Monsignor Palladin realize how tired he was. He longed for the day neither this priest or this Cardinal would be his concern.

"Good day, Father Elbi," Palladin said. Without sparing the sardonic priest another breath, Palladin turned and continued to his quarters.

In his bedroom he took a moment to change back to ecclesiastical dress. He put on all the vestiture of his office with it's colors of ancient origin and privilege: His black cassock trimmed in amaranth red, the color of love-lies-bleeding blossoms. He wound the purple sash of a protonotary apostolic around his waist, and placed the heavy gold chain and cross of Christ around his neck. It had been decades since he'd noticed its weight. Now, he wondered how he could feel anything *but* its weight around his neck.

Palladin placed a black biretta, with the red pom of a prelate on his head, without turning to look in the mirror. He knew what he'd see in the mirror was a lie.

Palladin swung a violet satin *ferraiolo* over his shoulders where it hung to his ankles. He tied a bow of its cloth strings at his throat. None of this served to restore him to the high place of self-regard he'd enjoyed previously. That would have been too much to expect.

He stood for a moment, draped in the vivid violet of all his authority, and never felt more helpless in his life. Palladin untied the privileged cloak, and hung it back in the armoire.

The Monsignor turned around and surveyed his room

with the big four-poster and Aubusson carpet. Late summer rain felt near; the air was grey-green and laden with static. He pulled money from his wallet and tucked it into his cassock pocket. He picked up his briefcase and walked to the bed where he emptied it of all its pieces of paper tumbling lightly onto the bedspread.

Now, he yanked a small brass key on a long, thin chain from around his neck. Kneeling, he fit the key into the keyhole of his armoire drawer and pulled it open. Inside was a white pine box. Inside that was a small, cloth bundle, the size of a newborn, which he carried to the bed. Palladin opened wide his empty briefcase and placed the bundle inside, then closed the satchel securely.

He searched himself for some small sign of relief, some indicator of redemption. He, sadly, found none.

At the same time, Noah pulled to the curb in front of 372 Broome Street. He and Abie flanked Cate up the stairs to the fifth floor landing. Their apprehension made them quietly hurry.

There had been nothing they could do to save Apollonia Leoni. They simply had not had enough information soon enough. This time, maybe they had enough to rescue Seraphia.

When Paolo, the oldest Nicolosi son answered the door, Cate momentarily didn't know who he was. She'd last seen him in early July at his mother's funeral; since then he'd changed a great deal. Not just the two inches in height; his eyes were older. They told Cate he knew exactly the danger his sister was in.

"I must speak to your father," Cate said gently. Paolo opened the door wider; Cate walked inside followed by Noah and Abie. When Cate saw Ercole Nicolosi, a cold wind blew through her.

He was in his big armchair, restrained by relatives, neighbors; Cate wasn't sure what was going on, except that Mr. Nicolosi was so agitated he looked deranged.

Cate stepped to him timorously. Signor Nicolosi was wailing, now angry, now frightened. Cate was sure he couldn't see or hear her through his hysterics. She knelt down by his chair. The closest woman, still speaking shotgun Italian, made room for her..

"Could you take the children out, please," Cate turned and said to Abie. He ushered the children, who were gaping at their father, down the hall toward the kitchen. He muttered awkward reassurances not to worry. We'll find your sister, he told them.

Cate turned back to Mr. Nicolosi and leaned in to him. She put her hands on his arms and held tight. She leaned in further, her face now directly in front of his and spoke calmly. "Signor Nicolosi, it's Cate Gallagher. I must speak with you about Seraphia."

At the mention of his daughter's name, Mr. Nicolosi would have come up and out of his chair, but for Cate's grip on him.

"*Scusami*," Cate said to the adults who stood by. "I must speak with Signor Nicolosi—*da solo. Scusami*". The others nodded their assent and moved like a small herd down the hall where they huddled. Noah withdrew after them but stayed close enough to be of aid to Cate. She reassured him with a small smile, then turned to the grieving parent.

"Signor Nicolosi, you must listen to me," she said clearly. "We are going to find Seraphia. *Capice*? We are going to go, and find her, and bring her home. Tonight. Right now. But you must listen to me. *Ascoltami*."

"Awright, Signorina Cate. I listen. You helpa my family. I will come too, and kill who hasa my Seraphia—"

"No, that is what you must *not* do. Do you understand? If you kill someone, even hurt them, you'll go to prison. Who will take care of your children then?"

"I am not a gooda father. I no protect my children. The nun, she say, the children musta have their *uniforme*. What musta I do?"

"Noah," Cate called. "Come listen. Tell me, Signor Nicolosi—this nun, did you know her? Had you ever seen her before?"

"No. I don't know the nuns' faces. She dress lika the nuns

at the school in the convent. Black. You know, everything is a black. And, white is here," he said putting his hand on his sternum, "a big *collare* white."

"Did you go to the convent?" Cate asked.

"No. The priest, he come here, witha the children."

"And who was that?"

"The new one. Father Costello. He says, he will look. In the church. In the convent. And come back. But I not just sit and wait. I tella to Officer Marino, on the beat. He says, go home and the *poliziotti* will come to you house. But they no come, Signorina. No one come."

"I've come, Signor Nicolosi. And I've brought friends. There is another priest, a Monsignor on his way now to St. Stephen's to find out what's happened. Do you understand? Help is coming."

"The Monsignor will help? He musta help!"

"He will help."

"We'll find her," Noah said with so much surety, it even calmed Cate, who was trying to hide from Signor Nicolosi her own fear for Seraphia's safety.

"We're going now. To find your daughter," Noah said.

FORTY-FOUR

A summer thunderstorm was coming. Warm, moist air rose and condensed over the entire island. *Mannahata* the Lanape and Algonquin had called it, from marshland to bedrock, their island of many hills.

The droplets falling in advance of the first autumn wind were small and priggish, drying by the time they reached the earth. But they were just the harbinger.

Large and bilious clouds hovered patiently, like alien visitors over the island borough. They clearly carried bilges of dark, heavy rain.

Monsignor Palladin was the first to arrive. He paid his cabbie, and stood on the sidewalk holding his briefcase tightly. He closely observed the priests' rectory, every window, door and ledge up to the roof; then he walked north toward the church next door. He mounted St. Stephen's smooth, grey-veined, marble steps and walked through the principal door of the sanctuary.

He was in a space he'd hoped never to re-enter. He held his breath and walked straight through. At the chancel rail, he genuflected to the presence of the Eucharist in the altar tabernacle, then opened the gate in the communion rail and passed through.

Palladin paused but did not look up at the stricken face of Christ on the crucifix above the high altar. Father Vincenzo's face had taught him statues reveal nothing. They are only the tortured figment of someone's imagination. Human suffering is to be found in the faces of humans.

Palladin turned left inside the rail and walked to the niche where St. Stephen was venerated. The reliquary with its shattered glass had long since been removed. In its place was a painted, plaster statue of Stephen, kneeling with arms outstretched as if to embrace the shower of stones about to hail down upon him.

Palladin opened his satchel and looked at the bundle inside. It was a loathsome thing now. He was as guilty as any ninth-century monk of imbuing bits of decayed bone with magical powers, making shamans of priests. On *these* the Church of Christ had been built.

He lifted the bundle from the satchel and laid it at the foot of the pedestal. He was done with it. He returned the bone relic of St. Stephen to the place from where he'd stolen it, so many years ago. *Let the dead bury the dead.* There is no magic in mortal remains.

Palladin snapped his briefcase shut and left it beside the wrapped bundle in the niche. He set off now to find the old man he knew would be waiting, and to put an end to the horror.

Monsignor Palladin entered the rectory hallway Immediately, he felt as if a cold, dry hand touched his spine. He remembered this place as he'd last seen it thirty-five years before; remembered it as being much larger. What he could no longer feel was the fear he'd lived with for so long.

He soundlessly tried the handle of the basement door, found it locked and wondered was it locked from the inside or out. Palladin moved up the hall toward the empty rectory office. He rounded the corner and climbed the staircase to the second floor landing, watching warily for who might appear.

He opened the first door he came to and found what he expected, a sterile room devoid of attachment to anything in either nature or humanity. He shut the door and moved on to the next. This room was also bare, save a narrow bed, and something which shouldn't have been there, laying in a heap on the floor.

Palladin turned it over with the toe of his shoe; it was the habit and veil of a Benedictine nun. This was what Mr. Goodwin said he'd seen in a closet. Palladin shut the door and moved quickly to the third room. The door was locked: was someone in there or not?

The Monsignor was going to find out. He backed up a step then rammed the door. The wood splintered. Once more, and the door flung open. The room was empty. Palladin stood still, listening for movement anywhere.

He moved down the corridor again, and at the far end, entered the narrow stairwell leading to the church roof. He climbed up and pushed open the heavy, metal door at the top.

The wind was stronger now, kicking aloft bits of grit like riled up flies. Palladin crossed the asphalt roof to the keystone set in the church's edifice arch.

There again is St. Stephen, large as life. Condemned by the *Sanhedrin* for speaking against Mosaic Law, Stephen about to be stoned to death by a legal mob, led by Saul of Tarsus. His bas-relief above the keystone holds a martyr's palm leaf in one hand, and a miniature church in the other. Its gaze is lost in a theophany.

So too, is the gaze of Father Kieran O'Malley as he touches the ecstatic face of the statue and wonders *Did you really offer yourself up to the stones like that? Your arms outstretched as for an embrace? I don't believe it! There had to be fear when you saw the murderous faces above you, the quarry rocks big as a strong man could hold above his head.*

O'Malley chuckled.

This was not the womenfolk throwing pebbles at the village trollop, was it? These were men who intended you to die. And the voice in your ears—was it the Son of God? Or was it the harangue of Saul, sent to Judea for just this purpose?

Didn't you bob about trying to protect yourself? Didn't you feel the cracking of your bones? Your skull? Of course you did.

And what say you to Saul—I mean, good Saint Paul, as you both stand before the Throne? How does he reply? Oh, I should like to know that. Doesn't seem sorry would be quite enough.

"Who has the girl?" Monsignor Palladin demanded.

Annoyed, O'Malley turned from the face of the saint, his reverie broken. "Well, I certainly don't have her," he said to his former foundling. "You of all people should know how unlikely that would be," O'Malley smirked. A low rumbling of thunder sounded over the river.

"You did well for yourself, boy," O'Malley continued. "Rising so very far through the ranks of the Church. Like cream to the top! I always knew you'd do well as a priest. But *such* a success—"

"Where is Father Costello?"

"Ah, now we come to the heart of the thing. *Where is* Father Costello? And what is Father Costello doing, heh? Don't you know?"

"Understand one thing, old man. You're going to tell me where Costello is, or your soul will stand in judgment for it—before the street lights come on. You don't have a lot of time."

"My soul?" O'Malley rolled his eyes. "You'd kill me? Is that what the Church has made of you? A Crusader?"

"You haven't much time."

"A hypocrite is what! *You* allowed him to be assigned here, when? Eight years ago? Eight years of not having to worry about *what do we do with Father Costello*. That's a nice long stretch, now. But the chickens always come home to roost. Eventually. Like you coming here tonight.

"He's been busy, our Father Costello. These last two years in particular. There're more, you know. More than the newspapers say. Many more. More than anybody knows about, including me. Why *did* you settle him here, Your Reverence?"

"Because you would have him," Palladin said.

"Because he'd be *safe* here! You knew his secrets would be safe, with me. That's the truth of it. You knew the Church's secret, your secret, would be safe here. Just another of Father O'Malley's boys. All grown up now. Like you."

"I am not like him! I have never been like him. Or, like you: a chancre on the Church!"

The old priest cackled mirthfully. "If I am, than Father Costello is surely its pus, wouldn't you say? Otherwise, the archdiocese would have left him where he was: at St. Mary's, or Holy Cross or St. Wilfred. But he couldn't be left there, could he? It wasn't safe after a time. So, he had to be kept moving. You remember, boy, what it's like, being sent from place to place? Like a badly posted letter.

The old man could see the remembering in the younger man's face. "So you moved him around; until you sent him here, with me. Back where you each started from. And, why not, both your bad apples in one basket.

"Oh, yes, and happy to have him, too, I was. Someone whose sins outweighed, by far, my own mountainous pile. I ought to know; he made *me* his confessor!" O'Malley hooted. "Why, my own appetites, as misguided and—*and nasty* as they are," the toothless old priest whispered, "pale next to the lethal unsavoriness of Father Costello's. Wouldn't you say?" His breath spewed like the opening of a grave.

"I had no idea he was as dangerous as this—" Monsignor Palladin said defensively. "That any *priest* could—"

"Don't play the *naïf* with me. You knew *something* was wrong with him. All those irate parents. And when the whispers grew too loud, *something odd about Father Costello*, you simply moved him again. And again." The old priest straightened up, his body rigid. "But it hasn't worked. The secret is out because good Father Costello turns out to be a bona fide madman! A genuine, homicidal maniac. While *I* am merely your garden variety— monster." The old priest doubled over in laughter until a deep, phlegmy cough overtook him.

"Where has he taken her?" Palladin demanded.

"Why, I really don't know, and that's a fact," he said as he hawked spit over the side of the church roof. "You *know* what he's doing, the loon!" O'Malley said with manic glee. The old priest staggered forward and lunged at Palladin, clutching him by the shoulders with fingers like rivets. "*You know*—"

Reflexively Palladin pushed him away and O'Malley fell back against the low wet parapet. The old man settled precariously against the edge. Rain fell in earnest now, it's patter faster and louder as it struck.

A white electrical flash split the sky, then a sharp crack of thunder signaled the emptying of the cumulonimbus overhead.

Palladin lunged forward, grabbed the old man by the ankles and upended him over the parapet. The old priest dangled head-first, fifty feet above concrete.

Palladin was the boy he'd once been, standing on a wooden perch before a roaring furnace fire. Only now, *he* had the power. He could let go; he could just let go, and this iniquity would drop like Lucifer expelled from Paradise. The shell of his head would crack like an egg on cement; its content would splatter and tomorrow stray dogs would come lick the stain.

Palladin let one scrawny ankle slip from his grip. Thunder smothered the screams this aroused.

"Where is she?" Palladin bellowed.

"He took her. The basement. Costello! Go to the basement!"

"It's locked," the Monsignor hollered.

"I have a key! It's here. Here it is," the old man blathered. "I'll give it to you," he said clawing at the chain around his neck. "Pull me up. Pull me up and I'll give it to you. Before it's too late! Too late for the girl."

Palladin grabbed for the old priest's belt, grasped it and roughly pulled O'Malley back onto the roof where he lay in a heap breathing heavily.

He clutched the hand holding the key to his chest as his face drained of all color. "I can—breathe, can't breathe," he gasped. "Help me. I ca— breathe. My heart." The old man grimaced first in pain then opened his eyes wide in sheer terror.

"Doctor. Get me a doc—" Another, stronger paroxysm shook him, then his head lolled back and his body relaxed. He was conscious but barely so. Father Palladin knelt next to him and, after a second of hesitation, made the sign of the cross and began the words of final absolution.

A froth like frog spawn burbled from the old man's lips as he looked into the face of the boy he'd so wronged. He extended the hand with the key. As Palladin reached to take it, the old man with his last ability, flicked his wrist and sent the key flying over the roof edge into the blackness of the street below. He whispered, fetch, boy. Then his eyes glazed and he was dead.

Palladin closed the dead man's eyes and dutifully finished his silent prayer for the dying. He stood and looked out at the open expanse of New York beneath a hot, heavy downpour of summer rain. His jaw slacked and he whispered hopelessly '*... hell has been emptied. All the devils are here*'.

FORTY-FIVE

Cate, Noah and Abie didn't pause when they left the Nicolosi apartment. Their sense of urgency was enormous. They rushed outside to the courtyard stairs where Noah surprised them by climbing up to the rooftop instead of following them down to the street.

"You two drive around to Mott Street," he hollered back. "I'll meet you inside the church."

"O.K.," Cate said clamoring down until she realized Abie's limp wouldn't allow him to keep up. "We'll meet you there," she said to Noah, pausing for Abie to catch up.

Noah nodded as he moved along the roof. It was slick beneath his feet from the downpour, but he covered the distance between himself and St. Stephen's at a fast clip, moving more cautiously as he neared. He flattened himself to the wall of the bell tower and peered around the corner. Twenty feet away in the mist, Noah saw a man standing over another.

Noah move cautiously forward, primed for the figure to run. When it didn't, he sprinted forward and saw it was Monsignor Palladin.

"What happened?" he asked as he crouched and felt for a pulse.

"I believe he's dead," Palladin said. "It's Father O'Malley."

"What happened?" Noah asked standing up.

"His heart, I believe."

"Come on," Noah said lifting the body by the shoulders. "We'll get him inside."

"Leave him," Palladin said. "We've something more important to do." He told Noah about the key to the basement somewhere on the sidewalk below. They trotted to the utility stairs and down to the second floor. "Wait. Look here—" Palladin said opening the middle room door and flicking on the light. "This shouldn't be here."

"It's the nun's habit I saw hanging in the closet," Noah said. "Like I told you."

"A nun comes over each day to keep house and bring the priests' meals from the convent kitchen. I tell you, only the two priests lived here. This," he said toeing the garment like a dead snake, "should not be here under any circumstances."

Noah pushed past Palladin out the door. "Let's get that key," he said.

They hurried to the first floor, crossed the dark vestibule and unlocked the front door. Outside, on the rain-soaked sidewalk, Abie and Cate were just getting to the church entrance.

"We've got to find a key," Noah said to them. "It fell down here somewhere."

"Is this it?" Cate asked. She pointed to something shiny under the water rippling in the gutter.

"Yes," Monsignor Palladin said snatching it up. "This is it."

They ran the few feet back to the rectory and fumbled for light switches. Noah followed the Monsignor down the hallway to the basement door.

Palladin used the key to unlock it and flipped on the light. They descended the steps and their eyes went immediately to the concrete slab by the uncovered hole in the floor. Monsignor Palladin took stock of his surroundings. He looked pale and fragile as if something had suddenly sickened him.

"Are you all right?" Noah asked.

"Yes, yes, quite all right," he said brusquely.

"You've been here before, haven't you? You know about this tunnel?" Noah asked.

"I do. I was a boy here." Cate, Noah and Abie exchanged

glances.

"You were a boy in this neighborhood, Father?" she asked.

"I was a boy in this room," Monsignor Palladin said.

FORTY-SIX

There was someone behind them on the basement stairs. They all turned to find a nun gingerly stepping down.

"What are you doing here?" she demanded. She might as easily have been demanding they hold out their hands for fingernail inspection. Then she saw the black cassocked figure in the background and his red pom biretta. "Your Reverence," she said. "I didn't see you there. May I be of some assistance? I'm Mother Frances, Mother Superior of the convent of St. Stephen's School." She stepped down the final step and folded her hands together neatly inside her long sleeves.

"Yes, Mother. Perhaps you can be of assistance," Monsignor Palladin said. A child has gone missing. And we're unable to locate Father Costello."

"A child?" Mother Frances looked stricken.

"Yes, Mother, one of the Nicolosi children," Cate said. "They're to begin school on Monday. Did you see them today—this morning?"

"No, I haven't. I've seen no one outside the convent today. I left there just a moment ago, to bring supper to Father Costello and Father O'Malley."

"Would one of your nuns have fetched the Nicolosi children here for school uniform fittings today?" Cate asked.

"Here? Oh, no. We size and fit all the students in the assembly hall on the first school morning. That would never be done here in the rectory. Oh, but this is dreadful."

"I need a flashlight," Noah abruptly said heading back up the stairs.

"You're going down there?" Cate asked.

"Of course," Noah responded.

"And then what?" she asked. "We need to figure out where to look for the girl."

"We already know where to *begin* to look," Noah said.

"O.K., but listen—we have to, I don't know—organize ourselves," she said.

Abie spoke up. "Cate's right. Let's all go upstairs. Figure out what to do. Eh, Ma'am," he said extending his hand to Mother Frances, "after you. Noah, you go on out to your car, get your flashlights. And, on the way, could you see the good Sister back to her convent?

"And, where's a telephone? Monsignor, they got one here?" Abie asked excitedly making for the rectory office. "Great," he said as he grabbed the telephone on the desk and flashed the switch hook. "Operator, get me the *Post*," he said in nearly one syllable.

"Hey, Noah! If you see Sgt. Simonov anywhere out there, send him in—or the beat cop!" he hollered across the foyer. "Gimme the rewrite desk— A girl's gone missing from St. Stephen's on Mott..."

A few moments later Mother Frances was back at her convent door and Noah had returned with flashlights, Sgt. Simonov, and Officer Marino in tow.

"Stand-by for the full report," Abie said hanging up. "O.K., let's figure this out."

"Where's Father O'Malley?" Cate interrupted. "Isn't he here?"

"He's here," Noah said. "On the roof."

"In the rain?" Cate asked concerned.

"Let me explain what's happened," Monsignor Palladin said. "Perhaps we should sit down a moment."

"Right," Abie said. "You sit down. Sergeant, down the hall there's a door to the basement. In the basement there's a tunnel. Anyone comes up through the tunnel grab 'em."

Sgt. Simonov nodded to Marino the beat cop, who hustled down the hall. The others found seats in the rectory's parlor office.

"Father O'Malley has had a fatal heart attack. His body is still on the roof," Monsignor Palladin began. "Before he died he told me Father Costello took the girl to the basement. I think we must believe him."

"Does that mean Father Costello is the priest Dollar Bill Baylor saw the night Mrs. Nicolosi was killed?" Cate asked.

"We don't know, and we won't know until we find him," Abie said.

"O.K., so here's what we *do* know," Noah said quickly. "A nun took the children from their home and brought them here this morning. We know it wasn't one of the nuns from the convent. Mother Frances said so, but the Monsignor and I both saw a nun's habit in a bedroom upstairs."

"Or, it wasn't a nun but a woman dressed like a nun?" Cate asked.

"Perhaps," Noah replied.

"We should have those clothes—the habit," Cate said. "We'll ask Mr. Nicolosi if it's what the nun who took the children was wearing. He said black with a large white collar."

"O.K., but don't they all wear that...?" Abie interrupted.

"I'll go get it now," Noah said.

"No. Some wear brown or white or grey. Anyway, Noah, while you do that—we know the feast of St. Seraphia is tomorrow. Monsignor, help me look around for a *Butler's Lives of the Saints*. There's one here, I'm sure. Perhaps there's some clue," Cate said.

"It's here," Palladin said plucking it from the bookcase. He settled at the small desk and turned on the lamp.

"*Saint Seraphia*," Monsignor Palladin began reading. "*Virgin and Martyr —born in Antioch in the reign of Adrian, the second century of our Lord. —orphaned, raised in Rome*, eh, let's see— Here it is. *Seraphia was denounced as a Christian and sentenced to death. She was first placed on a burning pile but was uninjured by the flames. Despairing of being able to inflict death upon her, the prefect Berillus ordered her to be beheaded—*"

"It's gone," Noah said rushing into the room.

"What's gone?" Abie asked.

Noah looked to Monsignor Palladin. "The nun's habit. On the floor, remember? It's nowhere in that room now."

"You must have gone into the wrong room," Palladin said.

"I thought so, too. I checked all three rooms," Noah insisted. "It's gone."

"Who else could have taken it?" Cate asked. "Officer Marino?"

"Hasn't left the basement," Sgt. Simonov said.

"Mother Frances?" Abie said incredulously.

Noah shook his head. "I walked her to the convent. She was empty-handed," he said.

A puzzled silence hung over them like a flaw in time.

"Where's the dinner tray?" Cate asked abruptly.

"What dinner tray?" Abie asked.

"She said she'd just come over to bring supper for the priests. She left empty-handed. Where's the supper?"

The four of them glanced around, then at each other. "Look all around. I'll check the kitchen," she said.

The searchers disbursed through the first floor of the rectory when Cate shouted from the kitchen.

"Come look at this—" The men heard the alarm in her voice and converged on the kitchen ready for battle. They found Cate standing stock-still staring at a small, brown bottle on the sink sideboard. Cate picked up the bottle and read them the label.

"*Teasdale's*. It's Chlorodyne. The dose is a teaspoon." Cate held up a sticky soup spoon. "He's drugged her. And there's no supper tray or food from the convent here."

Monsignor Palladin spoke up immediately. "We must go to the convent," he said rushing up the hall toward the front door.

"Someone should stay here," Abie announced, as he raced after the others.

"That's me," Simonov said. "I'm going to start a proper search of the building. And the church."

At the door of the convent, Monsignor Palladin banged an iron knocker several times. A young nun wearing an apron pinned over her habit opened the door and peered out.

She didn't know the Cardinal's chancellor by sight but she did recognized the red piping and purple sash of rank.

"*Urh Rev'rance,*" she cooed with a quick bob of her head. "Please, come in." The freckle-faced girl opened the door wide and ushered the prelate and his party into the vestibule.

"I must speak with your Mother Superior," Monsignor Palladin announced.

"Right away, sir. I'll tell Mother Frances, if you'll please to wait here just a moment." The young nun slipped quickly through the gap between a set of double doors. Her rush of excited words could just be heard in the vestibule. A moment later, the doors slid open and a diminutive nun, crinkled as old ivory hobbled forth.

"I am Mother Frances, Your Reverence. How may I help you?"

FORTY-SEVEN

Seraphia Nicolosi floated like a lotus broken free of its mooring. She sighed hoping the dark, pleasant dream would continue; but it didn't. There was only the vaguest sense of disruption in time and space. She couldn't remember having gone to bed but she must have, because now she was lying down in the pitch black of night.

What *did* she remember?

Being in the house of the priests. The dream was coming back again, lapping at the edge of her consciousness. Such a pleasant dream. If only she could remember; but she couldn't. She was too sleepy. Her eyes were open, or were they? It was dark and her eyelids so heavy. If only she could remember the dream. She drifted away again.

The darkness pulled her down, hand over hand into a deep, dreamless sleep where nothing out there could reach her; not the storm raging overhead, not the clamor of those searching frantically for any trace of her whereabouts.

"Officer Marino and I have thoroughly searched the rectory and the church," Sgt. Simonov said. "That girl is not here. Neither is Father Costello hiding here around."

The group had returned from the convent and automatically reassembled in the kitchen, a well-lit room in which to confront the worst of one's fears. The walls were white enamel turned the yellow of old bones. Hexagonal floor tiles from the previous century were grouted with black grime. The windows were frosted as though no one was to see in or see out. It was the last place of which they'd had the girl's trace.

Seraphia was awake again, this time, more so than before. The effect of the Chlorodyne was beginning to wear off. She realized now she wasn't asleep in her bed at all. It was a box of some sort but she was still too stuporus to be as frightened as she ought to be; as frightened as she'd be the next time she woke.

Mercifully, the girl sank again into the river Alph, awash in pleasant forgetfulness down to a sunless sea. The silence here created a sound of its own which drowned out everything else.

"There is one other place—" Monsignor Palladin's head jerked up. "Possibly the child is—" The priest dashed from the kitchen down the long hall where two doors faced each other. He snatched open the door on the left and stepped into the sacristy of the church.

In her dream, Seraphia broke the surface of an ocean raging in slow motion. She gasped for air and could get none. Her mouth was bound with a gag and when she tried to touch her face she found her hands tied cruelly tight behind her back. Then the ocean swelled again and she was dizzy. A sweet, tarry taste on her tongue made her retch. Her mouth filled with vomitus and she arched her neck, struggling to keep the bile from filling her nostrils. She choked the vomitus down and breathed rapidly through her nose, snorting to clear her airway. Then her stomach churned again. Her eyes were wide with panic.

"Come quickly," Palladin hollered.

When they entered the sacristy, Father Palladin was standing before the open doors of a large chifforobe filled with vestments on hangers. Palladin grabbed them by the armful and tossed the garments on the floor. He stared at a padlock attached to an eyebolt at the bottom of the chifforobe.

"That shouldn't be there," Palladin said.

"What?" Noah asked. "The lock? What's inside there?"

"A space. Beneath the chifforobe, between the floor and the sub-flooring. But it shouldn't be locked. There was no lock before."

Noah elbowed past Father Palladin and knelt to inspect the bolted false bottom. He handled the padlock, gauging its strength and heft. "Here," Cate said plucking long pins from her hat. Noah wiped his hands dry, took the pins and knelt over the padlock. He maneuvered the tips inside the keyhole feeling for the cylinder, torquing it just slightly. With the other, he felt for the tumbler pins pushing them down, praying to hear the click of the cylinder releasing. The lock shackle popped.

Noah pried the bottom of the chifforobe up on its hinges. Inside the dugout lay Seraphia Nicolosi as still and blanched as a discarded soup bone.

FORTY-EIGHT

R oll her over on her stomach," Cate said urgently.
Noah lifted the unconscious girl from the cubbyhole
onto the floor, and quickly undid her hands and gag.

When she was prone, Cate stepped in and folded the girl's
hands under her chin, shoulders spread, elbows bent. Cate
straddled her back, and began pushing with both hands against
the girl's lungs.

Finally, Seraphia gagged and sputtered as a gush of
stomach content worked its way up and out of her throat.

"Get some water," Cate ordered as she used her finger to
hold down the girl's tongue and clear her airway.

When Abie returned with a tin cup of water Cate was
upholding the semiconscious girl in her arms. She pulled off her
glove and flung a handful of water in the girl's face, then jostled
her by the shoulders and shouted her name.

Seraphia coughed and involuntarily drew a great lug of air.
Cate sat her up higher and vigorously patted her face with water.
She spoke softly now, telling the girl she was all right, she was
safe. She rubbed the girl's wrists hard.

"She needs hospital care," Cate said as Seraphia slipped
into a raspy doze.

"I called already for an ambulance from Bellevue," Sgt.
Simonov said loudly.

"Sergeant, can you go fetch her father. He'll want to know

she's rescued." Cate tucked her gloves under her belt and dug in the pocket of her suit jacket. "Take this," she said handing over a small coin purse. "Send him on to Bellevue in a taxi, and come back here. Can you do that?" she asked.

Sgt. Simonov took the money, and with a gesture that was either salute or tip of his hat, hurried out.

Cate pillowed Seraphia's drowsy head on the heap of vestments. A moment later, they could just hear the distant clang of the hospital's new ambulance service.

"Where are you going?" Noah asked when Cate jumped up.

"To wait outside for the driver," she said. "He should bring in an oxygen apparatus if he carries one."

"Good. Good idea," Abie said, kneeling clumsily to hold Seraphia's small hand.

"I must telephone the Police Commissioner," Monsignor Palladin said. "And insist he come here, immediately, to take charge of this investigation personally. I'm going to demand a city-wide manhunt for this madman. And you, Mr. Kahn, you must give an eyewitness report of all you've seen. The civil authorities will be forced to act!"

"And you'll be the hero of the piece I suppose," Abie said.

"Mr. Kahn," Palladin said calmly. "You are entirely correct. I have been complicit. Others as well, just as you have said. I cannot speak for them, only for myself. I was wrong. Turning a blind eye is *not* the way. Is *never* the way. Evil cannot be contained and ignored like a serpent in a basket. It has to be destroyed. We," he said including Noah, "have the power to do that."

"Wait, Monsignor," Abie said. "Before you tell the police, tell us. I don't want them getting their version of things out there before I can write the story. Tell us what you know, Monsignor. And start with the missing body parts. Just what is this guy doing? He some kind of religious ghoul or something?"

"I'll tell you," Palladin said. He was clearly distressed by what he was about to say and nervously wiped the damp sheen from his face with a large handkerchief. "I'll tell you what I believe, although it is a gruesome sacrilege only the most deranged mind could fully fathom."

"We'll be the judge of that," Abie said impatiently. "Spill."

Monsignor Palladin looked pained and thoughtful. "I believe this—this *maniac* is martyring these exemplary women, like saints; women and girls chosen not just because they are easily overcome, but because they are Catholic and named for a holy Roman martyr of the first or second century, a well documented period of Church history. It was the time of the *sancti cultus*, the cult of saints, which was the absolute foundation of early Christianity."

"The cult of saints," Noah said. "That's why he scavenges parts of the body."

"Yes," Palladin said. "You know of it—? I forgot; you're an archaeologist."

"I don't get it, " Abie said. " What's he want parts of dead bodies for?"

"Relics of the holy dead," Palladin said.

"What for? To sell?" Abie asked.

"No. He's not concerned with commerce. He doesn't lust for wealth, he lusts for power."

"You've lost me, Father," Abie said annoyed.

"Understandable, as there is not anything in your tradition which compares."

"So, explain it to me."

"Yes. Yes, I will. Most religions venerate the remains of the holy dead: a hair from the beard of Mohammed, his cloak, the tooth of Buddha. In Judaism, however, the tradition has always been, and remains today, the dead are *unclean*. Contact with the dead defiles the living.

"But Christianity—Christianity in particular, was built on the *miraculous* properties of the holy dead, beginning with the body of Christ itself."

"After Christianity," Noah interjected, "contact with dead bodies was no longer a defilement; but instead, in the case of relics, contact *sanctified* the living."

"You know about this relic *hazarai*?" Abie asked.

"I know about ancient cultures," Noah said with a shrug.

"Mr. Goodwin is correct. The plundering of the catacombs

of Rome was the height of this belief that the mortal remains of saints—particularly the martyrs—is a conduit between Heaven and Earth, between the living and the dead. To this day, it is held that the bone or blood of a saint breeches the barrier between the two worlds, allowing the dead to intercede on behalf of the living."

Palladin sighed deeply and for a moment Abie and Noah weren't sure he would continue. Outside, the ambulance was nearer. Palladin started speaking again and it seemed as if he was hearing the words himself for the first time.

"All those bodies dug up in the first two centuries of the Church," he said. "Dug up in order to possess the spiritual protection literally in each desiccated bit of bone. Fingers, feet, heads, organs, and bloody scraps of cloth—the smallest particle believed to embody *all* the power of the saint in Heaven. The possessor of a relic from the body of a martyred Christian has every expectation of miraculous intervention."

"Graves and tombs were opened," Noah said, "and the bodies of saints disinterred, dismembered and moved—or *translated* is the Church term—over the continents of the known world with the spreading of the faith. You see it even as far away as India, where the bones of St. Thomas the Apostle were plundered."

"So, you understand the implications," Palladin said to Noah. "The remains of the holy dead were no longer just carrion to be disposed of in graves outside city walls. Those remains could now protect even the least powerful from misfortune, from disease and death, ward off diabolic curses, even stop marauding armies in their tracks. And paramount of its powers: to grant indulgence from the flames of Purgatory; to redeem a soul from Hellfire. Father Costello would believe this utterly."

Abie needed a second to take it all in. "Yeah, well, good," he finally said. "Let him keep on thinking that way. Works to our advantage—you know?"

"Let's not make the mistake of thinking his insanity is irrational," Noah said.

"What do you mean?" Abie asked. "Of course he's irrational."

"Yes, of course. But he's been rational enough to escape detection for God knows how long.

"Well, he's got to know the jig is up now," Abie said conclusively.

"Yes certainly," Palladin said. "He knows. It makes him all the more dangerous, I would say."

Noah looked puzzled. "Explain something to me, Father. Couldn't he just go to Confession and be absolved of his sins? Saved from punishment?"

"Absolved, yes. But that does not remit the punishment. Even a confessed soul must suffer the fiery pits of Purgatory to atone for all mortal sins committed in life. The fire is no less a torment. The only difference between Hell and Purgatory is Hell is eternal. Purgatory, still, may last from a scant moment to centuries depending on the number and seriousness of one's sins.

"However, the Church holds that *anyone* who dies in a state of grace, sins absolved and earthly penance made, is held to be a member of the Communion of Saints, assumed to be in Heaven. They stand in the presence of God. Therefore, their relics can confer plenary indulgence: a *complete* remission from the fires of Purgatory," Monsignior Palladin rattled.

Then they heard heavy footsteps running inside the rectory.

FORTY-NINE

O utdoors, the intensity of the rainfall was increasing. There was little wind, so great sheets of water poured straight down. Three men ran through the wet onslaught along the Mott Street sidewalk and hurried up the rectory steps. A second later Sgt. Simonov thundered up the hall shouting *this way, fellas* to the two following him.

Inside the sacristy, Noah, Abie and the Monsignor froze as Simonov and the two men in white jackets burst in filling the small room with urgent activity.

"I must telephone Commissioner Waldo—" Palladin said again. Standing over Seraphia being tended to on the floor, he made the traditional hand gesture of benediction.

"Did you bring oxygen?" Abie asked the attendants, ignoring the priest's ritual.

"It's in the wagon," one of them said.

"Well, you should of brought it in. She needs it. Miss Gallagher's a nurse. Didn't she tell you?" Abie questioned.

"Who?"

"Where's Cate?" Noah asked suddenly. He turned to look at the sergeant. "Wasn't she waiting for the ambulance?"

"No, no one was there. The driver and the orderly were headed to the church when I got back from seeing the girl's father. I ran there and back the whole way, but I didn't see nothing of Miss Gallagher—"

Noah dodged in front of the ambulance attendants lifting

Seraphia on a stretcher and sprinted through the rectory.

Standing on the sidewalk, the rain pelted him as he looked as far as he could see, up and down the street. The heavy rain had driven the world to shelter and left behind a shrouded image like a fogged looking glass.

"Where is she?" Abie asked running up. "What do we do now?" Noah stood fixed, getting his bearings.

A few feet away Seraphia was being lifted into the ambulance. The orderly settled into the wagon next to her, while the driver and Sgt. Simonov climbed into the cab.

Noah paced, searching the sidewalk, up then down the street, loudly calling Cate's name. Abie turned up the collar of his coat and walked in the opposite direction hollering for Cate as well.

The ambulance pulled slowly away, and Noah moved off the sidewalk into the ambulance's wake. He squinted at a spot just ahead of him, then moved to the middle of the street. Between his feet, a manhole cover was just a bit out of place.

"Over here" Noah called to Abie.

Noah circled until the iron letters on the manhole cover were lit in the streetlight. Circled in the middle was the date 1863, and encircling that were the words Croton Aqueduct.

"The old Croton—it was torn down years ago," Abie said. "Hey, where are you going?" he yelled as Noah trotted away from the street toward the rectory.

"I need my equipment."

"For what? Wait—" Abie sputtered. A moment later Noah had returned with his oilskin haversack, short crowbar, the carbide lamp hung on a strap around his neck, and a large knife in a sheath on his belt. "You're going down there," Abie declared.

"Yep," Noah said peeling off his jacket and vest.

"What's happened?" Monsignor Palladin asked as he arrived under a great black umbrella.

"He's got her," Abie said pointing to the open manhole. "Noah is going to go after them."

Monsignor Palladin looked stricken. "Father Costello is a madman; you mustn't go alone, my boy."

"That's what I say," Abie insisted. "Wait for the police, at least."

Noah stuck the short crowbar inside the haversack. He pulled out his pocket watch, marked the time then dropped it in the sack as well.

"I can't lose that much time," Noah said. He dug in his haversack again, and pulled out a large piece of surveyor's chalk. "See this? I'll mark the tunnel wall every three-hundred feet. Tell the police to follow my sign. An X in a circle," he said beginning the climb down the manhole rungs.

"I shall go with you. You must not go alone," Monsignor Palladin said.

"Sorry, Father. You have to be here when the police and the Commissioner arrive."

"Then *I'm* going," Abie said starting to pull off his jacket. Noah stopped and stepped back up a rung.

"Abie, listen—that's no stroll through Central Park down there," he said gently. "Aren't you the guy who doesn't even like to ride the subway through a hole in the ground?"

"So, I'll make an exception. I'm coming."

Noah looked down for a moment. "Abie. Your leg— You're going to slow me down. I'm sorry." Noah ducked back down into the manhole.

"But, wait. *Where* are you going? You don't even know which way they went."

"I do know." Noah looked up through the manhole at Abie and the Monsignor huddled under an umbrella. "This tunnel used to carry water from the old Croton Aqueduct at 42nd Street to lower Manhattan. It's been converted for street runoff now. The water down there is rising. Fast. Flowing hard from north to south.

"There's only one way a man with a struggling or even unconscious woman could go. South with the flow, and fast before runoff fills the tunnel."

It was the last thing he said before letting go of the bottom rung and dropping into the dark rushing water below.

FIFTY

The late-night siren hadn't cause very much of a disturbance, though it was shrill and remarkably loud. It was not at all an unusual sound, particularly in Little Italy, so close to the expanding Chinatown where tong warlords battled nightly like feudal barons. But when the police sirens stopped in front of St. Stephen's Church, people got up from their dinner tables and peered out into the rain.

A dense, heavy drizzle persisted, leaving the air muggy and swampish. Three police cars emptied themselves, and a tall beefy man in a plaid suit directed uniformed officers to positions in front of the rectory and church. With a wave of his hand he indicated the locations for kerosene lamps to be placed. Only then did he march to the middle of the street where Abie and the Monsignor stood.

"Evenin', Monsignor. I'm Detective Lt. O'Keeffe."

"Where is Commissioner Waldo?" Palladin demanded.

"Pardon, urh Grace, the Commissioner sends his sorriest regrets, but he fears his personal presence would, *eh*—draw the wrong kind of political attention, you know. From the press and such. This being so close to Senator Sullivan's election and all.

"He says I'm to tell you, I'm his best boy, trusted with his deepest confidences. So, if urh Grace could just show me where the lass was confined, I'll have my men start having a look around for the culprit."

Palladin was livid. "This is outrageous! Where is Waldo? We have a much more serious situation at hand. A woman has been abducted—" Monsignor Palladin stopped himself before letting loose his full salvo of indignation. He reminded himself he was part and parcel of all of this. He took a deep breath then closed his eyes a moment as if in contemplation.

"My son," he said exhaling. "Forgive my outburst. Thank Heaven you are here."

"Well, sure, urh Grace, sir. No offense taken."

"Nevertheless, I really must make the Commissioner understand the utter necessity for urgent and substantial action. A woman has been abducted, taken down there," he said pointing to the manhole, "by someone we believe to be the same person who abducted the Nicolosi child, who is now enroute to the hospital. That person, as far as we know, is Father Costello of St. Stephen's Church. The woman is Cate Gallagher; I'm sure you recognize the name. By morning, not just Mr. Kahn's newspaper, *this* is Mr. Kahn—"

"Oh, I know who he is," O'Keeffe hissed.

"—*Not only* Mr. Kahn's paper, but every paper in the country will have this story as well as *all* of the political circumstances, which have brought us to this moment. It will be writ large across their front pages, you may be sure. That is what I must warn your boss of, Detective."

The policeman leveled his gaze on the priest's back as Palladin marched toward the rectory. O'Keeffe spit and rolled a toothpick from one side of his mouth to the other, then strolled up to the open manhole, where he stood in his best Colossus pose.

What Commissioner Waldo had told him was true. The Monsignor has lost his courage. Perhaps, is even out of his mind. As a matter of fact, Waldo himself sounded on the verge of panic. But, Big Tim's instructions were clear. He intended to win election to the United States Senate on November 5th, and nothing was to prevent it. This entire problem was to be contained, now, by whatever means. The killer, whoever he is, is to simply disappear. No arrest, no interrogation, no trial, no publicity. The police will mark the case closed with plausible and ballyhooed reassurances to the public.

Cardinal Bernard had already been pulled from his evening pinochle game and informed that Monsignor Palladin was having a crisis of faith bordering on nervous breakdown. He should be seen to immediately. At the Cardinal's request, Sullivan was sending a car for Monsignor Palladin. It would arrive any time now O'Keeffe calculated against his pocket watch.

As for the little Jew, Sullivan instructed a free pass. Not a single hair on his curly head can be touched—not yet. Killing a reporter, even this one, especially this one, right now would be the incautious, one-step too far. *For now*, O'Keeffe reminded himself.

"So, what're you going to do about all this, Lieutenant?" Abie demanded.

Eight weeks to Election Day. That's how long you've got, O'Keeffe silently promised Abie. Then you're all mine.

From his ample back pocket, O'Keeffe pulled a flashlight and aimed the beam down into the manhole. Faster than one would expect such a bulky man to move, O'Keeffe descended the rungs into the manhole, where he landed with a splash and a grunt.

Abie moved closer to the opening and watched the cop's flashlight beam bouncing about like river faeries until the tunnel grew dark again. Abie moved away, into a pocket of shadow beneath the overhang of a tree. He didn't want some flatfooted cop to usher him off to the sidewalk along with the growing number of rubberneckers. If the Monsignor did what he had threatened, it would be a crack in the Tammany machine heard coast-to-coast. When this story broke, it was going to break bigger than anything this town had ever seen, and Abie wanted the eyewitness exclusive. It was *his* story.

He slipped off his jacket then casually picked up one of the kerosene police lanterns. He moved quickly to the manhole while the cops chased away kids and herded citizens onto the sidewalk. Then, clamping the lantern handle between his jaws, Abie sidled down the rungs and landed in rushing water up to his waist.

Ahead of him, to the south was nothing but the sound of

flowing water and the pitch black of oblivion. Abie held his lantern high overhead and moved forward within it's yellow glow. He found, far from hindering him, the water buoyed him, making it possible for him to move ahead swiftly despite his gimpy leg.

FIFTY-ONE

The water moving through the massive brick conduit cooled Noah after the sticky heat above. Street runoff was still mixing with the rising overflow from city watersheds, leaving the water fairly clean. It carried the faintest odor of gasoline and horse waste, as though here flowed the common border of the old and new centuries.

The old Croton conduit was one of hundreds of tunnels and passages that are the municipal labyrinth below the streets of New York. Down here is unpredictable danger where solid granite abuts decayed rock and firm ground noiselessly gives way to treacherous drop-offs. Aquatic pools, even quicksand, shift as skyscrapers displace underground streams. This was the underworld, which Dutch settlers of *Nieuw Amsterdam* first breeched with the digging of a single well more than two centuries earlier.

The water was flowing higher but still well below the vaulted ceiling of the conduit. Dry roots and vines perforated the masonry at it's high water mark attesting to the dangerous flash floods of previous rainstorms and nature's determination to reclaim its own from decades of underground intrusion.

Noah moved quickly through the downstream of water, but not as quickly, he worried, as Costello might be moving. He knew the best chance of saving Cate would be to overtake Costello quickly, before he gained more head-way and disappeared into the underground sprawl.

He also knew city sewer workers used small skiffs with poles to punt these underground waterways quickly. When work was finished the skiffs were tied to the closest, rusted valve or iron ladder and left until needed again. Noah was sure Costello used these skiffs to move himself and his victims as quickly as possible away from pursuers. But where to? He had to have a destination. His executions were carefully carried out, then displayed. That takes time and seclusion. And, purpose Noah knew. The killer has to have a hidey-hole. A lair somewhere.

Noah slowed every three-hundred feet to chalk his mark on the tunnel's brick wall, and to *listen*.

Little was visible in the lamplight that bounced against his chest with each lunge forward. Above him, the muffled sound of automobile traffic occasionally echoed along the water surface. But now, there was only dense silence and Noah realized the course had veered west under a block of buildings.

The water continued to rise. He was winded from his fast stride through nearly thigh-high water. His face and the back of his neck were clammy with exertion. In front of him there was nothing but endless Stygian black. The thought of Cate, down here, in the hands of a monster was intolerable. He started again, moving faster. Now, no longer stopping to leave his chalk mark, praying to come upon an abandoned skiff before the water rose much higher.

FIFTY-TWO

A bie soon found the water several buoyant inches above his waist. He tucked up his legs and with one hand against the tunnel wall, allowed the flow of water to float him quickly along. Noah's chalk marks came more and more quickly, then abruptly there were no more.

Abie slowed himself, not wanting to overtake the leviathan O'Keeffe. He shuttered his kerosene lamp and peered into the darkness for several seconds while his eyes adjusted to the pitch dark.

He wasn't sure at first he'd seen it: a faint glow bobbing in and out of sight. Abie patted his breast pocket assuring himself he had his flint-lighter, then extinguished his lantern altogether.

He was plunged into darkness, but not the black wall of the blinded. There was depth perception in the diaminogen, and the grey surface of the water was clearly discernable flowing along the brick tunnel walls.

Abie moved ahead cautiously, knowing instinctively the corrupt cop was his stanch enemy. Slowly, Abie crept closer and the light ahead revealed more of itself. Then he saw O'Keeffe.

The policeman had come to a T-section in the tunnel, beyond which a cluster of small skiffs formed a log-jam. To the right, a second tunnel formed a roughly east-west fork in the water.

Abie watched as O'Keeffe's flashlight illuminated the mouth of the branch conduit, then swung back around to the skiffs bobbing straight ahead. To O'Keeffe they looked like a roadblock and immediately raised the hackles on the back of his neck. He pushed ahead through the water toward the skiffs, separating them roughly until he was certain no one hid amongst them.

O'Keeffe stood still awhile, staring down the gullet of the tunnel. Abie supposed the policeman was intently listening. In his own ears Abie's heart beat like a whirl-a-gig.

O'Keeffe glanced unknowingly in Abie's direction once or twice, then taking the measure of the situation, pulled one of the skiffs from the others. Using the punting pole for leverage O'Keeffe hauled himself aboard, grunting loudly. He stood, precariously at first, then got his footing. He pulled the pole from its ring socket and clumsily began to punt ahead.

Abie watched the skiff careen and weave until O'Keeffe was able to pick up a momentum which moved him smoothly along the flow of water. Finally, man, boat and light were swallowed by the gloom.

When he thought it was safe, Abie relit his lantern and began searching the tunnel wall for any sign of Noah's chalk mark. He moved forward until he stood at the mouth of the tributary tunnel where O'Keeffe had stood. Here the pitch was nearly level so there'd be no rush of water at his back moving him along. O'Keeffe had chosen the easier of the two routes down the throat of the tunnel. Perhaps Noah had done the same.

Abie felt a vague stab of panic as he cast his light around for a chalk mark telling him which way to go. *Why wasn't it there?*

Then he saw it, lower than he'd been looking, just above the waterline, an X in a circle, inside the tributary tunnel.

Abie rushed to the skiffs still bumping against the walls, and pulled one of them back with him to the side-tunnel. He set his lantern down on the skiff, then rolled himself over onto the flat bottom, centering himself amidship. Abie grabbed the pole and braced it against the tunnel floor stabilizing the skiff. Holding the pole tightly in both fists Abie stood up, and using his strong, upper-body, poled the skiff forward while he prayed somewhere ahead of him Noah was doing the same thing.

FIFTY-THREE

Noah had indeed come to the mouth of the branch tunnel some minutes before and saw the small flotilla of skiffs jamming the waterway ahead. He pulled off his haversack and rummaged around for a small, mahogany box with brass fittings. He opened the box and held it steady under his lamplight. Inside the box, the magnetic needle of his compass bobbed about aligning itself with the Earth's magnetic field. The ire-ore strata threw the reading off but it was sufficient to confirm that the tributary intersected from the west-southwest.

Noah stuffed the compass in his haversack and pulled out one of several maps and his pocket watch. Less time had passed than he'd thought. He calculated how many city blocks he would have traveled in twenty-two minutes of wading, and figured his distance at a half-mile, maybe a little more as the crow flies. He checked that against his surveyor's map, and thought somewhere near Canal Street was a good guess at his location.

The main conduit was pretty much a direct route to Bowling Green, where the body of Agnes Lombardi had been found, but not her head. The tributary, however, veered along a course to the city Municipal Center, near where Susanna Profaci was found, her body 'decomposed'. Noah tried to quiet his mind which was racing down two corridors at once.

Whom were the gods favoring today? Or is it all karma? He dug in a pocket, pulled out a coin and flipped it. *Heads, straight ahead. Tails, the tributary.* The coin flashed briefly like a silver fish leaping from the water. Noah swiped at the coin, catching it in mid-air, then slapped it down on the back of his wrist. He lowered his wrist to the lantern and looked. *The tributary.*

He was punting skillfully through the water now, staring into the dark, watching for any sign of light ahead. Noah plunged the pole into the water over and over until the rhythm of his movement had become a mechanical and forceful propeller.

He saw something from the corner of his eye. Something floated past. Noah reversed his body and swung the pole over the stern. He braced the pole against the bottom of the tunnel and stopped the skiff's momentum.

What was that? He leapt lightly into the water and waded back up the tunnel, carefully glancing his lamplight across the water's surface as he moved. There *was* something.

He lunged forward and grabbed the thing floating in the lapping water. A sheer white glove with a ruffle at the wrist. He remembered Cate had been wearing gloves in the sacristy, exactly like this one.

Noah scrambled back onto the skiff. He dropped the glove in the water where it could continue its journey to whatever rescuers followed.

FIFTY-FOUR

Abie was making good headway now. His lantern at the bow of the skiff cast an incandescent searchlight ahead of him. His nerves were settled but he threw frequent looks behind to assure himself Detective O'Keeffe had not doubled-back.

Earlier, in the main conduit, he'd passed a few sidewalk grates overhead and rungs leading up to covered manholes in the street. They had been comforting sights. However, since he'd turned into the side tunnel, he'd seen none, nor anymore of Noah's chalk marks. This was worrisome.

For the first time Abie began to examine the wisdom of having followed Noah down into an underground water tunnel. For Noah it was fine. Like a mole, Noah practically lived underground. But what did Abie know of this *Sheol*. Up there, on the streets of New York, he was a prince of Gotham. Down here, on his own, was a different matter entirely.

He continued to punt. *Was this tunnel simply endless? Maybe he'd find himself punting around in tunnel after tunnel, lost, unable to find an exit*—Abie felt the nascent stirring of panic. *What was he doing here?*

He had to calm himself. He wasn't too far along; he could still find his way back the way he'd come, probably. Abie took a deep breath; then softly, almost silently, he sang a little song from another time.

> *In dem Beis-Hamikdosh*
> *In a vinkl cheyder*

Ten more minutes, he promised himself, then he'd decide if he should turn back.

Unter Yidele's vigele

Shteyt a klor-vays tsigele

Abie punted the skiff with renewed determination, humming his childish, comforting tune. Noah *had* to be somewhere up ahead. Then he saw something which frightened him at first—a hand reaching up in the water just ahead of the boat. After a moment he recognized it was actually a flimsy, white glove. *Cate's?* It had to be. He used his pole to fish it out but in his excitement he fumbled and dropped the pole.

Abie felt vulnerable, exposed, and decided to dim the wick of his lantern. He floated ahead in the near-dark, paddling with his hands another ten minutes before his nerves got the better of him again. Without warning the water rushed now as the tunnel veered sharply right and widened out into deep shadow. The exquisite, artisanal brickwork of the tunnel gave way to a chamber hewn from granite bedrock.

The sound of water churning up ahead echoed off every creviced wall. Abie wished now he'd left the lantern bright. He desperately wanted to see what the skiff was plunging headlong toward. *Could it be a drop-off of some kind?* Noah had said the conduit emptied out into—*what, what had he said?*

Perhaps he should call out—just once. If Noah was there, he'd hear him.

Noah, he called softly. The only response was the echo of his own voice and the roaring rush of water. *Noah!* he called more gamely.

Perhaps he stood a better chance if he got himself off the skiff and into the water; he'd be safer in the water where at least his feet would touch the bottom. *Or would they?* The tunnel had ended; he was in a cavern now. *How deep could it be?*

Abie heaved over the side of the skiff, holding on tightly to the side, and in the process upended the bow. Too late he grabbed for his lantern which tipped over and slid into the water with a little hiss.

In pitch blackness, Abie struggled to his feet, in water not deep at all, only a little above his knees, but the bottom was impossibly slippery. Abie grasped the side of the skiff to maintain his footing. The accumulation of slick moss mucilage underfoot meant somewhere this chamber opened to the outside. Had to. Moss can't grow where there isn't at least, some miniscule amount of sunlight.

Abie balanced himself as best he could on the slippery bottom and craned his neck in the dark. He stretched his wet fingers in the air. It was there, the faintest breeze across his outstretched hand.

His eyes were dilated and when he looked up he could clearly see stars and pale street light through a sidewalk grate some twenty-feet overhead. He was in the world again or at least close to it.

Perhaps he could attract the attention of some passer-by. He'd have to holler loud he thought. He opened his mouth to bellow when something powerful seize him around the chest. In an instant, Abie was drug off his feet with a hand clamped over his mouth, down into the dark as if the cavern had swallowed him whole.

FIFTY-FIVE

D on't do that!" Noah roughly whispered in Abie's ear. "You have to be *quiet*," he said removing his hand from Abie's mouth.

"Godammit, Noah! You scared the life out of me. Thank God, it's you," he gasped. "Where the hell are we?"

"The Centre Street gate chamber. C'mon, stay close and don't make any noise. I saw a shadow move. Up ahead." Noah put his finger to his lips in a gesture of silence and they waded carefully ahead in the dark. The rush of water grew distinctly louder, and their footing increasingly slippery as the water level continued to drop.

Noah halted. Abruptly, he threw back his arm halting Abie as well. Immediately in front of them was an alpine plunge to an enormous weir where a half-dozen water mains converged and emptied far below with an uproar.

Both men stood stock-still on the slippery lip of the drop-off. Abie's abandoned skiff sailed swiftly past them smashing to splinters in the onslaught below. Beneath their shoes the slimy surface gave no foothold, only the promise of death at the first misstep.

With utter concentration, Noah inched himself and Abie sideways like crabs, across the slippery edge, through the moving, knee-high water and toward the chamber's concrete embankment. Their hearts pounded at each tiny step. Grasping with their fingertips, they finally grabbed hold of the concrete abutment and desperately climbed up and over. Had either lost their grip the plunge into the waterworks' mechanism would have been immediate.

At last, they were on dry footing. The two men stood with their backs against the bedrock wall gaping down into the powerful weir. It was several moments before they could look away and examine their surroundings. The gate chamber was a massive underground structure. The building of it had been contracted to the Empire City Subway Company in 1890, after one too many spectacular electrocutions forced the city to relocate all electrical, telegraph and telephone wiring underground.

This gate chamber was one of six in Manhattan housing floodgates, valve controls and relay switches for hundreds of underground corridors leased to New York Edison, Consolidated Gas, the New York Steam Company, and the IRT. They were the vortices of the city's entire underground foundation.

Noah tried to listen above the roar of the water. He couldn't hear anything except the whine of a turbine somewhere below, but then another sound. Abie heard it, too.

"That's a subway."

"The Broadway-Seventh Avenue line," Noah said.

Whatever moving shadow he'd seen earlier had by now fled. Noah used his lamp to slowly canvassed the chamber's dark corners. As they crept forward, he swept the light across a number of grates and vents, pipes and valves and hatches but found not the slightest sign Costello had ever passed this way with Cate. Yet, *someone* had to have been here—shadows didn't move on their own and he was sure he'd seen one move.

"There's no one here now," Noah said to Abie.

"*I seen 'em,*" a hoarse voice whispered. Noah swung his lamp around in the direction from which the voice had come but found nothing except a child's filthy mattress on the floor, heaped with rags like a nest.

"Who's there?" Noah asked in a calm voice. He scanned his light along the floor and scattered a host of German cockroaches, Croton Bugs they were called, swarming an empty food tin. "Show yourself," Noah said. "We won't harm you."

Noah and Abie stepped carefully over the debris and walked into the deeper shadows. "If you saw something—some*one,* tell us." They stood still, waiting for a response.

"Will you pay?" the voice asked from across the chamber. Noah swung his light in the direction of the voice quickly enough to glimpse a head with matted hair and greasy whiskers.

"Yes," Noah said quickly. "Yes, we can pay. Do you live here?" Noah circled around the backside of a pylon where a strong smell of old urine rose up to meet him.

"Sometimes," the scratchy voice said.

Noah handed Abie the lamp. He slowly reached into his pocket and rummaged for a handful of coins. He tossed one on the ground, several feet in front of him.

"Did you *see* someone? Just a little while ago."

After a moment, "Yes." The croak came from a different part of the chamber now.

Noah tossed another coin after the first. "Man or woman?"

"Both," the voice said nearer. "Together."

"Was the woman all right?" Noah asked.

"Maybe."

"Maybe—?"

"Maybe she were drunk."

Noah threw another coin. "Have you seen the man before? Does he come through here sometimes?"

"Sometimes."

"Which way did he go?"

When Noah got no response he threw the rest of his coins on the ground and shone his light on them.

"*Which way?!*"

For several seconds more, there was no response, then a loud banging behind them. Noah swung his lamp in the direction of the sound.

"There," the man said and scurried into the invisible dark. It was one of the hatched doorways.

"C'mon," Noah said sprinting toward the door. It was old and heavy, but when he yanked on the iron latch it swung open easily. Abie held up the lamp and revealed a long low corridor. A half-dozen rusted pipes ran just overhead. Paint of some indeterminable color peeled from the walls down to the grate floor. It looked to some extent like a very long baker's oven.

Noah grabbed the lamp from Abie and entered the corridor ahead of him. They were nearly twenty-feet in, when the door behind them slammed shut. The corridor at once became stuffy with ancient smells.

"Never mind," Noah said when Abie tried to scamper back. He swung the light forward again and followed its beam. Within another twenty feet they could clearly see the corridor was bricked closed at the far end. They hurried ahead, and at the the tunnel's end ran their hands over the old bricks and crumbling mortar as if searching for an invisible point of entry.

"Well, they certainly didn't come this way," Abie said. "We've been snookered."

"Hang on," Noah said examining the ceiling and grated floor in the lamp light that was growing steadily dimmer. Noah switched the lamp off to conserve energy.

"How are we gonna find her in the dark?" Abie asked, stretching out his hands to feel for Noah.

"Stand here," Noah said, "next to me—shoulder to shoulder. Now, put your other hand on the wall. As we walk, we need to feel along the wall for something we may have missed: a hatch, a recessed wall, a jamb—something. We need to do it carefully."

They paced their way back slowly, running their hands high and low along the walls and found no break in the peeling surface for fifteen feet or so. Then Noah abruptly stopped.

"It's here," he said bouncing on the balls of his feet. "Feel that? That *give* in this section of floor grate?" They both quickly stepped aside and Noah switched on the lamp again. He played its dim light along the edges of the grate. It revealed a set of hinges at one side, and a small handle at the other. Noah squatted and pulled open the trap door to reveal a steep stair descent, just as the lamp gave out, plunging them into utter darkness.

FIFTY-SIX

Cate recognized the cloying smell of chloroform as soon as the rag was smashed over her mouth and nose. It was the last thing she remembered clearly.

She was moving, and dizzy. Roughly *being* moved. Dragged off her feet, down. Like Alice down a rabbit hole.

Cate swam up through a pea-soup consciousness, and the chloroform rag was applied again, longer. For awhile, she seemed to be floating on water, and Cate wondered how long she'd been unconscious. She struggled to rise, but her mind could make no connection with her body, like a sleeper immobilized in a dream. She wanted to focus her eyes but they swam in her head.

Pain thundered at the back of her skull. She moaned and immediately a ham-like hand grabbed the back of her neck and, this time all but smothered her with the chloroform rag. Her last thought was that she was dying.

He was carrying her now, sometimes walking her upright with her arm around his neck as she stumbled along, sometimes pulling her by her hair, her arm, her wrists, sometimes laying her flat and dragging her. His pace was relentless.

Cate allowed him, even when she could have resisted, because resistance was futile. Her only hope was in compliance; the longer she could avoid his chloroformed rag, the more she was able to gather her wits and her strength. Breathe. Breathe deep. *Just keep breathing.* She had no doubt now she was going to have to fight for her life. *Just breathe.*

Now he lifted her over his shoulder as firemen do and she panicked. She instinctively resisted his pull and he slammed her to the ground with brute force. The stunning pain made her gasp, and the oily chloroform rag descended. Cate would not struggle again.

She was alone now. Alone in a bright, white limbo that receded to pitch black when she opened her eyes. She could see nothing, and calmly wondered if she were dead. Then she knew, in the most sickening way, she was alive. A smell. An overpowering, animal smell. The stench of blood, sweet and decayed. The loathsome smell of the abattoir. Even the floor on which she lay was sticky with it.

Cate was suddenly, heart-stoppingly grateful for the darkness. She was fully lucid now. She knew the last thing she wanted to see, *never wanted to see,* was the horror which the darkness concealed. She closed her eyes against the very possibility of what might be revealed, but her inner vision was filled with the terror of what she knew.

She knew what fate Saint Susanna had met.

FIFTY-SEVEN

"Light your lighter," Noah told Abie as they stood above the open floor hatch.

"*Light*—I don't have a light," Abie replied perplexed by their predicament.

"Your *flint* lighter. Do you have it?"

Abie patted himself and, exhaling, pulled the lighter from his breast pocket.

"Is it dry?" Noah asked.

Abie squeezed the side lever. Nothing happened. He squeezed twice more before the flint and rasp produced a small flame faintly illuminating their relieved faces.

"What are we going to do now?" Abie asked.

"I saw something down there before the lamp went out," Noah said stripping off his haversack and unbuttoning his shirt.

"What?"

"Clay," Noah said.

"Clay— What for?"

"Hold these," Noah said. "And give me your lighter."

Abie carefully handed over the precious flint lighter and watched Noah lower himself onto the metal steps which dropped below the grate hatch. "I'll be right back," he said.

Abie watched the small point of light move down the steep steps in Noah's hand. After a minute, Noah called up to Abie, "Here I come."

A moment later, he was back, holding a thick bundle of long branches.

"Dead tree roots," Noah announced. "Wherever you've got clay sewage pipes, you've got tree roots." Noah handed the lighter to Abie, while he bound two, thick root bundles with his bootlaces.

Noah held the lighter to a piece of torn shirttail and applied it to the brushy end of the roots. The cloth burned slowly. But right away, the dry wood crackled and popped as it caught. Now they each held a large firebrand.

"Let's get going," Noah said.

The bright light of his torch bolstered Abie's courage enormously. It felt like a weapon.

"Let's go!" Abie answered.

Noah buttoned what was left of his shirt and slipped on his haversack. Carefully they descended the sheer stair to a bedrock shaft no bigger than a few feet square.

"There must be an exit here somewhere," Noah said.

The two men held their torches high and low and quickly found a sturdy plank door with knotted rope for a handle. They pulled the door open and stepped through onto a concrete landing in a large excavated tunnel. Four wooden steps led down to narrow gauge railroad tracks in the dirt.

"It's a freight train spur," Noah said.

"So, do you know where we are? I mean, if we were up there," Abie said pointing his finger, "where we'd be?"

"Pretty much," Noah replied checking his compass.

The tunnel was a shambles of construction debris with a half-dozen lumber beams supporting the overhead. Small and large boulders lay everywhere, most exactly where they'd landed following the dynamite blast that had hewn them. Unused rail ties were tossed in a pile like a giant child's jackstraws. A discarded box of detonator caps sat half empty in the dirt.

Noah and Abie descended to the track where they stood looking up and then down the spur line.

"Which way, do you think?" Abie asked.

"Maybe neither," Noah responded.

Noah squatted and pulled out maps and his canteen. He

took a deep swig then offered it to Abie who was glad to have it.

Noah spread maps out on the tracks and studied it all by torchlight. "We're approximately here," he said pointing to a spot on one of the maps. "Near Lafayette and Chambers.

"According to the map, this freight track runs south to the Whitehall piers and north to 34th Street, the West Side Freight Line," Noah said looking south then north.

"Which way should we go? Should we split up?" Abie asked. "Personally, I don't think it's such a good idea we split up."

"It would be a very bad idea," Noah said gathering up his maps.

"So, south to the piers or north to West Side Freight? I say south, to Whitehall. It's next to Bowling Green where the Lombardi girl was found."

"Or," Noah questioned, "north where we just came from—where Mrs. Nicolosi was killed; or north*east* to the Bowery where the Ricci woman was killed? Or we could go north*west* to Broadway and Lispenard, where Lucy Mendoza was found. Or we can stay where we are, a half-block west of the Municipal Center construction site where Susanna Profaci was found. We're in the hub of it, Abie. All points of the compass lead to a death. This is the locus."

"So, which way do we go? There're only two ways here, up or down the track."

"Maybe not," Noah said advancing across the track.

"Where are you going?" Abie asked exasperated but following close behind.

"To someplace not on the map."

FIFTY-EIGHT

He was making preparations to kill her. Cate knew that. She could smell the sulfur as matches were struck, many matches, then the heat and smell of good wax candles burning. She could hear his busyness, like Abraham, his preparation for the shedding of blood. Something was being dragged across the floor. And now hammering. But still she couldn't make herself look.

Inside the vacuum of her terror, she was losing her relationship with time. The past was present: *Her mother and the sisters at St. Veronica's school so satisfied to see little Catherine tucked in a corner, poring over her Butler's Lives of the Saints. Such a reverent and studious girl, as she slowly turned the pages.* No, not reverent at all, she muttered.

She was, in fact, studiously fascinated by the details described in the martyrdom of the Saints. *Mesmerized by the black and white etched illustrations of ecstatic virgins and pious youths, kneeling in prayer at the approach of their executioner and his hideous instruments. She turned another page.* Cate struggled to stop her mind from going where she desperately wished not to go. Susanna.

...nobly born in Rome about the year 285 AD and said to be the niece of Pope Caius. Having made a vow of virginity on which account she refused to marry, she was impeached as a Christian and made to...

Cate focused on laying deathly still, the way a opossum does. Imperceptibly she tested the strength of the tie around her wrists. She'd long since lost any feeling in her hands except a bee-stinging numbness. The rope, swollen with water, held tight. She took a deep breath to fend off panic.

Just keep breathing.

Ever so slightly, she shifted a foot and was thankful to find her feet were still unbound. But to where could she run?

...suffer with heroic constancy the cruel martyrdom ordered by Diocletian in the beginning of his reign...

Escape. If she had the strength to stand she could try to run, perhaps hide or defend herself some way. But she'd have to open her eyes, she'd have to see what she didn't want to see.

...and was flayed alive thus receiving her crown from the hands of Christ.

Cate, trembling, turned her bruised face ever so slightly and opened her eyes a slit. Candles and votives burned everywhere, their light steady and unwavering.

It was a cross-beam the priest had hammered together in the shape of an X.

Where am I?

A wench and pulley hung from the ceiling anchor of a grand chandelier that now lay in dusty smithereens on the floor.

What is this place? Cate struggled to fit the jig-saw pieces together.

Dry-rotted, velvet drapes hung against trompe l'oeil windows. Overhead was a fresco of gold stars on a field of peeling blue. And carefully laid out across the lid of a grand piano was an array of butcher's tools.

Escape.

Her kidnapper stood quietly, just staring at her expressionlessly, as if he were the one wondering what would happen next. Then he grunted and turned away.

Cate continued to survey the space she was in and finally saw something which gave her heart. Train tracks and a tunnel entrance. She saw clearly now that this was a subway stop, an abandoned station.

Across the room the priest gathered a length of rope from a pile on the floor. This was her chance; she saw he was occupied cutting the rope into arm-length pieces. His back was to her.

Down the tracks, inside the tunnel, somewhere to run, to hide—

Cate took a deep breath then leapt to her feet. In less than a second he was on her. She hadn't gotten three feet, before he'd bounded ten and had her by the back of her neck in his crushing grip. Cate tried to wrench herself free, kicking at him uselessly. He pulled her toward him and gripped her neck harder. The pain was paralyzing. She reared back, grunting like an animal, ready to attack his face with her teeth and nails. She no longer feared him; she hated him, *hated* him with a fury she hadn't known existed. It coursed through her like an explosive chemical. He tightened his grip on her neck and she was stupefied with pain.

His face was pinched like a snake's, black eyes wide, glassy, his focus on her so concentrated he twitched. An unbidden thought took hold of her now. She whispered, as so many others had before her, *just let me die quickly.*

He pressed her down, forcing her head toward the floor, the floor Cate could see clearly now. Her eyes darted taking it in like powerful uppercuts: small puddles of fly-blown blood everywhere, footprints and drag marks, bits of bloody pulp and bone chips. It was the killing floor of a human slaughterhouse.

Cate dropped like dead weight and he lost his hold on her sweaty neck. She tried to scramble away through the gore, on her elbows and knees, but he caught the back of her hair and yanked her, screaming, to her feet again. He grabbed excitedly in his pocket for the chloroform rag.

Cate arched and twisted in his grip. She screamed differently now, in that dark, forgotten place. She cried out the only prayer she had left in her. *God, oh God! Help me—*

FIFTY-NINE

A bie followed Noah across the freight train tracks where the ground was loosely packed dirt, smooth and undisturbed by foot traffic except for a single trampled path leading to the farthest wall. It was a carefully constructed brick wall, old and sturdy. Here the disturbance to the dirt on the ground was chaotic.

Noah lowered his torch and saw what he was looking for. A boulder on the ground partly obscured a small burrow chiseled through the brick. The opening was barely shoulder-wide. Noah dropped to his knees and thrust his torch into the entrance.

"Come on," he said standing up and slipping off his haversack. "It's only a a couple of feet to the other side." First Noah, then Abie got down on all fours and cautiously slid into the hole. They crawled on their bellies to the other side and found themselves in a concrete room.

"What's this place?" Abie asked. He brushed at his damp clothes crusted in grime. Noah lifted his torch. What they saw was a room-size apparatus encasing an enormous fan.

"What is it?" Abie asked. "Some kind of ventilator?"

"Sort of," Noah said. He used his elbow to wipe the dust off the manufacturer's plate. *Roots Patent Force Blast Blower.*

"*Force Blast Blower?*" Abie asked. "Like a pneumatic fan. Maybe an early experimental type? The thing must weigh ten tons."

"More like fifty tons," Noah said. "Come on." He

squeezed past the huge fan and into a long narrow concrete shaft where they had to pass in a bent duck walk.

"I think this is the fan's air flue," Noah said.

"Some kind of utility?" Abie asked inching along in a crouch.

Noah was silent a moment until the flue opened into a cylindrical brick tube less than ten feet wide. Down the center ran a single set of railroad track. The ties were mostly rotted into the brick track bed; but the rails and spikes looked as durable as they must have when they'd been laid forty-two years before.

"Hear that?" Abie asked. He pointed upward and cocked his head to listen. "That's traffic up there. Listen— Horns. And horses!"

"We're only about twelve feet down. Ever hear of Alfred Ely Beach?" Noah asked.

"Yeah. A bit before my time. An eccentric inventor, supposed to have secretly built a subway somewhere. Just to show Tammany Hall it could be done. You thinking this—?"

"Do you recall how it was powered?" Noah asked in a hushed voice as they crept along, their backs to the tubular wall.

"Some cockeyed idea, what was it? Some kind of—*That was it!* Back there. A giant pneumatic fan—

"So, it's true. How come you know so much about it? Even most New Yorkers now never heard of it or think it's some kind of myth."

"Not a myth. Just neglected and forgotten," Noah said. "The City Engineer's office thinks they have the location fixed at Broadway between Murray and Warren. That's pretty much where we are. I was supposed to scout the location. They want to run the BRT Broadway Line through here. I was sacked before the assignment started."

Noah stopped to look back at Abie then down the tunnel ahead of them to a tall pile of crumbling wood. "There it is, what's left of Beach's subway car," Noah said. He squinted beyond the rubble. "Abie, look there. It's lit up ahead!"

"I don't see any light."

"Put your torch down."

Abie set his torch on the ground for a moment and

stepped into the middle of the track bed. "Yeah. You're right. There's some kind of glow ahead."

Noah moved at a quicker step than before. Not wanting to lose the element of surprise, he dropped his torch to the ground as the glimmer at the end of the tube increased. He pulled his knife from its sheath and was already at a dead run when he heard the shrill cry of a woman.

"—*God. Help me!*"

"Let'er go!" Noah bellowed as he sprinted out of the tunnel.

The priest flung Cate directly in Noah's path, and ran like the devil in the opposite direction. At the far end, where the station and track bed ended, a smaller opening in the station wall swallowed him in a dark gulp.

Noah heard Abie yell as he, too, ran as best he could into the station, waving his firebrand.

"The son of a bitch is getting away!" Abie hollered, but Noah was kneeling by Cate, who was struggling to her feet trying also to flee.

She didn't see Noah, only the knife in his hand, and tried to run on legs too abused to obey. Cate collapsed but continued to crawl across the floor like a worm inching through muck.

It's me, Cate, Noah whispered setting the knife on the ground. Noah spoke to her like someone coaxing a jumper from a very high ledge. "It's Noah. You're safe now. We found you—"

"You've got to kill him!" Cate cried hoarsely. Her mouth and chin were blistered from the chloroform; blood dried in her nostrils.

Noah slowly picked up his knife and carefully cut Cate's hands free. He rubbed her wrists and attempted to put his arm around her, but she was too agitated and wouldn't be comforted.

"You've got to go after him and *kill* him!" she insisted snatching her hands from his. "Go after him—!"

"Noah, you better come look at this," Abie called from the passage entrance where the priest had fled.

"We're getting out of here, as fast as we can, the same way we came in! Cate needs medical attention," Noah said.

"*No!*" Cate screamed. She pushed against his chest.

"You've got to follow him! Kill him," she insisted hysterically. "He's a monster! An evil, *evil* monster."

"Noah, there's wires everywhere," Abie said holding his torch down low. "What are all these wires? You better look at this."

Reluctantly Noah turned his attention toward Abie, and then abruptly pulled Cate along as he raced to the spot where Abie stood.

"Quick! In there," Noah shouted pushing and dragging them into the tunnel. Scarcely a second later a percussive wave at their backs knocked them to the ground as a series of explosions erupted caving-in the station and the way back, behind them.

SIXTY

O'Keeffe halted when he heard the blast. He wondered that construction would be going on so late, then assumed double-shifts were in place to make political hay before election day. O'Keeffe's skiff had finally run aground where the conduit ended and the last of the water was absorbed by a cavernous expanse of what looked to be dry loam. The smell was horrific. Decades of decaying, organic waste from street runoff formed a noxious murk that hung visibly in the air. All around him the high walls of ice age rock formed a natural grotto

.

O'Keeffe swung his flashlight, seeking a way forward and out, and disturbed what roosted high above him. Thousands of hog-nosed bats frenzied, flapping their hideously webbed forelimbs. Their screech was earsplitting as O'Keeffe desperately waved his arms to fend them off until he finally had presence of mind enough to switch off his flashlight. After a minute more, the bats settled to roost again. They hung upside down, enfolded in their wings like little men in opera capes, their yellow eyes never leaving the intruder who'd stumbled into their midst.

Sweat and blood from his scalp trickled into O'Keeffe's eyes stinging them badly. His pawing only made it worse. He was parched now too, from so much exertion. He needed water. Perhaps he could make it back to the skiff, back to where water flowed. Wash his hands and eyes in the runoff. Couldn't *drink* that water though, he realized, so what was the point, even if he could stumble blindly back? He stood frozen like an etching, unable to return or move ahead.

O'Keeffe opened his fly and exposed himself. He carefully relieved his bladder on first his left, then right hand. He shook his hands dry and wiped them on his sleeves. Now he could gently flick the bat dust and dirt from eyes, and wipe away blood and sweat with his shirt cuff.

The policeman stood squinting into pitch blackness. He adjusted himself, picked up his flashlight and, careful to point it away from the roosting bats, switched it on again.

That was when he saw something moving among the big, craggy rocks ten yards ahead. A flash of black. Perhaps just a swooping bat. O'Keeffe slowly raised the beam of his light laterally sweeping the rocks ahead. He saw it again. Something moved. He could hear the little shower of stones as the man, and what else could it be, leapt from rock to rock. O'Keeffe pulled his Webley and cocked the hammer.

"Show yourself," he demanded. Another small shower of stones fell among the boulders. O'Keeffe trained the flashlight beam along the sandy ground in front of him. It was flat and even, dotted here and there with stagnate pools of water.

He realized he was a sitting duck in the open space of the grotto. He crouched and moved ahead quickly. Now muck sucked at his shoes. With the next step he sank in a puddle of water to his ankles and cursed under his breath. He stepped ahead to what looked to be firmer ground and instead found himself now up to his knees in foul, putrid water. The slimy mud at the bottom released his shoes only with his strenuous effort, but after the next step sucked his shoe and sock from his foot. The slime was thick and warm between his toes.

When with his next step, the sludge gave way beneath his feet, O'Keeffe felt the first stab of real fear. He was sometimes a brave man. Now he steeled himself against panic. Panic would not kill Dermot O'Keeffe, he vowed.

He was sunk in water only to his waist, but the underlying layer of muck immediately encased him to his knees. He realized it was possibly a sinkhole. How deep or far around he had no idea.

Again he heard pebbles sifting from the boulders above, closer now. O'Keeffe stood as still as a salt pillar. Very slowly, so as not to shift his weight abruptly, he raised his right knee and allowed muck to gently ooze down underfoot. As that firmed up the hole, he lifted his left foot and did the same. After repeating this three times, the pool was again only ankle-deep and he'd gained enough purchase to move forward.

He brought his two hands together and gripped the Webley and the flashlight straight out in front of him. The beam danced from rock to rock but never high enough to rouse the bats again. He saw no one in the fast bounces of light until he just glanced a face ducking behind a rock. He fired off a round but too late, realized the reverberation would rouse the restless bats again. They flew in all directions like a plague.

O'Keeffe's arms flailed as he beat the squeaking animals from his face. He lunged forward and was immediately mired to his waist in fluid mud. The water floating on top rose to his Adam's apple. Only his head and hands were clearly above water. Now there was no remnant of bravery in him.

"Throw away your gun," a calm voice said from just above.

"Help," O'Keeffe bleated. "Whoever's there, help me. I won't shoot you, I swear "

"Throw away your gun and relax. Relax and in a few minutes you'll begin to float on top the water."

"I'm tossing the gun, see," he said. O'Keeffe's revolver fell with a thud near the rocks less than a yard away. Now the voice from behind the rocks stood in plain view. His clothes were brown with grimy dust and dirt. Only a fragment of his celluloid collar identified him as a cleric.

"Father. You have to help me, Father. And, a good Catholic I am, too. Just—if you could just climb down a bit and stretch out your arm, Father." The priest scrambled over several large rocks until he loomed right above the wide-eyed panicked face.

Fearing to move anything but his fingertips O'Keeffe waved at the air like a child after a sweet on too high a shelf. The priest descended slower, never stepping from the firm bed of rocks. O'Keeffe begged again and the priest stretched out his arm. Cautiously, his fingers wrapped around the butt of the discarded hand gun.

"Help me. For Gawd's sake and all the saints—" A surge of terror made O'Keeffe lurch and he tasted the first splash of fetid water. It was surprisingly greasy. He held his head back bringing his chin just to the water's surface. He dared not open his mouth to speak again.

The priest stood examining the Webley in the beam of the flashlight, which O'Keeffe still clutched like straw, above the water. O'Keeffe's eyes followed the priest's every movement, wide and terrified. He looked almost relieved when the priest pointed the weapon square at the center of his forehead. The priest suddenly raised his aim and fired three fast rounds into the overhead. The bats frenzied with such fury the priest had to take cover on the ground between the boulders.

When he stood, all that could be seen of O'Keeffe was his quivering hand clutching the flashlight, and the smallest little island of forehead and hair. In a moment more, all went black as his hand finally stilled and the flashlight slipped underwater.

The priest needed no light in his cathedral. He turned and mounted two city blocks of boulders as sure-footedly as a billy goat leaping, even as his heart leapt, with gratitude and joy in his chest. Once again, through the divine intervention of his saints, he had survived. He was the most blessed of men. He approached his hidden alcove shrine on his knees, joyfully singing the *Te Deum Laudamus*. Here was light enough, a candle burning at every rocky niche. And here, too, his prizes, his protectors, his invincibility. He sang praises to their names before a head in a bell jar, a pair of breasts resting on a silver salver, a pair of eyeballs on a gold plate. The flayed skin of a woman in framed glass. Hands and feet and bloody organs encased in a dozen glass reliquaries like jewel cases. He prayed and praised them and thanked his divine intermediaries for having again saved him from what would have been his downfall.

Once again, he was saved in this life as surely he would be in the next. Just so long as the flames—*the flames! Don't think about the flames* his relics called to him in angelic voices. *The Serpent shall not have you.* They whispered sweet reassurances and told him there was only one *more* they wished to join them. One more task and he'd be safe to return to the upper world where none could ever gainsay him. One he must still go back for.

SIXTY-ONE

Noah, Abie and Cate lay face down in the dirt passage. Behind them, Beach's station was a smoking cave-in. Noah was the first up; he moved quickly to Cate. When Abie began to struggle to his feet coughing, Noah said, your torch—don't let it go out, and Abie scrambled for it.

"Keep your eyes open for Costello," Noah warned. "He could be anywhere." He pulled the canteen from his backpack, then slapped Cate's cheeks gently bringing some color back to her face. She mumbled a little and Noah held her upright trying to get her to swallow a bit of water.

Finally, Cate opened and closed her eyes several times, then took a gulp of water from his canteen. Only then did she seem able to focus a bit.

"Noah!" she wailed and clutched him lest he suddenly disappear. That's when the tears came unleashed, great racking sobs of pain and relief.

"Shhh," he said holding her, rocking back and forth. "You're safe. I've got you now. We'll get you out of here. To a hospital."

"Don't leave me!" Cate begged. "Please, don't—"

"I won't leave you, Cate. I promise," he assured her. "I will never leave you."

"Noah, can she walk?" Abie sounded panicky. "We've got to get out of here. That maniac could have this whole passage booby-trapped with dynamite."

Noah pulled Cate's hair back from her face and dusted some of the grime from her skin. "Do you think you can stand?" he asked feeling her arms and legs for injury.

"I think so," she said. "I'll try." Noah slowly stood with his arm around her. "Easy," he said. "Are you hurt anywhere?"

On her feet, Cate felt a little of her assurance return. "I hurt *every*where," she grimaced, "but I think I'm all right. I can walk. Are you going to follow him?" she asked urgently. "He's got to be stopped, Noah."

Noah took a good look at their surroundings. "I think this was Alfred Beach's staging area; the way his crew moved the machinery in and out in secret. There must be a way out up ahead. Let's hope Costell took it."

"So, we should get going," Abie said emphatically.

"Not that way," Noah said. "We're *not* following him."

Noah led Cate to a spot where she could sit with her back against the tunnel wall. He set the canteen by her hip then pulled out his pickaxe. He hefted its weight in his hand, then tossed his Bowie knife to Abie who gratefully wrapped his fingers around its handle.

"I'm just going over there to look at the entrance," he said calmly to Cate. "To see if there's a way out, over the rubble."

"But he's getting away," Abie said.

"Look at your torch," Noah said." Abie was holding little more than a stub of root threatening to burn out with each flicker. Abie realized that when the flame died they'd be plunged into a darkness from which they had no hope of remedy, completely at the mercy of the madman who was somewhere up ahead of them.

"You really want to go after him?" Noah asked.

"So—what *do* we do?" Abie asked.

"We stay here. We stay calm." Noah positioned himself at the top of the rubble heap blocking their escape. He pulled some of the top rocks from the pile blocking their side of the entrance. "A sizable chunk of Broadway just imploded up there," he said. Already they could hear urgent shouts and the clanging of approaching alarms above. "Hear that; rescue's on the way.

Get ready to start yelling for help. Meanwhile, we just need to hope that madman doesn't come back to finish us off before it gets here."

SIXTY-TWO

The hoopla began. Minutes after the underground explosion, a crowd of gawkers swarmed around the gaping hole at Broadway and Warren Street. The police roped off Broadway between Murray and Warren, and firemen from Engine Company No. 6 trained their hoses into the smoking ruin.

Traffic slowly backed up in both directions from Wall Street to the Bowery; and it was discovered a significant portion of the tip of Manhattan was now without electrical service.

Press photographers had a heyday as rescuers made their way down into Beach's demolished station amidst shouts of *someone's yelling down there.* It took a brigade of city workers and volunteers a little more than an hour to dig through enough rubble to pull Cate, Abie and Noah to safety.

On hand, by that time, was Mayor Gaynor, who made a short speech and posed for press photographs with the battered and hapless victims.

Police Commissioner Rhinlander Waldo hailed the trio as lucky not to have been blown to Kingdom Come, and saw to it they were quickly hustled away by police: Cate in an ambulance to Bellevue Hospital, Noah and Abie to the grotesquely baroque, police headquarters at 240 Centre Street.

As yet, the public knew nothing of Father Costello or his mayhem. The letter of alarm, promised by Monsignor Palladin in *The Morning Messenger,* had not appeared. By noon, however, every city daily had an extra on the street reporting the mysterious implosion at Broadway and Warren Street, the dramatic rescue of two men and a woman from an underground passage, and most fantastical of all, the re-discovery of Alfred Ely Beach's fabled subway station.

The story had everything, including a hint of scandal once the police identified Cate to the press as the recently convicted Catherine S. Gallagher, notorious Greenwich Village birth control advocate, and author of a pamphlet whose title could not be re-printed in the pages of a reputable newspaper.

The identity of her two male companions was being withheld by police, pending investigation of any possible criminal violations. What they were doing, slinking about in the sewers of New York, setting off explosives, endangering the lives of citizens, was yet to be determined, announced Waldo's stooge, Deputy Commissioner Dougherty. Although, it most likely had to do with unearthing the old, legendary subway station, as one of the gentlemen was a known journalist and the other an archaeologist.

Nevertheless, that the adventurous trio might be in league with foreign anarchists would not go uninvestigated: so Deputy Dougherty reassured the public via the press.

Abie and Noah were released, without charges, ten minutes after *Post* publisher Oswald Villard showed up at police headquarters with an attorney bearing two writs of habeas corpus.

Abie lost no time getting to his office in Villard's car, while Noah stayed to give police his detailed statement. He repeated the recitation of events from the Nicolosi girl's disappearance, to the explosion in Beach's station: first to a police captain, then to Deputy Police Commissioner Dougherty, who decided the sooner Noah Goodwin was out of headquarters the better. Noah received a stern admonition not to discuss the case with the press.

Noah made the same promise to Dougherty he'd made to Abie. Not a single reporter got a word out of Noah as he sped out of police headquarters and into the snarl of traffic on foot.

When he got to the hospital, Cate was under heavy

sedation and deep asleep. Noah sat and held her hand and occasionally nodded off in an exhausted doze.

Lemuel came to the hospital on his lunch hour, but didn't see Cate because children weren't allowed. Noah came down to the lobby and thanked him for coming. The boy was excited about something he'd discovered on his own in the *Post's* morgue files, just like a real reporter.

It took Noah awhile to decide what to make of Lemuel's discovery, then decided to make nothing of it before he could speak with Abie.

Abie came a few hours later. His editorial was filed, part one of a series. The latest news: the discovery of the body of New York cop, Lt. Dermot O'Keeffe, killed in the line of duty. He'd lumbered into quicksand down there and drowned himself, Abie said. No loss to humanity. Abie popped a piece of Dentyne in his mouth.

"Governor Dix is threatening to send in state troopers if the Fire Pit Killer isn't caught soon; Waldo's cancelled all vacations and off-days to put close to five hundred uniforms into the manhunt. Personally, I don't think he could find his own ass if it were on fire."

After another hour, Abie said goodnight; he was heading home to Henry Street and sleep. They hugged as kids do when summer camp is over. Abie remembered to give Noah back his Bowie knife.

"You lied to me," Noah said as a matter of fact. "It wasn't about the dead women at all. Not really. It was about Gaynor."

Abie looked quizzical for a moment, and then nodded.

"Your brother's drowning was no simple accident. The boys from the high school, from Saint Boniface— Gaynor was the judge who let those boys off. The ones who roughed up your brother, pushed him in the river, let your brother drown."

"My brother." Abie stared at the ground. "Horseplay, Gaynor called it," Abie said. "How'd you find out?"

"The kid. Lemuel. Found the story in a press morgue clipping. Maybe there's a good reason you didn't want me to know what really happened."

"There is." Abie pulled out a cheroot and lit it. "They *shamed* us. Gaynor and those boys. Do you know what shame is? Dehumanization. I didn't want you to know how hurt—how much they damaged me." Abie puffed a large cloud of smoke. "I'm glad you know, though. Someone should know. It was about all of that: the living and the dead. It's done now," Abie said flicking ashes to the ground.

Noah offered him a lift home but Abie declined. "Think I'll take the subway," he said. "See who's reading the *Post*."

Sgt. Simonov came by twice, said little and wandered out again. There was a telegram from Mrs. Stanton Blatch, and a telephone message saying Cate's father and brothers would be there by morning; but there was nothing from Monsignor Palladin.

A worried Noah sat and watched Cate sleep until the strictly enforced visiting hours ended, and a dragoon of a nurse named Blomqvist insisted he leave. He unwillingly did.

When Noah stepped onto First Avenue, newsboys were hawking the headlines of the *New York Evening Post*:

CRAZED KILLER AT LARGE
CHURCHMAN ACCUSED
TAMMANEY COVER UP
Eyewitness Account of Kidnap Pursuit,
Mayhem & Attempted Murder
Series Part I
by
Abraham B. Kahn

No one knew it yet, but Abie's series would toll the death knell for New York's Democratic Party machine for the next two election cycles, after which Tammany Hall would never fully recover.

Noah bought a paper and three hot dogs with everything from a street cart, and headed back into the hospital lobby to finally get some shuteye.

SIXTY-THREE

As uncomfortable as the lobby chairs were, Noah slept hard across three of them. He went mostly unnoticed as the traffic through the city's only night hospital increased. Once, after midnight, a nurse had fluttered around him while he slept. She covered him with a spare patient blanket.

When Noah woke, it was the lull between the nighttime rush and the morning-shift change. Noah stretched and wandered into the deserted corridor in search of the men's lavatory.

He looked in the sink mirror and saw how badly he needed a wash, a shave, and a change of clothes. It would be another three hours before visiting hours resumed. Noah considered retrieving the Cadillac, and heading to the NYU faculty digs he was still making use of. But when he saw how empty all the corridors were, he decided to chance slipping into Cate's room unnoticed.

Noah walked unseen to the stairwell and up three flights. He slipped past the nurse's station where two figures in starched white head veils were busy stacking charts.

Along the corridor, the patients' doors were all ajar. It was silent as a blank sheet of paper, here and there writ with a moan, an alarming snore, a conversation being held in hushed tones.

Noah saw the conversation wasn't coming from Cate's room and was relieved. It was the room just before hers. An early morning doctor making rounds probably. As Noah passed, he could see Mr. Nicolosi seated beside his daughter's bed. He and Seraphia were both listening raptly to another figure in the room. Noah stopped in his tracks when he saw it was a priest.

He gently pushed the door farther open and spoke to Mr. Nicolosi. "I hope you remember me, sir," he said. "I helped find your daughter."

Mr. Nicolosi was startled to see Noah, but immediately rose to shake his hand heartily.

"I'll take my leave of you, now," the priest said stepping from a shadow.

"Ah, this is," Mr. Nicolosi said gesturing to the priest, "Father Elbi, who has come from Cardinale Bernardo."

"*Bernardo*—from Cardinal Bernard," Noah said. "At four in the morning?"

"You will excuse me," Father Elbi said, waiting for Noah to clear the doorway. "Or I shall be late for *Lauds*."

"Of course, Father," Noah said. "I was just wondering, about Monsignor Palladin—"

"Yes?" Elbi asked tersely.

"I was just wondering, if you could tell him, for me, I'll be stopping by to see him later. My name's Goodwin. If you could let him know."

"As a matter of fact, I cannot," Father Elbi said. His smirk was poorly masked. "His Holiness has recalled Monsignor Palladin to Rome. He sailed four hours ago."

Noah attempted to hide his dismay. "Well, that was swiftly done."

"The miracle of modern telegraphy," Father Elbi said, as he pushed past Noah. He turned in the doorway and held Seraphia and her father with a long gaze before tracing the gesture of benediction in the air. With a curt nod to Noah, Father Elbi swept down the corridor.

Noah turned to the girl and her father. "Is everything O.K.? You look a little scared," he said.

"*Che significa*, scared?" Mr. Nicolosi asked Seraphia.

"Reassure your father," Noah went on. "Tell him, the one who took you—Father Costello—the police know who he is.

They will find him. You needn't be afraid."

Seraphia began to translate, then stopped suddenly. "Father Costello? No. He is not the one," Seraphia said with her eyes wide in fear. "It was another man. Not Father Costello."

Seraphia paused a moment to explain to her father in Italian what they were saying. Mr. Nicolosi gasped and crossed himself.

"Not Father Costello," he said as Seraphia had, and wagged his finger in Noah's face. "No," he said again.

"Father Costello is my friend," the girl whimpered. "He brings candy for us sometimes when he visits us. And a dolly for my little sister once." Seraphia was clearly upset at the idea Father Costello was being accused. "You have to believe me," she said on the verge of tears.

Noah was taken aback. "I believe you, I do. But, you know—Miss Gallagher, she helped find you, too. And, and someone hurt her, as well. She's next door, in the next room. Did you know that Seraphia?"

"She is? I didn't know," the girl said sadly. "Is she going to be all right?"

"Yes. Yes, she is. She's sleeping now, I'm sure. But when she wakes up, the police will come, and she'll have to tell them it was Father Costello."

"But, *I* can't tell!" the girl insisted breaking into tears, followed by a flood of Italian to her father. Mr. Nicolosi stood and addressed Noah. "Go, *per favore*," he said not ungently. Seraphia will sleep, *subito*. No more *agita*, heh. O.K.? *Per favore, Signore*. I will take a good care now. Me," he said with his hand over his heart.

"Of course, yes, she should rest," Noah said backing out of the room. He wondered for a moment, was it possible Monsignor Palladin had been wrong. Had Father O'Malley lied. Palladin was sure Costello was the kidnapper, but only because the old priest had said so.

Noah was disturbed by Father Elbi's visit, and Seraphia's absolute insistence Father Costello had not been the one who snatched her. Noah didn't believe it, yet he himself couldn't swear it was Costello. All he and Abie had seen in Beach's station was a figure in black running away in the dark. Seraphia had seen— Had seen a man dressed as a nun! Perhaps she really hadn't recognized him. Or, more likely, perhaps this priest, Father Elbi, had intimidated the girl and her father into silence.

But Cate had been trapped with him for hours. With the Monsignor shipped off to Rome, and the Nicolosi girl's denial, only Cate was left to reliably identify Father Costello as her abductor.

The hospital ward was waking up; there was a nurse pushing a patient in a wheelchair up the hall, and another arriving with a cart of medicines to be dosed out. There were baleful moans from two rooms. Someone was calling for help and someone else for a bedpan. Gradually, there were nurses everywhere.

Noah was uneasy. He hurried to Cate's door and rushed in. Something was wrong. The nurse by her bed was frantic; Cate was coughing and heaving badly. The nurse had pulled the pillow from under her head and was laying her flat.

"I'll get oxygen," the nurse said. "Stay with her. Keep her flat," she said as she headed out the door.

Noah took Cate's hand and bent low to hear what she was trying to say, —*smother me. That nurse. Costello.* Noah dropped Cate's hand and rushed to the door. He hollered for help needed in room 409.

Two nurses and an orderly immediately ran toward Noah, while a third nurse kept rushing toward the open elevator doors. Noah sprinted down the hall but not in time to stop the nurse from pulling the grate closed and pushing the lever to *down*.

Noah banged on the closed grate but could do nothing as he watched the cage descend and the arrow indicator drop to the third, then second floor.

"Room 409! Now!" he shouted at the nurses' station. "Call the police!"

SIXTY-FOUR

Noah bolted into the stairwell, and leaped down the steps three, four at a time. At the first floor, he raced into the lobby, but by the time he reached the elevator doors, the lift was passing to the unmarked level beneath the main floor.

"Call the police," he shouted again at the admissions desk. He darted back to the stairs, and down the last flight. Noah rushed out of the stairwell, and found himself in the one hundred seventy-six year old hospital's basement where the city morgue was located.

He was instantly wary. He pulled his knife from its sheath and crept along the dark, back corridor. The only light was from the elevator standing open and empty. Opposite the elevator was a swinging door that had not entirely settled.

Noah pushed the door open with his foot and went in slowly. His eyes adjusted to the dark and he saw light fixtures overhead with hanging pull chains. He knew to kill a snake you had to grab it by the head. He'd flush Costello out the way you would an animal. Noah pulled a light on, making himself a lure.

The white tile room was empty except for a gurney and some enamel cabinets. Through the glass front of a cabinet, Noah saw an array of nickel steel autopsy tools: scalpels, saws, oversized scissors, hammers, forceps, and other instruments he couldn't even guess at.

He picked up something which looked like a long, slender breadknife, except, instead of a serrated edge, its blade was razor sharp. It was twice the length of his own knife. Perfect for taking the head off a man-sized serpent. Noah wrapped his handkerchief around his sweaty palm before grasping the knife handle firmly.

Keeping his eyes on the open door in front of him, he walked to the next cabinet. Nothing useful there. Then, one more to check, more like a pantry. He tugged on the door and suddenly it was on him, knocking him back, and spilling out the body of Nurse Blomqvist. She was stripped of her uniform and headdress. A ligature was tight around her purple neck.

Noah saw in an instant she was dead, and immediately returned his focus to the frozen shadows in the next room. Nothing moved, no shadow stirred.

He reached up quickly, pulled the light off, and rushed the entrance using the gurney as a barrier. As soon as he was in, he grabbed a dangling chain and pulled on the light, revealing Father Costello was cornered in a room with no exit. His body, grotesquely dressed in the dead nurse's clothes and starched hair veil, was coiled on the floor, head down in a submissive pose.

"Don't hurt me," he groveled. "You mustn't hurt me. I've done nothing."

"Don't move," Noah said, and stomped down on the side of the man's head. He held the long knife in one hand like a scimitar. Suddenly, Costello jerked his arm and stabbed Noah with a scalpel, clean through the backside of his knee bringing him down like a house of cards.

Costello scrambled out from under Noah, and grabbed the long knife from Noah's fist. He raised it with two hands over Noah's head, ready to strike, and grunted loudly.

Noah reacted slowly looking up to see Mr. Ercole Nicolosi's prosthetic hand clamped on the back of Costello's neck, lifting him until his toes danced on the floor.

"I kill him now," Mr. Nicolosi said. His eyes were clear and focused. "I say so and I do it. I am nota scared of these *sacerdoti*. I break his neck."

Costello was rigid with pain and his eyes bulged horribly.

"Don't do it," Noah shouted. He twisted himself up onto one knee but couldn't manage to stand. "Listen to me. Senior Nicolosi, who will take care of your children? They're going to go to school. What will happen to them if you go to prison?"

"I do a father's duty—"

"This man is my prisoner," Sgt. Simonov said stepping in ahead of a small crowd of orderlies and nurses. The sergeant drew his service revolver and placed the muzzle against Costello's temple. He cocked the hammer.

"Set him loose now, please," he said to Mr. Nicolosi gravely.

Slowly, Mr. Nicolosi released his grip on the deranged priest and took a step back. "I am nota scared of these priests no more," he said again.

"It's all over, people," Sgt. Simonov announced. "You there," he said to a burly orderly. "Put these on him." Simonov pulled manacles from his belt.

The orderly expertly took the whimpering Costello to the floor with a nerve pinch and then cuffed him behind his back. Sgt. Simonov holstered his pistol. He nodded back at the sprawled body of Nurse Blomqvist. "She's dead," he said. "Don't touch her 'til the coroner gets here."

Simonov bent low over Noah and slipped his arm under Noah's shoulder lifting him onto his good leg. "I think you had the angels on your side, this time," he said to Noah matter-of-factly.

Noah braced himself between Simonov and an orderly who lifted him onto the gurney. "That's one way of looking at it," Noah said wincing, then grinning. "A fine way, actually. Angels on my side."

EPILOGUE

Noah's leg required surgery but healed well after that. He managed smoothly on crutches for the next couple of weeks. The university was happy to have him stay on and recuperate, and suggested he might wish to consider a staff position. He didn't.

Cate used the Cadillac, as Noah couldn't drive, and it made it convenient to get back and forth between the Family Aid office and NYU. She was doing so much driving she felt obligated to get licensed.

She and Noah went to City Hall where drivers' licenses were issued, and Noah suggested they get a marriage license, as long as they were there.

Cate laughed it off until he hobbled over on his crutches, and stood in that line. When Cate had registered as a New York State driver she joined Noah and tugged at his arm. "What are you doing?" she asked.

"Waiting in line.

"But this is ridiculous."

Noah convinced her, ridiculous or not, they should get a license, and just look at it for a while, put it on her mantel and decide if they liked the way it looked.

Meanwhile, a New York Supreme Court judge ordered Father Costello to undergo thirty days observation at the state asylum on Blackwell's Island. The Cardinal's new chancellor, Father Urs Elbi was given permission to visit him there, and brought all the sacerdotal items for hearing his Confession and celebrating a Mass in Costello's small padded cell.

The next morning, Father Costello was found dead; there was glass in his mouth from the tiny ampoule of cyanide someone had passed to him. Much to the relief of many people, there would be no trial.

Then came election day. "Big Tim" Sullivan won his election to the Senate as promised, but before he could take office, Abie Kahn reported on the following events: At a dinner honoring Sullivan as Catholic Layman of the Year, his paranoid, syphilitic delusions permanently got the better of him. Sullivan insisted his food had been poisoned and tried to stab the Cardinal's chancellor, Father Elbi.

On August 31, 1913, "Big Tim" escaped custodial confinement. Early the next morning he was run over by a train in Eastchester. The train's engineer testified that Sullivan, laying across the tracks, appeared to be dead before the train struck him. The press, including Abie, cried foul play. The Bronx coroner declared it a suicide and closed the case.

Police Commissioner Waldo, having captured the Fire Pit Killer, rode the crest of a brief wave. Tammany Hall was again in favor, and hurrah for the red, white and blue was heard throughout the land. But on November 5th, the splinter Progressive Party swept into office taking not only the Presidency, but the entire New York state ticket including the office of Governor, Lieutenant Governor, Secretary of State, Comptroller, Treasurer and State Engineer.

Mayor Gaynor, and his appointees: Police Commissioner Waldo, Deputy Commissioner Dougherty, and Manhattan Coroner Hellenstein all managed to dodged the political abyss, until fate stepped in.

Mayor Gaynor had assumed office in 1910 and had yet another two years to his term. On September 10, 1913, Gaynor's son Rufus found him dead of heart failure in a deckchair, aboard the steamship *Baltic*. It was a family vacation off the coast of Ireland. A death mask was made, and the body was shipped home aboard the RMS *Lusitania*.

On January 1, 1914, John Purroy Mitchel was sworn in to replace Gaynor as Mayor of New York City. Mitchel was a reformist. The first to go were Commissioner Waldo and his deputy, in a hail of investigative charges.

Waldo lived off his wife's fortune for the next thirteen years before drinking himself to death. The death certificate said *septicemia*.

Coroner Herman Hellenstein's multiple, grisly charges were held up for particular scrutiny by the public. The newspapers tagged him *a ghoul*. He was the last man without a medical degree to hold the post of Manhattan coroner.

By the end of November, Noah was sufficiently healed and able to travel. He could stay away from his work in India no longer. His father would have insisted he go, now that the rains had passed. He and Cate looked at the marriage license sitting on the mantel every day for weeks. Every day, it lost a little of its allure. In the end, it was just a piece of paper.

What grew instead, was a kind of shelter, which enveloped them. Whatever it was, it existed whenever and wherever they were together. Soon, neither of them could imagine stepping outside the shelter of each other.

But, he had to go and she had to stay. What they had spent their lives building was on two separate continents. They didn't talk about this dilemma; it was already well understood by each of them.

Noah cranked the gramophone and set the needle to a recording. The premiere of Mahler's *Symphony #1* slid like moonlight into the bedroom.

Noah told her stories about other women. He said there are over three-hundred million women in India; millions die in childbirth every year.

"That's a terrible number," Cate said.

"Old women tell young women to use crocodile dung and honey for birth control."

"You know, that's actually an effective contraceptive, which primitive women have used for centuries—" she said.

"In the far flung villages, Moslim mothers perform circumcisions on their daughters."

"It's horrible. I've seen it here, in the Ethiopian community." Cate looked sad.

"A girl who shames her family can be doused in pitch, set on fire, and nothing will ever be said."

"Please don't tell me anymore," she said.

"I have twenty-four thousand dollars in the bank."

From the Victrola speaker horn, a hundred and four musical instruments converged into eight octaves of harmonics. It was sheer Heaven.

The next day, Cate arranged with Mrs. Stanton Blatch to announce to the suffrage community: Cate would be moving up to President of the Family Aid Society. She intended to open the Society's first women's shelter overseas, in India, where the need is greatest.

Nurse Dora Adler will assume the position of Director of the Family Aid Society, immediately. It is to be a salaried position, thanks to a small endowment from an anonymous donor.

A week later Noah and Cate were married at St. Cecilia's by Father Leoni. Eventually, they would become the parents of eight children, whom they would raise on several continents.

As for Monsignor Palladin, he was subsumed into the inner workings of the Vatican. The events that transpired in New York City were never discussed with him by anyone. It was as though nothing had ever happened.

AUTHOR'S NOTE

The Death of Saints is historically accurate, although the story is fictional. The saints and their martyrdoms are real, if you believe they're real. They are referenced by their correct feast dates; so, anyone wishing clues in advance, may put the dates and names together and consult your copy of Butler's *Lives of the Saints*. I recommend the 1881, seventh edition, to read the unexpurgated texts.

The one Saint I have taken liberties with is poor Susanna. Her manner of martyrdom was never recorded, but as she was removed from the Church's calendar of saints in 1969 as only legendary, I exercised a writer's creative prerogative, and chose flaying, a common form of Roman execution.

The circumstances surrounding the deaths of William Gaynor and "Big Tim" Sullivan are factually represented, except that, in reality, there are additional details even more bizarre than the few recorded here. To anyone interested in reading more about political corruption in 1912 New York, I recommend the excellent *Satan's Circus* by Mike Dash.

The text for the speech delivered by Mrs. Emmeline Pankhurst was taken from her own pen, as recorded in *Shoulder To Shoulder A Documentary By Midge MacKenzie*, published in 1975.

Julia Solis's brilliant *New York Underground: The Anatomy of a City* is a trove of lost pre- 9/11 images to be found, now, literally nowhere else.

ACKNOWLEDGEMENTS

A most sincere thank you to Hali Abdullah & Don Rodriquez, Leslie Cooke & Alan Aiken, Lori Roane, Ann & Bill Kahn, Joy & William Pryor, Nigel Lesmoir-Gordon, Kendal & Elgin Grant, Neville C. King, Esq., Neville E. King, Audra Whaley & Mendal Reuben, Johnny & Cynthia Simmons, Sacha Simmons, Chela Simmons, Sancho Simmons, and Tallulah, a more supportive network of family, friends and canine one could not hope to find.

www.ingramcontent.com/pod-product-compliance
Lightning Source LLC
Chambersburg PA
CBHW020047180626
46812CB00006B/2217